MAIN

WITHDRAWN

W9-CEJ-619

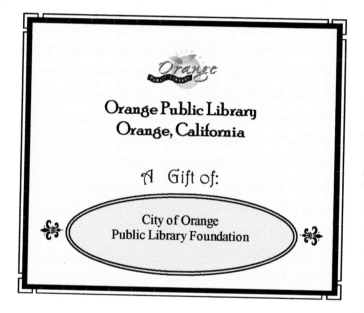

Orange Public Library
Orange, California

A Gift of:

City of Orange
Public Library Foundation

THE DRAGONS OF NOOR

THE
DRAGONS
OF NOOR

JANET LEE CAREY

City of Orange
Public Library

JAN 27 2011

Orange, CA

EGMONT
USA
NEW YORK

EGMONT

We bring stories to life

First published by Egmont USA, 2010
443 Park Avenue South, Suite 806
New York, NY 10016

Copyright © Janet Lee Carey, 2010
All rights reserved

10 9 8 7 6 5 4 3 2 1

www.egmontusa.com
www.janetleecarey.com

Library of Congress Cataloging-in-Publication Data

Carey, Janet Lee.
Dragons of Noor / Janet Lee Carey.
p.   cm.
Sequel to: The beast of Noor.
Summary: Seven hundred years after the days of the dragon wars, magic again is stirring and three teenagers join forces to help bind the broken kingdoms of Noor and Otherworld.
ISBN 978-1-60684-035-1 (trade hardcover) —
978-1-60684-237-9 (eBook)
[1. Dragons—Fiction. 2. Fantasy.] I. Title.
PZ7.C2125Ds 2010
[Fic]—dc22
2010011311

Printed in the United States of America

CPSIA tracking label information:
Random House Production · 1745 Broadway · New York, NY 10019

All rights reserved. No part of this publication may be reproduced, stored in a retrieval system, or transmitted, in any form or by any means, electronic, mechanical, photocopying, or otherwise, without the prior permission of the publisher and copyright owner.

To Anjani Desiree Hubbard,
who danced by the sea when we were sixteen,
and made her home in the mountains.
And to Dreamweavers:
Katherine Grace Bond,
Margaret D. Smith,
and Rebecca A. Chamberlain,
for story and song.

PART ONE:
THE FALL

PROLOGUE

To the future High Meers of Othlore Isle, guardians of the dragon treaties and the Sylth King's scroll, I pen this letter, which is my greeting and my warning. As meers you will have studied my dragon histories in three volumes, but the scrolls locked away here with this letter tell a part of their story not revealed elsewhere. In brief, I trace the history of my last meeting with the Damusaun, our Dragon Queen, the journey I took to Oth on her behalf, and the dire secret regarding the Sylth King's decree writ here on his scroll, a secret each High Meer must guard with his life.

✝   ✝   ✝

After the hundred years of war ended between men and dragons, the Dragon Queen summoned me. I was the only man who'd sided with the dragons in the war to bind the worlds, and it was an honor to be called before the queen. The night was clear on the eastern shore when we met, with a trace of moon like an eyelid over the sea. I bowed to Her Majesty.

"Rise Mishtar, friend of dragons," she said. "We have fought together these many years. I know your wounds as you know mine."

Her scales shone in the firelight, a fire she'd made with her own breath when I arrived at the beach. On her broad chest plate I saw the jagged scars: the names of the dragon dead, blood-written on her scales.

I rose to address her. I was in my fortieth year, and the muscles in my arms and legs ached from battle. "Damusaun, Queen. It has been an honor to fight with you."

She was silent then, perhaps counting up her many losses. "You have fought well, Mishtar, but I would ask one more thing of you," she said.

A wave washed up, the white foam touching the tip of her tail. She flicked off the moisture. "Mishtar, you know it is against the law of the Old Magic to kill," she continued.

I nodded. I also knew all who lived in the Otherworld of Oth were bound to follow the law of the Old Magic. The dragons had broken it when they went to war.

Wind bowed the bonfire, slanting the flames toward the sheer cliff, where more dragons waited for their queen deep in the cave.

The queen said, "For breaking the law of the Old Magic, the Sylth King exiled us from our homeland."

"For how long, Majesty?"

"We have not been able to return home for the last hundred years."

I'd not seen dragons using the deeply rooted Waytrees to leave our world of Noor, but I'd thought this was due to battle, that every tooth, talon, and fiery breath was needed for our fight.

"Surely the High Sylth King of Oth understood the need to fight to keep the Waytrees alive? If they died, there would be nothing strong enough to bind the worlds. Noor and Oth would split apart."

The Damusaun shook her head, her neck scales rattling. "The Sylth King rules by the law, Mishtar." She flicked her tail, smacking a thin glaze of seawater on the sand. "Go to him for us. Tell the High Sylth King the way between worlds has been secured by our blood. The worlds of Noor and Oth remain bound together as before. Now that the war is over, the treaties signed, ask if he will grant us passage back to Oth. We are war-torn. We long to go home."

And so I took the treaties we'd forged between dragons and men and traveled to the Otherworld, with the help of the deya spirits in the Waytrees.

In that beauteous land, I was escorted to the fairy palace of the High Sylth King. Bright sun sparkled through the glimmer walls of the palace dome room. I was made to stand in the glare until I was damp with sweat, squinting up at the Sylth King where he sat in judgment on his jeweled throne. I came to him proud to be the dragon's Mishtar. He treated me as a beggar.

The king's lip curled as he scanned the treaties. "Tell the dragons we do not forgive them for slaying men."

"Sire," I said, "if the dragons hadn't fought, the men of my world would have taken the wild lands. I tell you the ancient Waytrees are nothing to these men but logs for building and wood for their fires. If they had

THE DRAGONS OF NOOR

succeeded in felling the deep-rooted trees that bind the worlds, Noor and Oth would have been severed forever."

The king tossed the treaties on the floor and called his scribe, bidding the man write the words he whispered in his ear. What was this? A new treaty? The ones the dragons signed with the rulers of Noor were binding and needed no addition. I stooped to retrieve the treaties from the floor.

The Sylth King spoke his final judgment as the scribe handed me the new scroll. Hearing the king's sharp words, the very ones writ in the scroll, I was stunned to silence. Before I could argue, I was taken from his sight. Sylth guards marched me to the Waytrees of Oth where the roots are deep, and threw me out of their world.

Three days I walked through storms in my own world of Noor before I reached the Dragon Queen again. We took shelter under the boughs of an azure tree.

"The Sylth King said if you do not kill any men for seven hundred years, your exile from Oth will end. Then you can return to your homeland." I showed her the king's scroll.

The Damusaun's eyes burned with fury. "Seven hundred . . . years?" she roared. "How can he expect us to abide by this?" She stepped beyond the shelter of the boughs, lifted her snout, and sent angry red fire skyward. The flames hissed and fizzled in the falling rain.

The exile was long, even for dragons, who live more than a thousand years. Some of my friends would die before they would see their homeland again. But the Damusaun saw the real peril.

In her hour of burning anger, I waited under the branches. She would not turn her anger on me, her messenger, but still she released it until the rain cooled her scales and her rage was spent. She stepped back under the tree and wrapped her tail about her legs. "The king's judgment endangers both worlds," she said at last. "We must keep our exile from Oth secret, Mishtar. If men know we can no longer fight to defend the Waytrees, they will break our hard-won treaties and come again to cut them down."

I left the dragons then and sailed back to Othlore Isle, a lone island set apart in Noor's West Morrow Sea. On Othlore I built this school where the meers of Noor study the lore of Oth and apprentices learn the ways of magic. In the High Meer's river house, I locked the scrolls away. Five scrolls in all, the treaties between men and dragons signed after the war, and the Sylth King's scroll. This last scroll is to be kept secret. Only the magician appointed as High Meer shall know why the dragons live in exile: that if they kill a single man in seven hundred years, they will never again be allowed to cross back into Oth. So I have guarded these scrolls for the last fifty years. I am old now and a dying man. The scrying stone the Dragon Queen gave me when we parted shows me much. As the centuries pass, I foresee a time when prideful men will break the dragon treaties. If men return to the ancient woodlands to fell Waytrees again, the dragons cannot kill a single man to save them. We are all in great danger if men should cut the azure Waytrees of the east, for if these offspring of the World Tree fall, the splitting worlds will pull farther apart, tearing deep roots in every land, and all Waytrees in Noor will die. Sever these most ancient azure trees, these dragon bridges that stretch between the worlds, and there will be no way between.

The dragons say there will be signs if the worlds begin to split. First, the Waytrees will begin to fall across the forests of Noor. Second, men will forget how to dream. Third, a black hole will be torn in the heart of the Old Magic, awakening a Wild Wind.

If these things should come about, I compel the future High Meer who guards these scrolls here on Othlore to use all you know of magic and take what action you must to save the Waytrees that bind the worlds.

Signed,

Kiram, founder and first High Meer of Othlore

Musician, scholar, the one the dragons call Mishtar

ONE

STEALING WIND

Children fly when worlds are shaken,
Now the children are Wind-taken.
Seek them there, seek them here,
before the children disappear.

—FROM THE GAME CALLED "BLIND SEER"

The fat bumblebee rammed against the kitchen window again and again. Hanna would have carefully put aside the green glass platter she was drying to free the little creature if the shock of the enormous golden wing spearing the white clouds above the trees hadn't made her drop the precious platter. The loud crash as it hit the floor sent her leaping back as shards flew in all directions.

"Now look what I've done!" She dropped to her knees, cursing her clumsiness. Three generations of Sheens had cherished the beautiful green platter. It was the finest thing the family owned, and her mother's favorite possession. The sight of that golden wing high in the sky had sent such a jolt of fear and wonder coursing through her body, she'd forgotten what was in her hands.

Tymm must have heard the crash. Racing into the kitchen with his glue pot, he hurriedly unscrewed the lid as Hanna put the larger shards on the table. Each broken bit made a gentle clinking sound like abandoned keys. Above the rim of the table she caught Tymm's ready eyes.

"You won't be able to fix this one, Tymm."

"I will, Hanna. See if I don't. And I'll have it done before Mother comes home," he added.

She watched Tymm dip the brush into the glue pot. Hanna's eight-year-old brother loved attacking broken things. With concentration he assembled like a great round puzzle the pieces she rescued from the floor.

The bee still rammed the window with fixed determination. Had she imagined what she'd seen just now? Hands still shaking, she opened the window a crack to let the bee out, brushing the insect in the right direction. Only then did she have the courage to look above the trees again. New clouds brown with rain had blown in. The golden wing was gone.

Terrow dragons are golden, she thought, catching her breath. Dragons? Here? Dragons lived in eastern Noor in sunny places like Jarrosh or Kanayar. She'd never heard of any flying as far west as Enness Isle, not since the days of the dragon wars, and that was seven hundred years ago.

She looked up, wondering if it had only been a flash of sunlight cutting through the clouds, and caught sight of a giant form swimming through the air. The creature gleamed like polished coins, and it was . . . enormous. Hanna's body quivered. First the Wild Wind a week ago screaming into town, stealing children right out of the market square, and now a dragon had appeared. Magic was stirring on Enness Isle, and there was no one here to help her.

Wing and tail disappeared into the brown rain clouds drifting toward the mountain peak. Hanna curled her toes inside her boots. She'd heard voices, low and keening, coming down the mountain this morning. The deya spirits calling from the trees: another sign of the growing magic, of the wildness of the Otherworld reaching into Noor. She'd wanted to go to the deyas, but she'd promised to stay home and watch Tymm while Mother went to market. Tymm couldn't be left alone with a Wild Wind blowing in, stealing young children.

There was no call from the woods now. Only a

brooding silence. Still, Hanna felt the magic rising in a slow and relentless wave, engulfing her, trying to draw her deeper in.

When her older brother, Miles, went missing last year, the deyas in the trees had helped her cross into Oth in search of him. And she'd ridden with the wind spirit, Wild Esper.

Hanna had seen no wind spirit in the gales that battered Brim Village and swept three children from the market square, none of them more than nine years old. *A spiritless wind*, she thought uneasily.

She flung her apron on the chair. A week had passed since the children were Wind-taken. Seven days too long for the grieving mothers and fathers down in Brim. Seven days too long for her to be kept in the house looking after Tymm.

"Pass that piece here, Hanna." Tymm's eyes gleamed with pleasure, as if he could see the broken platter whole again, and indeed he'd already glued a fourth of it back together.

Hanna pushed the shard across the table with her forefinger, then slipped on her cloak. "I have to go out. I won't be long."

Tymm jumped up from the table. "I'll come, too."

"No. You'll stay here."

"Miles wouldn't make me."

"Miles is away at school. And if he were here," she added, "he'd tell you to obey your older sister. You may eat my piece of crumb cake while I'm gone."

She was out the door and through the garden before he could argue. The familiar sound of wooden wheels rumbled up the lane. Hanna ducked behind a pine tree as the wagon turned the corner. Good, Mother was back. Tymm would be safe now. She'd worry about Mother's response to the broken platter later.

Hanna took the steep trail heading for Garth Lake, which was cradled in a valley halfway up Mount Shalem. The oldest Waytrees on Enness Isle grew there. The deyas in them would know more than anyone else here on the isle about the rising magic that had come. If they'd helped her to find Miles last year, they might help her to reach the missing children now. She was the only Dreamwalker on Enness, and should do all that was in her power to find the ones who were gone.

It took her more than half an hour to reach the first plateau. Sweaty even in the morning chill, she stopped to take a breath. No sign of the dragon since she'd left the house. She quickened her pace, still dizzy with wonder at what she'd seen. What was a terrow doing here, so far from its homeland in the east? The thought of pairing up with a dragon to find the village children thrilled her, but it was a thrill mixed with fear. Dragons were dangerous.

Mist crept in on cat paws through the underbrush and stirred about her feet in rings. At last she reached the trail that wound up the ridge high above the lake. She stopped by a mossy boulder, hands on her knees to catch her breath. The woods seemed too silent.

Her skin began to prick. She hadn't been able to come when she'd first heard the deyas' calls. Had she missed her chance to ask their help? Still out of breath, she started off again.

> *Children fly when worlds are shaken,*
> *Now the children are Wind-taken.*
> *Seek them there, seek them here,*
> *before the children disappear.*

The first lines of the Blind Seer game haunted her as she circled the ridge. They seemed to foretell what had

THE DRAGONS OF NOOR

happened down in town. Blind Seer was a game she'd played when she was younger, skipping off to hide from the seer, who stumbled about wearing his blindfold. Back then they'd thought nothing of the rhyme.

Snap. Hanna spun around. Who was following her? She slipped into the foliage.

Another snap. "Tymm? What are you doing here?"

"I finished up the platter and sneaked away from Mother. You can't make me stay inside for always." His short blond curls bobbed as he ripped the leaves off a slender twig.

Hanna pricked her ears, listening for a breeze. "Come on. I'll take you home." She thrust out her hand.

Tymm brushed her away. "I want to stay with you. You're going to see Taunier, aren't you? I know you like him."

"I'm not going to see Taunier." Impossible that her little brother could make her blush, but there it was.

"Then why'd you come up here?"

"Why should I tell you? And anyway, there's no time to argue. I've got to get you home before the wind blows in." She tugged him more forcefully.

He thrust out his chin. "I won't go. I'm not afraid of no wind."

Tymm was used to playing outdoors, roving with Da and Taunier tending sheep or mending pasture fences. He was too young to understand the horror of what had happened in town: everyone shouting, running after the wind-blown children; mothers and fathers crying out. One of the children was Tymm's friend Cilla, a beautiful girl with red curls and a singing laugh. Hanna and Taunier had fought the gusts, climbed a tree, tried to grab Cilla's flailing skirt as she blew higher and higher. In the end she and the other two were no more than three black dots sweeping east over the sea.

"Listen to me. The wind came after children and no one else, Tymm. It scoured through the crowd, knocking everyone but those three young ones flat, and it swept them away. You have to stay inside!"

Tymm resisted a little longer, but when she tried to pick him up and carry him back, he said, "I'm no baby!" His footfall was heavy as they made their way back along the rim of the gorge. If Tymm hadn't come along, she could have found the deyas in another ten minutes. He was *always* getting in the way, always . . .

A little breeze stirred her hair. Hanna trembled. No one knew where the Wind-taken children had gone. Not the grieving parents nor the rest of the terrified villagers who'd sworn to keep their young children indoors or tethered to their sides if they had to step out of the house.

"Why didn't you know that bad wind was going to come ahead of time?" Tymm asked sulkily. "Great-Uncle Enoch told me you can see the future in your dreamwalks."

"He told you that?" Hanna gripped his hand tighter. "I can, sometimes, but not always." She crushed a mushroom underfoot. It had upset her, too. She'd not felt any sense of danger when she'd gone to Brim with Da and Taunier that day. All she'd cared about was whether she could sit next to Taunier in the cart, close enough for her arm to touch his shoulder.

Taunier was sixteen and strong. He smiled little and talked even less. Still he never called her witch-girl like the other boys in town, never teased her for her strange miscolored eyes. That in itself would have warmed her to him, even without his tall muscled form, his smooth brown skin, dark eyes, and the slightly crooked nose that made his handsome face all the more real. Miles had boasted that he'd been the one who had given him that crooked nose in a fight, but she wasn't sure it was true. Boys down in Brim liked a good fight, too, especially with the outsiders like Miles and Taunier.

That day in the market, she'd been so preoccupied with delicious thoughts of riding home next to Taunier that she'd had no inkling of the storm. What good were dreamwalks if they didn't warn her of danger?

"Wait a moment, Tymm." She stooped to uproot a few handfuls of long grass. She'd weave a sturdy tether, tie Tymm to her arm, and keep him close to her side.

"What are you doing?"

"Making a rope."

"I can do that better than you." Tymm swiped the grass. He would not have been so greedy if he knew what it was for. Still, what good would grass be in such a strong wind? She sighed.

They were nearly to the fork in the path that led back down to their cottage when the midday mist thinned enough for them to see the water below. Hanna paused and pointed down to the valley floor, at the little island poking out of the water in the center of Garth Lake.

"Can you see those giant trees?" she asked.

Tymm glanced up from his braid. "They're all ugly

and burnt up," he observed, his fingers moving nimbly as he spoke.

Hanna didn't blame Tymm for dismissing them. She'd felt the same way the first time the Falconer had brought her here. She smiled at her ignorance now. The Waytrees were likely more than a thousand years old. There were few trees like them in all of Noor, wise enough to bridge the way to the magical world of Oth. More Waytrees grew on the mountain, but none so old as these.

Only the ancient Waytrees housed deya spirits, who held the wisdom of the two worlds and helped the trees bind Noor and Oth together. The deyas' magic was strong. She needed their help to find the Wind-taken children. But she couldn't take Tymm down there. A rook flew past, its wings beating the air. She followed its flight and caught sight of a long golden spear shooting through the sky—the terrow dragon. Hanna's neck tingled as the slender tail slipped into the clouds again.

"Tymm?" she breathed, her voice thick with wonder.

"Aye?" Tymm's eyes were still on the grass rope. She would have told him about the dragon sighting if she hadn't heard a wind rustling through the bushes.

What was she thinking, standing here on the trail with Tymm fully exposed?

"Let's go." Hanna tugged him down the path. This time she would tell Mother to *lock* the door, no matter how much Tymm complained.

A haunting sound drifted up the hill behind her. Soft at first, it slowly grew from one voice to two and three. The voices mingled with the dove cooing in the evergreens, the croaking frogs in the water below, but the deya song was deeper and richer than these.

> *Come, Dreamwalker,*
> *Come, Hannalyn,*
> *Before our roots are broken.*

The deyas in the Waytrees were calling again, and she wanted to go, had to go.

I'll come back, she silently promised.

"Hear that?" asked Tymm.

"Hurry," she answered, though she was surprised Tymm could hear the deyas' call. He had never been attuned to magic the way she and Miles were.

"Frogs in the lake," Tymm shouted happily. "Dozens

of them. I'll catch some." He suddenly broke free. Spinning round, he dropped the grass rope and started running down the steep hill toward Garth Lake below.

"Stop, Tymm! You can't go down there!"

Hanna retrieved the rope and ran after him. A cold gust slapped her face as she raced downhill.

"Come back now! It's too dangerous! The wind is rising!"

He'd nearly reached the bushes.

"I'll just get me a frog!" he called back. "I won't be long." He raced straight into the sill thornbushes, their thick red branches hiding him from her view.

"Get out of there, now! The wind is picking up!" She threw herself into the swaying thicket.

"Tymm? I'm just up the hill. Walk toward my voice."

"I can't. I'm stuck!"

She heard the panic in his call. "Hang on. I'll get you out!" Hanna tied the grass rope about her middle. She'd need it once she reached him. Breaking off a branch, she swung it left and right, thrashing the tangled bushes. A sharp wind gusted through, rattling the sill thorns.

"Anteebwey!" she swore. Miles should be here to help her! He was learning magic on Othlore, but what good were books and study when a fierce magic had come here to Enness Isle to steal the younger children?

She had to reach Tymm, get him safely down to the Waytrees. Once there, the deyas might be able to use their magic to protect him against the rising wind.

"Help us," Hanna screamed.

Help us, the deyas echoed back from across the lake, desperation in their voices. Something must be happening to them, but she couldn't see their island through the thick bushes.

From the sky above the terrow suddenly spewed a line of bright orange flame. The bushes along the shore caught fire. Wind whistled through the thorns. The whistle rose to a scream, whipping the branches.

"Tymm! Drop to the ground if you can! Hurry!"

The sudden gale uprooted burning thornbushes and sucked them swirling into the sky.

Tymm called, "Tesha yoven!"

"What? What are you saying? Tymm?"

No answer.

"Help me!" shouted Hanna.

Another heavy gust swept down the hill. It blew Hanna into the air and slammed her down again. Sill thorns slashed her as she fell and hit the hard ground. She groped her way to her knees and shook herself. A loud cracking filled the air, followed by thunderous sounds. Was the wind blowing down the Waytrees?

"Tymm! Get down. Hold on to the ground! Don't let go!"

Hanna managed to pull herself upright, but the next gust tore her farther away from Tymm. This time she landed full force on her back. She tried to breathe, to scream, but she couldn't.

Swooping down again, the howling gale swept Tymm over her head.

Hanna jumped up, clawing at the sky. "No! Don't take him! Let him go!"

Arms out, legs flailing, Tymm screamed as he blew over the pines. The wind drew him east above the foot-hills and sped him toward the sea.

She hadn't reached him in time. Rage flooded through her.

"Why take Tymm?" she screamed. "What do you want with him?" She wept until her throat was raw.

A long while later, when she'd cried herself out, she stumbled through the ravaged bushes to the shore. The dragon's fire had died down. Smoke rose to meet the swirling fog, brother to sister. There were no flashes of gold. The terrow had disappeared again. Hanna gripped Tymm's grass rope, still strung about her waist. It hadn't done any good. She hadn't been able to save him.

The storm had blown the Waytrees down, and the little island in the lake was strewn with wood. Even in the mist she could see the broken trees split down the middle. The trunks and branches were bone white. The deyas were gone.

TWO

When the Waytree bridges fall,
Roots die binding all to all.

—Dragons' Song

Bone-white marble walls surrounded the meers' school at the base of Mount Kalmeer, whose great forest grew in all directions from its snowcapped peak. The first High Meer had chosen to build his school on Othlore, for the lone isle in the western sea of Noor was a place deeply rooted in magic.

A ray of sunlight broke through the clouds as Miles left the western gate with his bearhound, Breal, and crossed the creaking footbridge leading to the forest. It was risky to sneak outside when he should be in Restoration Magic class, but he'd heard a call coming from the Othlore Wood. A magic beckoning, he was sure. The sound had haunted him all day, though no one else seemed to notice, and so at last he'd come.

In the green canopy, pale light fell through the boughs, painting yellow circles on the forest floor. Already he and his dog were too far in to see the school. Apprentices from every land yearned to study magic here. Few students were accepted, and fewer still earned the right to be initiated as meers, with Othic symbols emblazoned on their palms. Miles was still proud to have been chosen. He would study hard, become a meer, and someday even become the High Meer. That was his secret desire. He'd never told another soul, though he'd almost let it slip once with Hanna.

Boughs swayed overhead, washing him in cold shadows as he crossed the spongy turf. He wished Hanna were with him. She'd understand the risk he might be taking by following the call into the woods this afternoon. But Mother and Da hadn't let her come. They still believed in backward island ways: girls were to be at home, not gone away to school, and no amount of argument on his or Hanna's part had persuaded them otherwise. Even knowing she was a Dreamwalker, that she'd been the only one able to rescue him last year, hadn't made them change their minds.

Beside him, Breal's ears pricked.

"So you hear it, too." Breal looked up, brown-eyed, panting, before trotting ahead, drawn by the summons. It was a sound past human hearing, but not past Breal's, who knew the call of magic, having lived under a curse for many a long year, and not beyond Miles's own hearing.

Miles hadn't shape-shifted since leaving Enness Isle a year ago, but each animal shift had left him with a mark or gift. He bore an ugly scar on his neck from his first wolf change, and sharpened vision from his falcon shift, but the heightened hearing from his shift into the Shriker was the strongest of them all. He clenched his teeth, thinking of the Shriker: his giant bearlike body, his claws, his bloody fangs. The demon beast had killed many innocent folk on Enness Isle before he and Hanna had broken the curse.

When Miles first arrived on Othlore, he'd been relieved to learn that shape-shifting was forbidden at the meers' school. The word *meer* meant "one who wields magic," but the school taught discipline and was firmly against any misuse of power. Miles hadn't been ready to handle the shape-shifting gift the Sylth Queen had bestowed on him so he could do her dirty work. He knew the Old Magic forbade those who lived in Oth to kill, and she'd had to choose a human boy to slay the Shriker for her.

Miles shivered, remembering how he'd become the beast to do the deed. In his Shriker's form, he'd killed, relished in the killing, and nearly lost himself in a dark shape-shift. He was keenly aware that he'd come out of the beast form only with Hanna's help, and with the faith his teacher, the Falconer, had shown in him.

Pine needles crunched beneath his boots. His skin itched with anticipation as he followed Breal through the bracken. No matter what or who was calling him into the woods now, he would not use his shape-shifting gift again until he learned how to handle such powerful magic.

Miles stopped for a moment to finger the tender green needles. The pines in this part of the forest were too young to be Waytrees. But Othlore Wood had groves with Waytrees of many kinds. It was not so much the type of tree, but the tree's age that mattered. A Waytree must be ancient, a deep-rooted tree large enough to house a deya spirit.

Miles felt himself expanding as he walked beneath the boughs. When he was not in class, or serving his

Music Master, he would come to the forest often and in all weathers to play his silver ervay flute. The Falconer had given him his prized ervay before he died, and Miles kept it safely strapped to his side in a beaded leather pouch Hanna had sewn. The decorative beads were blue and green, the colors of his sister's eyes.

Zabith, the Forest Meer, dwelled in this part of the forest, but she'd sailed away last winter. The meer had often seen him come and go, and she hadn't seemed to mind his walks, for he always came alone.

Shadows darkened. Miles began to sense the deya spirits hidden in the massive trunks. He could almost feel their wakefulness as they nourished the Waytree roots that bound the broken worlds. As he followed Breal from pine to oak, birch to redwood, the haunting call deepened to a wind song, soft and slowly changing. He wanted to let down his guard, to tell himself the sound was only the breeze troubling the leaves. In Othlore Wood he could very nearly believe that. Still, he stopped in the birch grove where Breal circled round an elder tree, and sat thumping his tail against the soft earth.

Miles ran his hand along the white bark, paper smooth and cool against his palm, and heard the wind-blown notes like a mourner's cry. "What's troubling you?" he whispered. The tree stirred beneath his fingers. Miles stepped back.

He'd not meant to waken anyone by the question, but with a shudder, the deya stepped out from the heart of her tree. The tree spirit was twelve feet tall at least. Her body and gown were the white and black of a birch, the silver and green of living leaves, and she shimmered before Miles as leaves do when touched by wind and sun.

Miles bowed his dark head. He'd met deyas last year on Enness Isle when he'd been given his shape-shifting power. But he still felt awed in her presence.

"You honor us, Mileseryl," the deya said, her voice a welcome breeze.

Miles touched his forehead. "And you me."

She'd used his deya name, Mileseryl, and he waited to hear hers, but she gave him none.

He glanced at her brown roots extending from her silver gown. Breal came close as if to sniff them, then backed away to stand by Miles.

"You have brought us word," she said, with such assurance that he glanced up again, startled to see how drawn her face looked. She wavered, insubstantial as a candle flame. He sensed that she was very ill, maybe even dying. His throat tightened.

"What word are you seeking?" he asked. He suddenly felt he would do anything to help her. The deya's gown fluttered; her arms rose and fell again like wings. But she stayed close to the earth and to her Waytree.

"We few deyas who still remain await news from Meer Zabith."

Miles knew last winter Meer Zabith had sailed to Jarrosh in the eastern lands of Noor, where dragons guarded the oldest Waytrees in the world. He'd carried her trunk down to Othlore Harbor and helped the old woman aboard her ship, but he hadn't asked her why she was bound for Jarrosh. Meer Zabith was a seer and a recluse who kept counsel only with the High Meer himself.

"There's no news from Meer Zabith that I know of," he admitted.

The silver gray figure thinned like a parting mist. "We hear this, and we drink it into our roots now." The Waytrees behind her seemed to shudder.

"The dragons must have flown. We fear the strongest Waytrees in Jarrosh have begun to fall. Our roots are not as deep as theirs. Without them we do not have the power to bind the worlds."

Slowly she drew back. "I will tell the others," she said.

He saw her fading as she leaned into the birch tree, and reached out, as if to pull her back. "Wait. Where have the dragons gone? Why do you think the Waytrees of Jarrosh are falling?" Breal stood alert, tail lowered, ears pressed back.

"Our roots die with the azure trees. We cannot stay."

Hissss. A sound not made by wind or trees.

"But the Azures are far away in the east. Why do your roots here have to die? I don't understand."

"Too late," the deya said. "Soon we will be gone, and you will forget."

"Forget what? Please tell me!" He reached for her, but she pulled back, into the tree. "You can't leave," he argued. "The deyas have lived in these Waytrees for thousands of years."

The deya spirit was a ghostly wisp-woman now, her fading presence more a lingering fragrance than a vision.

"You will all forget," she said again, and was gone.

Miles leaped forward. "Come back. I call you from

your Waytree—" But Miles faltered. She had not given him her name.

A hissing sound sped through the wood from above and from below. A thick, dark line grew up the birch trunk. White bark peeled away like curling paper. A long black fissure suddenly split with a resounding crack!

Breal circled, barking. The birch tree shuddered, its branches raining down. The trunk split wider and toppled to the earth, just missing Miles.

Miles lurched back, stunned, then he flew forward to find the deya. "Are you hurt? Where are you?" Gripping the shattered trunk, he tugged with all his might. Breal dug about the base of the trunk as they both struggled against the heavy weight, but they could not budge the tree.

The forest floor rose and fell, as if heaving in a breath. Miles stumbled against Breal and fell backward on his hands. The birch to his right split open with another loud crack. Miles pushed himself up, trying to find his footing on the heaving path.

The trees swayed and buckled as if riding a stormy sea. Small black fissures grew up an oak trunk, splitting wider and wider.

"Watch out, Breal!"

Boom!

Ahhhh! Ahhhh! The sound of voices knelling. *Hissssss!*

Branches rained down from all sides, from oak and birch and pine. Breal took off. Miles covered his head and raced behind his dog. His breath came hard as he sped down the trail. Dodging branches, it took another half an hour to reach the bridge. Across the river on the crest of the hill, he stopped at last and turned again. Hands on knees, he sucked in ragged breaths and gazed toward Othlore Wood, where a singular storm was raging.

The school gate had opened, and meers and apprentices flooded through. In the glade across the river more trunks darkened; thunderous sounds echoed down the foothills as trees buckled and hit the earth. Deep mist rose above the collapsing canopy, rolling in gray waves toward the center of the wood.

Miles stood in the blowing grass with all the others. The earth was still, the evening sky dark but clear. A light breeze crossed his skin. The Waytrees were not toppling in a wind, not falling in a quake, but in some raging magic beyond their ken. A flock of crows flew upward like a black cape tossed into the air. More birds abandoned the wild woods, screeching and twittering with terror as they darted past. Deer and foxes raced over the bridge into the long grass.

The Music Master, Meer Eason, began to sing the *Kaynumba*, and others joined him in the ending chant, knowing they could not battle a magic storm coming from the heart of the wood.

Miles's head was filled with sound; he felt as if his bones were breaking. Centuries ago, the dragons had fought a war to protect the Waytrees. The birch deya said they'd flown. Where had they gone? Miles reached for a branch that had blown clear of the forest, leaning his full weight on the staff.

The birch branch was not yet blackened by the sickness that was taking Othlore Wood. Miles wrapped his fingers around it and felt skin to bark as if he held the hand of one who was dying. His granda's hand had felt like this—dry, slender-boned, cool to the touch, just before he passed.

"*Kaynumba, eOwey, kaynumba.* The ending comes, O Maker, the ending comes." Meers and students from every discipline sang as the trees passed away. Miles tugged his ervay from its leather bag. His fingers passed along the sylth silver as he played the Y-shaped flute along with the chanters.

On the topmost point of the hill, Meer Ellyer appeared, his russet cloak sweeping out behind him. The High Meer's lips did not move, for silence was his offering, but his hands were held out to the storm so all could see his meer sign—the Othic symbol for wind-fire—dancing blue on his left palm.

"*Kaynumba.* The ending comes."

Just before dawn the breaking was at an end. A few small saplings still stood, down by the shore and on the far side of the mountain, but the ancient trees lay flat and smoldering on the forest floor, all pointing inward to the place that was once the heart of the wood.

THREE

When the two worlds broke apart,
Noor folk lost touch with the Old
Magic and forgot the way to Oth.

—*The Way Between Worlds*

Breal raced up to the house of river stones and sat before the front door, thick tail wagging. Miles should have taken it as a good sign, but he couldn't shake off his fear. Last night the great forest had fallen. This afternoon a fierce wind had screamed across the school yard and swept three young pupils into the sky. Soon after that the High Meer had summoned him to his house.

Miles tried to calm his nerves. He'd been the only one to enter Othlore Wood yesterday. Did the High Meer think he had something to do with the destruction? Or with the children—some of the youngest in the school—stolen by the wind? He hoped the High Meer wasn't planning to expel him. He didn't want to go home.

39

He wanted to stay here and study to defeat whatever dark magic had come to the meers' isle.

Crossing the porch, he stood with Meer Eason, in the low, circling mist. To his right, just beyond the piles of dead trees, the river shone deep blue with twilight. They'd not spoken a word walking here. Meer Eason drew back his hood, his black face wrinkling with concern as he stepped up to the threshold. Miles wiped his damp hands on his cloak. Eason adjusted his long braid worn down one side in the fashion of a Music Master. No ringing of bells or knocking, just a moment's wait, and the door creaked open. Inside, Miles removed his muddy boots and slipped on a pair of rush sandals.

The High Meer, Ellyer, was seated on a meditation cushion across from the Sea Meer, Kanoae. Pillows were strewn across the floor, and three walls out of four were lined with bookshelves. The room would have been very simple, almost stark, if it weren't for the pale blue, dome-shaped stone on the corner table. The scrying stone: it must be that and nothing else. He'd read about this stone in history class.

Long ago the Dragon Queen gave the scrying stone to the Mishtar, the first High Meer of Othlore, for his service in the dragon wars. The blue amber was said to have been made from the sap of the great World Tree itself, hardened over millennia. No images danced on its surface now, but then only the High Meer knew how to call visions from the amber.

The old man caught Miles's questioning look and smiled. His golden skin wrinkled like fine silk about his upturned mouth and beside his almond eyes. The thin white hair crowning his otherwise bald head showed a few black strands.

Miles shifted from foot to foot, unsure if he was supposed to sit or remain standing. The rich scent of thool drifted from the steaming teapot. Miles saw Kanoae watching Breal curl up near the crackling fire, head down on his flattened paws. Meer Kanoae had captained the ship that sailed him to Othlore last year. The thick-set meer had cleaned up before this meeting, tied back her brown hair, and traded her wind jerkin for her formal robes. Miles's mood darkened. The powerful woman was here to escort him home, no doubt.

Meer Eason nudged him. Miles quickly joined Eason in a formal greeting, left hand to forehead then bowing heads once and twice. Meer Ellyer and Meer Kanoae returned it.

Kanoae patted a green cushion on the floor beside her. Miles sank down, feeling like a prisoner awaiting his sentence. Why such formality? Why not just get on with it and accuse him, if that was what they were here to do? But these were meers, and things would be done in an orderly manner. He licked the sweat from his upper lip, his foot twitching with agitation.

The High Meer poured four cups of thool, and Kanoae passed them around. The window was open a crack. Outside the river's voice sang in low and high tones down the mountain's throat, its song sounding thin in the absence of the usual sounds of wind whispering through green branches.

No wind blew here now. He clutched his cup, heat stinging his hand as he remembered the young apprentices wrenched out of the school courtyard. The wind had taken only three students, chosen them, it seemed, for it had blown Miles and the rest of the students aside, knocking some into the west pool, smashing Miles and a score of others against the courtyard wall.

He'd caught one of the boys by the ankle as he was being sucked into the storm, but the wind was stronger. The boy flew out of reach, calling *Tesha yoven*, words used in a binding spell, as he spun higher and higher with the other two above the eastern wall. In a moment's time they'd vanished in the clouds.

"You worry for the Wind-taken," said Meer Ellyer.

Miles started. Had the High Meer read his mind?

"Aye," he admitted. "The children who were stolen were so young." He paused. "Only three out of all of us, as if they'd been selected."

Eason said, "Meer Ellyer, do you think the wind that took the apprentices has something to do with the fallen trees?"

"The images in my scrying stone showed other lands where the forests have died," said Meer Ellyer. "In those lands other children have been Wind-taken."

"So you *knew* it would happen here on Othlore?" Miles heard the irritation in his own voice and added a quick, "Sir?"

"I hoped the trees would stand here, Miles. This isle is protected for a reason. It's the one place in Noor where the Old Magic of Oth is still taught."

Miles sipped his sweet drink. There was something about a Wild Wind in a passage he'd read in one of his books, but he couldn't recall what it said. "But why were the children taken?" he asked. "Why is this all happening at once?"

Meer Ellyer frowned. "The scrying stone does not show me all. But I saw the wind sweep the children east toward the dragon lands, where the oldest Waytrees grow."

Miles thought again of the boy he'd tried to save from the tempest. He was not much older than his brother, Tymm. Why hadn't he been able to keep hold of the boy's ankle?

"What brought you to the woods yesterday?" asked Meer Ellyer.

Miles's spine stiffened. The interrogation had begun. Just what *had* he been doing in Othlore Wood before it began to fall? Miles put his cup on the floor. Watched the steam rise.

"I heard a calling sound."

"What sort of sound?" the Music Master asked. Miles rubbed the bridge of his nose and tapped the floor nervously. If he said he'd heard the deyas calling, wouldn't they ask why? He'd not told the meers about the acute hearing gift he'd gleaned from his last shape-shift. Shape-shifting had been prohibited to the students here ever since an apprentice named Yarta had misused the gift thirty years ago. She'd shape-shifted smaller and smaller until she vanished altogether.

Yarta had gone too far and died, and the practice had been banned to all apprentices ever since. Only those in the Wielder's Order knew the shape-shifter's art these days, but they never spoke of it. If the High Meer knew Miles had heightened hearing because he was a shape-shifter, he'd have good reason to expel him. And if that happened, he'd never be blue-palmed, never bear the magic sign on his hand that proved he was a meer.

Meer Ellyer sliced an apple, waiting for Miles's answer.

"A sort of music. Wind in the trees, I think. I went inside the forest to listen more closely to it." It was not the whole truth. He'd guessed the sound had been more than wind in the trees, and his acute ears had picked it up from as far away as the school buildings. But he wouldn't tell them that.

Meer Ellyer asked, "What happened then?"

Miles looked from meer to meer. Even Breal's large brown eyes watched him from his place by the fire. "A birch deya came out of her Waytree."

Meer Eason scooted closer. "Go on."

"She asked if there was any news from Meer Zabith. She seemed to think I was a messenger"—he paused a moment—"but I'd not heard of any news. She was disappointed then, and she said something about azure trees and dragons."

The word *dragons* felt like fire coming off his tongue. He hoped to catch a glimpse of one someday.

"This is important," said Meer Ellyer. "Try to remember exactly what she told you."

Miles frowned, thinking. "The deya said the Waytrees of Jarrosh are falling. She said the dragons must have flown away." He looked at the High Meer. "I've been wondering what she meant by that."

Meer Ellyer stirred his thool. "You have studied the Mishtar's dragon books, have you not? The part about the dragons and the World Tree?"

Miles fidgeted on his cushion. He remembered the description of the great World Tree, Kwen-Arnun, towering thousands of feet over NoorOth. A tree so sacred it was guarded by dragons. In the second age when Kwen-Arnun split in the quake that tore NoorOth in two, when Kwen crashed down in Noor, and his tree-wife, Arnun, shattered in the magical world of Oth, the worlds split with their falling. After the split, dragons waged war with the men who came to chop down the World Tree's descendants to use as timber and fuel.

"I think," he said, "if they have flown from Jarrosh, the Waytrees there have no one guarding them."

"They would not fly away," argued Meer Kanoae. "Dragons have always protected the ancient azure groves from harm, whether it be men with axes or any other kind of threat. It's in their blood."

Meer Eason said, "Still, the Waytrees fell here in Othlore Wood, and we saw no dragons flying overhead."

"We can't be hasty in our judgment," warned the High Meer. "We did not see dragons when our forest fell. But there is more at work here than we can see."

He refilled Eason's cup. "The birch deya told Miles the azure trees of Jarrosh are in trouble. Meer Zabith came to me last winter with the same concern after she had a warning vision. Our Forest Meer knew the ancient azures have the deepest roots. All the other Waytrees of Noor can't hold the worlds if the azures die. They are not strong enough. She sailed east for Jarrosh after that."

"And has not been heard from since," added Kanoae

bitterly. "Now if she'd listened to sense and gone on my ship—"

Meer Ellyer held up his hand to silence her complaint.

Miles looked out the window. The river flowed dark outside with the coming night. "What will happen if Oth splits all the way apart from Noor? Not just a rift like the one that happened in the second age when the World Tree fell, but if there is . . . a complete split?"

The High Meer answered in a low voice. "The Mishtar warned us long ago. If the worlds split completely, all magic will go out of Noor. People will forget how to dream. Then Oth itself will disappear."

Miles's mouth went dry. He'd been to Oth, a place so drenched in magic that even the air sparkled with life. If all the magic were to go out of Noor with the vanishing of Oth . . . "We can't let it happen," he said. "How long do we have?"

"I cannot say, but if all the azures fall, the break will be complete."

Miles stood, overturning his cup. "We have to stop it. You said the wind took the children east. We have to follow. Find the children. Find out what's wrong with the trees. I'll go." He knelt and tried to contain the spilled thool spreading across the hardwood.

"Sorry," he whispered. Heat climbed up his neck. The cup was chipped. If his little brother Tymm were here, he could mend the chip, but this was the High Meer's house. No Tymm with his handy glue pot. The High Meer padded to the kitchen, returned, and tossed him a cloth.

"Jarrosh is near my homeland," said Meer Eason. "If the azures are in trouble, and the Wind-taken children were blown there, Miles is right. It's clear we must go."

"We need to set sail now and meet this problem at its source," agreed Kanoae. "But Miles has no reason to come. He's just a boy of, what, fifteen?"

"Sixteen," corrected Eason.

"Still," she went on, "he's not even been blue-palmed."

Miles's back was to her as he wiped up the spill, but he felt her eyes on him. The High Meer said, "Why else would I have summoned him today, Kanoae?" He looked down at them, a short, lean man made taller by their positions on the floor. "The deyas sent out their call, and Miles heard it and came. We all know they rarely speak to men. I, for one, would not want to go against the deyas' choice."

A thrill raced up Miles's spine. He hadn't been summoned to be expelled. Meer Ellyer had called him here to give him a mission. He rinsed the cloth in the kitchen, wiped his hands on his trousers, then crossed to the fireplace and hugged Breal's furry neck to hide his trembling.

The High Meer lit the oil lamp and took a large black bowl down from the shelf. The bowl had intricate patterns cut into the sides. Sitting down, he turned the dark bowl over and held it above the lamp like a helm. Light shone through the tiny holes in the bowl and lit the ceiling with a thousand stars.

"Can you see the prow star of Mishtar's Ship in the night sky?" asked Meer Ellyer.

Miles pointed to the star pattern, shaped like a great seagoing galleon. "There," he said.

"That's the star Meer Zabith followed. The seer took the same seaways the Mishtar followed east when he chose to fight alongside the dragons."

The High Meer did not move the bowl, but let his guests gaze upward as if he were bringing the night to them, a gift you could not touch, nor claim, but one that filled the eyes with pleasure.

"The journey will not be an easy one," he said. "The Boundary Waters are well guarded by the king's ships, for there's been a history of piracy in the east, spices mostly, but other goods as well, and the seas between here and Jarrosh are treacherous."

"My ship is sound." Meer Kanoae seemed offended.

"Still, you should prepare yourselves to face tempests. And if the gulf between the worlds grows wider, there may be earthquakes."

"May the Old Magic send us favorable winds," said Meer Eason.

They spoke together for another hour as the night drew closer in around them. And when the hearth fire was burned down to red coals, they made ready to leave.

Slipping off his rush sandals, Miles crouched by the door to put on his boots. The High Meer touched his shoulder. "One last thing," he said. "In the scrying stone last night I saw a girl with sqyth-eyes. She was walking in a dream."

Miles left his boot unlaced and stood. "Sir?"

Meers Eason and Kanoae had also stopped by the door to listen.

Meer Ellyer took Miles's cloak from its peg and held

it out to him. "The scrying stone is often dark. When images come, I pay attention." He took a breath, the crease lines on his forehead deepening. "Dreamwalkers have all but disappeared from Noor. I sensed when I saw her that she is to come with you. But I was given no clue about where she might be. Did the deya say anything about a Dreamwalker?"

Miles felt the air between them expanding. "No, sir, she didn't. But I know the girl you saw," he said. "She is my sister."

FOUR
BLACK BRANCHES

Who will sound the song when we are gone?
Who will hear the way to begin?

—SONG OF THE DEYAS

The sound of children's laughter drew Hanna out her window. In her dreamwalk she did not feel the cool night breeze blow against her skin or sense the damp grass at her feet. She passed through Mother's garden, where rose petals lay in the grass, following the sound across the dirt road.

The moon hung pale as an oyster shell where the starry night crowned Mount Shalem's peak. More laughter. Moving through her dreamwalk, Hanna crossed the dirt road and entered the place that had only a week ago been Shalem Wood. All down the mountainside, the elder trees lay dead, their branches pointing up at the sky.

Near a fallen log a little sapling trembled in the wind,

but Hanna was warm as she moved deeper into her dream. She stepped around the giant logs. Dead. All dead. A week ago, after Tymm was taken and the Waytrees in Garth Lake toppled, the rest of the Waytrees in Shalem Wood began to fall. Thunder had rumbled along with their falling. Hanna had fled the lake, the timbers nearly crushing her as she ran. More ancient trees fell that night and more in the days to come. Seven days and nights they fell. No one had dared venture into the forest then. Hanna had stayed by her mother. Neither of them had slept more than an hour at a time. Grief for Tymm kept them awake. Stunned, they walked empty-handed from room to room.

Along with Mother's grief and her own, Hanna bore Da's anger. Da blamed her for losing Tymm and wouldn't speak to her. Taunier had tried to cheer her a little, but she was deaf to his encouragement. She, too, blamed herself.

Tonight the wood was empty, the mountain bare but for a few small sapling groves.

More ringing laughter drew Hanna up the trail until she reached a broad, grassy meadow where a colossal black tree stood in the very center of the field. It seemed as if all the trees in Shalem Wood had gathered into one and swept up from the earth to touch the moon and stars. The massive trunk was curved like the body of a woman, gowned in silky, black bark. There were holes in her trunk as if she were only half finished, yet as Hanna moved closer, she felt the hairs rising on the backs of her arms. This tree was very much alive.

Children's voices came from above. Hanna peered upward. Figures were moving high in the boughs. A small blond head poked out between the branches.

"Tymm! It's you! I've found you!" Hanna's heart sang as she shouted to him. He was back!

Far above, Tymm clung to a bough with one hand as he ran his other hand along the smooth black trunk. As his fingers moved, pressing, shaping, a face began to form.

"Tymm, you're too high up. Come down from there, now!"

Laughter trickled down the dark branches. If he wouldn't climb down, she'd have to go up. She leaped for the lowest branch. The black wood was as slick as wet glass. Curling her fingers around the lowest limb, she swung her right foot upward. Her hand slipped; she grappled, fell, and hit the ground below. The fall knocked the wind out of her, and she awoke with a start, struggling to breathe.

Still dizzy from the fall, she jumped up, shouting, "Tymm!"

The enormous tree was gone. Falling to her knees, she let out an angry sob. She'd almost had him, if she'd been able to climb up the branches and wrap her arms around him.

"It was a dreamwalk," she whispered, wiping her eyes. Even if she'd reached him, he would have faded with the dream; she couldn't have brought him home.

Hanna brushed blades of grass from her sleeping gown, her hands moving rhythmically as she made up her mind. The dreamwalk had told her Tymm was alive. The wind had blown him and the other children high up into a tree. She would go after him. A tree that massive could not grow in Noor. She'd seen trees close to its towering height only once before, when she'd crossed into the Otherworld. The wind must have blown the children into Oth.

Hanna tried to picture the tree again. Where in Oth would a giant black tree grow? Not anywhere near Enness Isle, she knew, for the tallest Waytrees here had been the ones in Garth Lake, and they were nowhere near that tall before they fell.

The Falconer used to say Oth was as close as breath and just as invisible. She'd seen the maps in his book, the mountains and valleys of Oth reflecting exactly those in Noor, though the names were different. Still, no one could see Oth or reach it without the aid of magic. She would need help to cross over and find the place where such a tree could grow.

The dewy grass chilled her bare feet as she made her way to the far edge of the meadow. She'd flown world to world with the wind woman, Wild Esper, last year. Esper might carry her to Oth. In fact, she would have to if Hanna asked it of her. Wild Esper owed her a boon.

She climbed onto the broad boulder Miles called the watching stone. From its top, one could see Brim Village far below. She curled her toes against the rock. Beyond Brim Harbor, the ocean gleamed red with the rising sun. The sight troubled her. She'd never awakened from a dreamwalk to daylight before. What if she began to dreamwalk in the morning hours, or in the middle of the day? It would be harder to keep her dreamwalks a secret from those outside her family. She tasted the possibility of future humiliation, then forced herself to turn those thoughts aside. She couldn't worry about that now.

Arms up, fingers spread wide, she shouted, "Wild Esper, if you're here on Mount Shalem, show yourself to me!"

Orange-capped waves rolled in on the shore far below. She would let herself be blown to the place Tymm and the others had gone.

She wiggled her fingers, testing the air. *I will make her come,* she thought, *I am sqyth-eyed, and my blue eye gives me the power to befriend sky spirits.* Even as she thought this, she knew how small she was against the elements. How old was the wind, the earth, the sky? She was nothing, and no one to command a wind woman.

Gathering her courage, she shouted again. "Wild Esper. Sky kith, come now!"

She called a third time and a fourth. At last, the wind woman swept up from the sea, cold blue as morning, with the smell of the ocean in her hair. The sudden gust blew Hanna backward. She caught herself with her hands, her palms scraping against the rough stone.

The wind woman swirled overhead as Hanna scrambled to her feet. "Wild Esper, take me to Oth."

Wild Esper breezed nearer, her giant face clear and untroubled. "Why?"

"My brother has been Wind-taken. I have to find him."

The wind woman swirled to the left. "Can a sister find a brother?"

"I can, and you know it." The wind woman knew that well enough. She'd helped Hanna find Miles in Oth last year. Wild Esper sent out tickling breezes and toyed with Hanna's hair.

"Miles and I took care of the Shriker for you and the Sylth Queen, and freed Oth from his curse," Hanna continued. "You told us then we could ask you for a boon for all we'd done. Have you forgotten?"

Wild Esper whisked higher above. "Does a wind spirit forget?"

Hanna didn't know how to answer. "Will you take me to Tymm?"

"Ask for another boon."

"Why?"

"The Old Magic has awakened. No wind will blow against it."

"Can't you carry me to Oth the way you did before? I've had a vision of a great black tree. I think that's where Tymm was taken. I don't know why that is, but I saw—"

"The Wind-taken were not blown into the western lands of Oth. They were carried east."

It was true enough. Hanna had seen Tymm and the others blown east over the sea. She'd been to the Oth lands here in the west—the Oth that matched her own island, for one place mirrored the other. She'd seen maps of eastern Noor and eastern Oth in *The Way Between Worlds,* the handwritten book the Falconer had given her before he died. But she'd not traveled east when she'd gone to the Otherworld. How far had the Wild Wind taken Tymm? How long might it take to get there?

"Do you know how can I reach the Oth lands of the east?"

"Ask your great-uncle Enoch and Old Gurty."

"Why ask them? They've never been east." She might borrow Great-Uncle Enoch's little sailboat. But it would take weeks and weeks, maybe months, to cross the Morrow Sea in that old rickety thing.

"I need you to blow me east, Wild Esper. You have to take me now!"

Wild Esper gusted down the steep hill and up again. "Now, now," she echoed. "I ride only the west wind. Ask Noorushh, who rides the sea winds, to take you there."

"But . . . I don't know that wind spirit! And he doesn't owe me a boon."

Wild Esper shrank down to ride a playful breeze and spun behind Hanna's back. "I do not go where the west wind does not blow."

Hanna dug her nails into her palms. "Can't you change course this once, Wild Esper? Are you so completely powerless?"

At that, Wild Esper's wind rose from breeze to bluster. The wind woman swelled to an enormous size with the powerful wind. Rushing at Hanna, she swept her off her feet, blew her sideways, then flung her onto the ground.

Hanna lay stunned as the wind woman drew back again, her face gray with rage.

"I didn't mean to offend you," Hanna called. "Come back." She got up, stood unsteadily, and waved her arms wildly at the vanishing wind. "Surely we can find a way. Only please, come back!"

FIVE

WILD ESPER'S REVENGE

*I sailed from Othlore to Enness Isle. The day I
arrived on Enness, Wild Esper blew in a storm.*

—*The Way Between Worlds*

Come back she did, and with a vengeance. Hanna
was halfway down the mountainside when the
wind woman blew in on a great black cloud. It had not
taken her long to gather a storm in her skirts. Soaring
overhead, she released a torrent of rain.

"I'm sorry!" Hanna shouted. "Really, I didn't mean
it!" But the rain only battered her harder, drenching
Hanna's hair and gown. She could find no shelter in the
fallen forest, so she stumbled down the path, slipping in
the mud. She was not much closer to home when she
heard Taunier calling.

Mother found my cot empty and sent him out to look for me,
she thought bitterly. *And here I am in my sleeping gown!* She

crouched behind the blueberry bushes, hoping he wouldn't see her as he passed, but his eyes were too sharp for that.

"What are you doing out here?" Taunier's words were harsh and biting as he helped her to stand. When he saw what she was wearing, he looked away and offered her his cloak.

A blush burned up her neck, but she didn't explain herself. Taunier had been working with her da long enough to know that she sometimes disappeared at night. He was the only one outside the family who knew she was a Dreamwalker. Her parents were ashamed of her "night rambles," but Taunier had caught her walking through the woods at night three times since he'd come to work for her da, so he knew.

"Come on, then," he said more gently. "You're soaked through." Draping his wool cloak over her shivering shoulders, he was about to slip off his boots when she said, "I can walk barefoot, really I can."

"You're sure?"

"I am a mountain girl," she said with pride.

"You are that," he replied, laughing.

Rain slapped their heads and backs, drumming the ground. Hanna peered up through her wet bangs. The wind woman was not visible in the clouds, but she was somewhere near, riding the storm and probably delighting in their misery down below. What would Taunier think if she told him what, or rather *who*, was behind this storm?

Hanna's teeth began to chatter. She had to find a way to travel east and follow Tymm.

"Here." Taunier pointed to an overhanging rock. "Let's wait out the worst of it."

At sixteen, he was no older than Miles, yet he was as tall and strong as a grown man. He'd fished with his grandfather as a young boy, worked as a blacksmith's apprentice, then later for the wool merchant, all before he'd come last year to herd sheep for Da. Hanna followed him under the sheltering rock. Taunier's experience fishing with his granda might help if she had to sail east, and it was looking more and more as if that was what she'd have to do. Taunier knew more about boats than she, though she'd fished a few times with her own granda before he had passed away.

Taunier's smooth brown arms shone with rain as he gathered kindling. He'd inherited his dark coloring from his father, a spice trader from Kanayar. Taunier's father had died when he was young, and he rarely spoke of him.

Taunier knelt under the overhanging rock, his brow tilting with concentration as he laid the branches for the fire. She needed to ask him if he knew anyone with a small boat. But before she could go into that, she would have to speak of her dreamwalk and tell him why she needed it.

Intent on the fire, Taunier seemed not to notice Hanna's intense stare. But then why should he pay attention to a girl with one blue eye and one green, a girl some people in town called a witch?

Lightning flashed, shooting silver streamers across the clouds. Hanna wrapped Taunier's cloak more tightly about her. Feeling suddenly tired, she sat and moved in closer until the flames sent delicious waves of heat across her body. She'd hiked a long way in her dreamwalk last night. Rain sprayed around the rock. A sharp wind dislodged a branch in the fire. Sparks flew up as it tumbled from the burning pile, setting the corner of Taunier's cloak alight. Startled, she scooted back against the boulder, furiously trying to untie the knot about her neck and free herself from the burning cloak.

Taunier leaped up, put out his hand, and waved it over the flame. The fire moved under his palm from cloak to branch and joined the central blaze again. Smoke rose from the scorched cloth. Hanna squinted at Taunier and coughed. Had he moved the fire without touching it?

"How did you do that?"

Taunier sat again. "Do what?"

"Herd the fire."

"I didn't."

"You did. I saw you. Did you use magic?"

His shoulders stiffened. "What makes you think that?"

"I was just wondering . . ." She fingered the burned edge of Taunier's cloak.

"My granda taught me how to tend a fire, and he was an ordinary islander like yourself," he instisted.

Ordinary? She'd never been called that before. She laughed, then blushed.

The fire spilled ruby light across Taunier's face and reddened the tips of his black hair. Why wouldn't he admit he had a gift? What was he afraid of?

She peered at the storm. With or without Wild Esper, she had to go east across the sea. Beyond their small shelter, rain pounded the fallen pines and firs.

"What are you thinking about?" asked Taunier.

"Of this." Hanna waved her hand at the dead Waytrees along the hillside. "And of the Wild Wind that took the children." Tymm's name caught in her heart; she couldn't say it aloud.

Taunier cleared his throat and stood up. "This storm won't end any time soon. We'd best be getting home before your mother goes into a panic. You know how she's been since Tymm—" He offered his hand to help her up.

"There's something I have to ask you." Hanna rose, the low fire burning between them. "It wasn't all that many years ago when you used to fish with your granda."

"So?"

"So, do you know anyone down at the harbor who can loan me a small boat?"

Taunier stomped out the fire. "Why?"

"I need to look for Tymm."

Smoke coiled about his legs. "Hanna," he said, "you know all the sailors in Brim went out to sea after the children were blown over the water. And you know as well as I do that they didn't find any of them."

"They didn't know where to look."

"And you do?"

Back on the trail, the slippery mud chilled her feet. Taunier said, "I know you found Miles last year, but this is different, Hanna. Miles was lost here on Mount Shalem. Tymm and the others . . . they were taken far away from us by some—"

"Magic," Hanna finished. "Some magic. That's why I have to go."

Taunier shook his head and said something under his breath. It sounded like *stubborn girl*.

"What did you say?"

He shrugged. "Nothing."

She should have told him where she'd found Miles last year. Miles was on this mountain, yet he was in Oth, a place invisible to all who didn't have the magic to enter in. She'd kept last year's adventure to herself. Only the Falconer, Old Gurty, and Great-Uncle Enoch had known the whole story. It might help to show Taunier the maps of Noor and Oth in *The Way Between Worlds* so he could see how one world mirrored the other. It would be a place to start; yet she'd never shared the Falconer's magical book with anyone but Miles.

At last they came in sight of the cottage. She could see Da working down at the sheep pen. There was no time left. She should tell Taunier now. Whether he admitted it or not, he seemed to know something about magic, and if that were so, she could really use his help. She didn't want to have to sail after Tymm alone. "What do you know of magic?" she asked cautiously.

"Only what I've been taught."

"And what's that?"

"Trouble. And those who practice magic are trouble-makers."

"You can't really think that!"

He thrust out his hand. "Come on. You're to be home, and your da's waiting for me below."

She pulled back. "You go on. I won't be slowing you down anymore."

"And now you're mad at me? When I came to fetch you?"

"I could have gotten home on my own!"

"Fine, then. Suit yourself!"

"And here's your cloak!" She tore it from her back and hurled it at him. It slapped wetly against his front. He glared at her as he put it on, then turned on his heel and marched down to Da.

When Hanna reached the yard, Da said, "Go in now

and comfort your mother. The poor soul thought the wind had stolen you, too!" His voice was cold with anger.

"I dreamwalked, Da. I couldn't help it. I'm sorry."

In the cottage, Mother sat on the bench near the fire.

"I'm sorry, Mother. I didn't mean to worry you."

Mother shook her head, speechless over losing Tymm, and then this morning thinking Hanna, too, had disappeared. Hanna felt her Mother's confused sorrow all the more in the silence.

"I'll make us some thool," she offered. A few minutes later, bringing her mother the steaming cup, she wanted to say she'd caught sight of Tymm, but Mother had been raised to distrust any kind of magic, and she feared Hanna's dreamwalks.

Hardly able to bear the troubled silence, Hanna found herself wishing her mother would shout at her. Mother had always kept busy, spinning wool when she wasn't scrubbing the floor, milking the cow, cooking stew, or making candles. Now her hands were empty. She hadn't even picked up her cup.

"I'll find him, Mother. Remember how I found Miles last year?" Hanna was desperate to believe it herself. But she'd had more faith in magic when the Falconer was alive to guide her. The great meer had traveled all over Noor and had crossed into Oth many times before he came to spend the last years of his life on Enness Isle. Hanna missed her old teacher terribly.

"Won't you drink your thool, Mother, before it gets cold?"

"I don't want it."

Hanna sat on the bench. The fire was warm, but the warmth didn't reach her. With her arm about her mother, she watched the tilting flames.

SIX

You will learn to find great magic in ordinary things.

—*The Othic Art of Meditation*

It is not easy for a girl to run away, especially an island girl, but Hanna's granda had once had a small sailboat. It belonged to his brother, Great-Uncle Enoch, now, though it was little used and in ill repair.

She had to borrow Da's wheelbarrow to haul the Falconer's trunk and other supplies down to the harbor, and then she had to steal the boat itself. It shamed her to do it, but she couldn't stay on the island any longer.

Before dawn, she'd hefted the trunk aboard the boat and stowed it down below. She'd filled it with needed things: the Falconer's book, which she needed for its pages on magic, herbal healing, and, most of all, for the hand-drawn maps of Noor and Oth. She'd also packed the

Falconer's healing tinctures, his knife, and Tymm's grass rope—the very last thing he'd made before he was stolen. Last she packed her own precious lightstone, which had glowed even in the darkest realm of the shadow vale last year when she'd gone into Oth after Miles.

Trunk stowed and water barrel battened down, she slipped her hand in her pocket and felt the cool glass vial. Great-Uncle Enoch had given her the vial last evening when he'd come to the cottage with Old Gurty to treat Mother with mountain herbs that would ease her anxious fears and help her sleep.

Hanna had asked Great-Uncle Enoch to help her draw water from the well, hoping to get a word with him alone. As she'd hauled up the water bucket, he'd said, "After your da came by our cottage to tell us Tymm was stolen, I went to Garth Lake to sit by the old roots and listen."

The bucket shook in her hand. She hadn't gone back to the lake herself the week after Tymm was stolen, when the whole forest was toppling down. Nor had she tried to reach Great-Uncle Enoch's smallholding, with so many trees falling between her cottage and his. She marveled at the old man's courage. Still, her great-uncle had a deep understanding of trees. Most folk thought Enoch had lived in Reon for fifty years before coming back to Enness, but Hanna knew the real secret of his past. He'd angered the Sylth Queen long ago, and she'd taken her revenge by imprisoning him in a stunted oak for fifty years.

She'd helped Miles and Gurty free him from the oak after they'd returned from Oth, and she remembered how Enoch had cried with joy when he'd been freed.

Hanna peered into his eyes, light blue even in the moonlight.

"The roots are dying," he said. "The Waytrees all across Noor, who hold the mysteries of Oth in their roots, are falling. If the last of the Waytrees fall, the way between the worlds will close."

Hanna's throat constricted. "I spoke to Wild Esper," she blurted. "She said the wind blew Tymm and the rest of the children to eastern Oth. If the way between the worlds closes, how am I . . . how can we get Tymm out of Oth before it's too late?"

Great-Uncle Enoch shook his head. "The roots did not tell me that. But you went to Oth last year and found Miles."

"Here on the mountain," she reminded him. "Tymm was blown cast."

Enoch took the bucket from her to fill a pitcher. "You were in Brim when the first wind came, and later you saw Tymm taken. Tell me what you saw, Hanna."

"The wind stole only three children out of the crowd: Cilla, Brand, and Darlee. It seemed to pick them out. To *choose* them. If you had been there, you would have seen how it knocked the rest of us down. First it happened in the market square; then Tymm was taken, but I was not." She'd not said this aloud before. She hadn't let herself even think it. Her brother had been chosen. She'd been left behind.

Hanna leaned against the cold well stones. She'd crossed over into Oth and knew something about magic. Hadn't the Falconer entrusted her with his important book before he died? Hadn't she and Miles helped free Enoch from the oak? Wasn't she a Dreamwalker whose dreams often foretold the future? Why would the wind steal children too young to know anything of magic? What could the wind possibly want with *them*?

She looked up at her great-uncle. "Why take Tymm, Uncle Enoch?" she asked. "He's so young."

"So young, aye." He tipped the dipper this way and that. "The wind is choosing, as you say."

"But why?"

Enoch could speak the language of the trees. He'd been to Oth, was old enough to know, but he only shook his head, his tangled hair a white nest in the starlight.

"You'll go after him, just as you went after Miles."

"Come with me. Can you come?" Her hand was on his threadbare sleeve.

Enoch shook his head. "I'm too old to go as far as that. You know it, Hanna." He hung the dipper on its hook, then pulled a small, brown bottle from his pocket. "This is for you."

She cupped the cool glass in her hand. "Is this a healing tincture?"

Enoch smiled. "You might say that, but it's only a bit of salt water."

Hanna wanted to say, *What's the use of that?* But Great-Uncle Enoch touched the corner of his eye. "Tears," he whispered. "And not sorry ones, but glad ones that came on the day you, Miles, and Gurty freed me from the tree."

His wrinkled face cracked to a full smile. "Gurty helped me gather them after you left us on the mountain."

Hanna remembered how he'd come out of the oak tree the Sylth Queen had enspelled him in, waving his arms and weeping happily after fifty years of imprisonment on the high cliff.

"What am I to do with them?" she asked.

"The roots told me the Kanameer will know what to do with them."

Enoch picked up the pitcher and turned to leave. His soft-spoken words had confused Hanna more than ever. "Wait," she said. "Who is the Kanameer?"

It was then Da had thrown open the back door, calling, "What's taking so long with the water, girl? Must I come out myself?"

A gull landed on the dock and folded its wings. Hanna slipped Enoch's vial back into her pocket and looked out across the bay. It was time to go. She climbed on the deck of the creaking boat. The cloudy sky held the threat of rain, but the rising sun sent arms of light across the sea. As the time for departure drew near, she grew more anxious. Why hadn't she paid closer attention to Granda's instructions the last time he'd taken her to sea? Frowning with concentration, she checked beneath the narrow seats, where the extra rope was stored, and found the stash of candles, the life floaters, and other gear.

Footsteps sounded on the dock, and I Iauna turned. Taunier leaned against the piling, arms crossed, the burnt edge of his green cloak flapping in the breeze.

She rose to face him. "What are you doing here?"

"I might ask you the same question."

Mother and Da must have found the note she'd written before dawn this morning and sent him down to stop her. "Tell my parents I can't come home," she said. "Tell them I won't come."

"I know that."

His calm answer infuriated her. Was he so self-assured that he thought he could leap on deck and muscle her home against her will? When they'd walked back down the mountain yesterday morning, she never should have told him she was in search of a boat or mentioned her reason for wanting it. But Taunier's next words made her draw in a breath.

"I thought I'd better come along."

"Come along?"

"Aye, it's better than sailing this little ship alone, isn't it?"

She adjusted her hood to conceal her red cheeks. "You know it's bound to be a long journey," she challenged.

"Would you rather I stay behind so you can look for Tymm on your own?"

"No, I—" Now what had she done? A half smile appeared on his face. He was teasing her, and she'd fallen for it.

"I was out for weeks sometimes with my granda. Twice we sailed as far as Reon to sell our catch, and our boat wasn't much bigger than this one."

She didn't want to argue, and the next few moments were a flurry of activity as they readied the boat for launch. The sun glinted on the choppy water, and gulls circled overhead. Hanna's heart felt lighter. It would be a long journey, but she didn't have to cross the East Morrow Sea alone.

Before she helped Taunier hoist the sail, she touched Enoch's small brown bottle for luck, though some would say the liquid treasure inside was only a bit of salt water.

SEVEN
MIST AND MUSIC

*After a long sea journey, the Mishtar returned
home to the isle of Othlore. There he wrote his
dragon history, scored the* **Dragons' Requiem,**
and taught young meers his magic.

—*A MEER'S HISTORY OF NOOR*

S alt water splashed the *Leena's* prow. On the foredeck,
Miles cleared his raw throat and shouted into the
wall of fog. "Hanna! Taunier!"

No answer. The torches hissed. They'd lit two here on
the prow and two at the stern, hoping to send a guiding light
into the thick mist. How could she have run away like that?
They'd sailed all the way to Enness Isle only to find Hanna
had gone the day before. Another delay, after it had taken
them nearly two weeks to sail from Othlore! He spat over the
side. Pigheaded girl. If she'd waited just a little longer, they
would have taken her aboard the *Leena.* But she'd gone off in
Great-Uncle Enoch's excuse for a boat, a one-man ship that
would never make it across the East Morrow Sea.

Miles shouted their names again. How could they hope to find Hanna in this wretched, endless fog? It was a wonder Captain Kanoae could steer at all in this soup.

He put his hand up to his neck. Shout much more and he'd lose his voice altogether. Deep down, he understood why Hanna had left in such a hurry. He leaned into the rail, remembering how horrible he'd felt when Da told him Tymm was Wind-taken, like he'd been hit in the gut with a shovel.

He knew something was terribly wrong when he'd walked up the long dirt road toward home and saw all the old trees of Shalem Wood felled, the great forest of his childhood gone. But the second blow was worse when he'd reached the cottage with the meers to find Mother, her face swollen from tears, and Da, with his utterly lost expression.

"They're gone," Da said while Mother paced, sobbing. "Both of them. First our Tymm, then Hanna thinking she could sail after him." He choked the words out, his voice thick with anger. "We sent Taunier down to fetch her back. Stubborn girl wouldn't come."

"Where's Taunier now?" Miles had asked.

"The boy went with her," Da said. He sat on the

bench and looked up at Miles. "At least the lad's familiar with the sea."

"Taunier will look after Hanna," Miles said, hoping to ease his da's fears. Meer Eason had brewed some thool while Miles tried to get his mother to sit down next to Da.

"He was always so clever with his hands, was Tymm," Da said, his own rough hands cupped over his knees as he looked into the fire. It took a long time to make sense of the whole story with both his parents so lost in grief. Miles found his own inner storm taking on more power at the sight of Mother's hopelessness and Da's rage.

Over and over Miles had said, "I'll bring them home. I promise," trying to convince them—to convince himself.

"We'll do all we can to find your son and daughter, Mr. Sheen," said Meer Eason. There was no consoling them. They both had a hollow look, like the expression Miles had noticed on the Brim townsfolk; only his parents' faces were lined with a heavier, more personal sorrow.

The ship heaved. Find Hanna. Find Tymm. He wondered if he could keep either promise he'd made to his parents. If they couldn't locate the small sailboat in this fog, how could the meers go east without the Dreamwalker? And if they did turn east without her, how could he go with them and abandon his sister?

Breal trotted up, his nostrils flaring.

"Have you picked up a scent?" Back at the cottage they'd held one of Hanna's scarves to Breal's wet nose. A great hunter, Breal had followed prey from Noor to Oth and back in his darker years, when the Shriker's curse was on him. Now Breal thwacked Miles's leg with his heavy tail, confusion in his large brown eyes.

Miles leaned over the rail. Maybe it was time to use his power. Just this once he could shape-shift into a bird, fly over the water, and spot his sister's boat. What was the harm in that? His heart pounded just thinking of it, and his mouth began to water. It would have to be a large bird, like the giant falcon shape he'd taken last year, for he wouldn't consider shifting into anything smaller or less powerful than himself. A great bird, then, with a six- or seven-foot wingspan. His breath quickened. He gripped the rail tighter, then Breal tugged his shirttail so hard it nearly pulled him over, bringing him back to his senses. Squatting down, he put his face against his dog's neck to breathe in the familiar smell of his fur and calm himself. The falcon's warning last year had been right. *Change thrice and you free dark power.* His third shift into the Shriker had freed dark power all right. And he'd nearly lost himself when he'd become the beast. What might await him if he should shift a fourth time?

"Sorry, Breal," he whispered. "It's only . . . so much has gone wrong, and we need to find Hanna quickly."

When he stood again, Meer Eason was crossing the deck. A sudden wave sent a white spray across the meer's face, leaving droplets in his gray-black braid. He gave a laugh of surprise, adjusted his damp robes, then tipped his head and hummed. Miles wondered how his Music Master could remain so cheerful.

"What notes are the wind playing?" he asked.

"Why?" asked Miles.

He should have listened, then answered his teacher with respect, but he was too worried about Hanna to think of music now.

"I ask because it is important."

Miles frowned. "Sir?"

"Music goes back to the first song lines of eOwey. The Old Magic of that first song is still here. Listen, play, and we will keep in tune with it." Eason drew out his alto flute. "We must do all we can to keep in touch with the Old Magic."

It would ease him to play a song. Sometimes he lost his anger when he played, or his fear, but how could he take any solace with Tymm gone and Hanna in jeopardy? It didn't seem right. And anyway, his mood was too heavy now for music.

"The magic is already going out of the world," Miles said. "Haven't you felt it?"

Meer Eason nodded. "I feel it."

"Even when we passed through Brim's market square on our way back to the boat, everything seemed different. No one was haggling over prices, and the children just stood there. They seemed to have forgotten how to laugh or play." He gripped the rail, not sure what he was trying to say.

"It takes imagination to play," Eason said. "The High Meer told us that, as Oth splits away from Noor, people will forget how to dream. I, too, saw the emptiness. They had the look of those who sleep but cannot dream."

"I still dream," Miles said.

"In color?"

Miles stared into the fog. "Gray dreams."

"Fading dreams," Eason said. "We're lucky still to have some magic in us from our music and from our time on Othlore."

"Will it be like this all over Noor from now on?" The mist seemed to flood into him, saying this. It was as if all the children had been stolen, not just those who were Wind-taken. And it wasn't only the children who had lost their liveliness. The grown-ups were worse: gray-faced, deadened. What happens to people who cannot dream? What kind of world would be left in Noor if all the magic were gone?

"Maybe Oth's already too far from us," Miles said despondently. "Maybe we're already too late to stop the rift between the worlds."

Meer Eason leaned into the wind. "I don't think the High Meer would have sent us to Jarrosh if it were already too late, Miles." He polished the silver flute with the soft lining of his cloak. "This heavy feeling you have, I won't tell you it's not real, but you have to try to fight it. Keep hold of the magic that is in you. We can't be of any help if we lose hold of that in ourselves, can we?"

Bringing the conversation back to its beginning,

Meer Eason continued, "Music will help you feel better. How is the *Dragons' Requiem* coming?"

"The Mishtar's score is hard to play, sir."

"That it is," Eason said with a knowing smile. "You can practice it with me now."

"But, sir."

"What is it now? Did you leave your ervay down in the cabin?"

"No, I have it." Miles lifted his cloak, revealing the leather pouch hanging from his shoulder. It was a part of him, always there. "It's just . . . the *Dragons' Requiem*. Do you think it's true what we heard about the dragons when we landed in Reon?" There had been some ugly rumors flying around the harbor and at the sellers' stalls last week, when they stopped to get supplies.

"That the dragons are at war with men again?" Eason said. "It's hard to say. They're wild creatures, after all."

"But why would they break the treaties after so many years?"

"I've wondered that myself." Meer Eason stared out into the nothingness, the sea and sky one solid color. Miles felt the ship moving forward into the gray.

Breal interrupted the conversation, nudging up against

Miles and lifting his snout. "Breal's been sniffing the air. He might have found Hanna's scent."

Meer Eason looked pleased and patted the dog's head.

Miles said, "He has a brilliant nose."

Meer Eason laughed. "I hope you're right." He played three notes, catching the wind's eerie tune. "We can't see Hanna's boat in this mist. Play with me. We will let our music speak across the water."

Miles wasn't at all sure Meer Eason's idea would work, but he tugged the ervay from the beaded pouch. The sylth silver of the Y-shaped flute felt cool against his fingers.

"Begin," Meer Eason said.

Throughout the sunless day, the sea air remained gray as an empty room. Torches hissed orange on the prow, their light barely piercing the fog. Miles leaned against the rail. His lips were numb from hours of playing. Still, as they'd practiced the *Dragons' Requiem*, he'd felt a tingling in his core, the sense that the Old Magic was everywhere around them, invisible yet there, as Meer Eason had said. In the music, he'd found the assurance he'd needed so much just now.

More hours passed, with still no sign of the little

sailboat. Mist thinned enough for them to see the moon rising ringed with clouds. Music drifted across the endless dark. Then Breal began to bark, and a voice called across the water. "Hello?"

Miles lowered his ervay, trembling. He knew that voice. "Hanna?"

A small wavering sail appeared ghostlike ahead. Miles made out a tiny boat with two figures huddled on the deck. One stood suddenly on the wobbling boat, peering through the gloom.

"Miles?" Hanna called excitedly. "We heard the song. Taunier sailed toward it. I can't believe—"

Breal barked and jumped up and down on the deck.

"Breal?" Hanna reached toward the *Leena* recklessly, tipping her boat even more.

"Keep your craft steady," ordered Captain Kanoae. "You'll see your brother and your dog soon enough. Let us come up alongside you."

Kanoae deftly maneuvered the *Leena* toward the small boat on the choppy water. Breal bounded across the deck as Miles and Eason unlashed the climbing ropes.

"Give me your hand," Miles called down to Hanna. She scaled up the side, and her small cold hand gripped his. He pulled his sister onto the deck, her round face nearly invisible in the dark.

"What are you doing here?" she asked breathlessly. They were alone for a brief moment as Meer Eason helped Taunier on board.

"You're crazy, Hanna. Do you know that?" He hugged her, then pushed her away, relieved to find her and irritated that she'd sailed off with Taunier.

Meer Eason called, "Where's your hospitality, Miles? Our guests are cold and wet. Why don't you take these seafarers down below and get some hot thool into them?"

"What about Enoch's boat?" Taunier asked anxiously.

"Don't worry about that. Captain Kanoae and I can rig up the towline ourselves."

"Come on." Miles led them to the stairs. He had a word or two to say to them both in private.

FIGHT
BELOW DECK

Tesha yoven *is "Bind the broken"*
in DragonTongue.

—THE MISHTAR, *DRAGON'S WAY*, VOL. 2

Hanna took the pan down from the hook and lit the stove in the ship's galley. "Where's the thool powder, Miles?"

Her brother was too busy glaring at Taunier to answer her. They were the same age, but Taunier was taller and broader shouldered; still, Miles looked poised to start a fight. "Just what were you thinking, taking my sister to sea?"

Taunier narrowed his dark eyes. "I didn't take her to sea. She was leaving on her own, so I—"

"He's right." Hanna wedged her way between them. "I was going to leave Enness anyway. Taunier came along to help, so I wouldn't sail east alone."

"Mother and Da are worried sick," snapped Miles, pacing, his face angry in the candle's glow.

The ship tilted, and the pans hanging from the ceiling clanged together. Hanna spread her feet to keep her balance. "I knew they would be upset, but I left a note telling them why I—"

"You should have stayed home, Hanna. Mother and Da were already frightened enough after what happened to Tymm."

Her brother's words stung, and Hanna blinked back sudden tears. "It was because of Tymm I had to go. You know that!"

Tymm's name had been invoked but twice. Still, Hanna felt it floating in the air between them like a spell. And it seemed that the table, the hanging pots, and the spice bundles grew dim with the sound of it.

Miles wiped his nose on his sleeve. "Da told me you were with Tymm when . . . when it happened."

Hanna sat on a bench and wrapped her arm about Breal's thick neck. He panted and licked her cheek. "We were out by Garth Lake when the wind came. I tried to catch Tymm as he was swept away, but I couldn't reach him." She hugged Breal harder. "I tried, Miles; I really did." She was crying now, wiping her cheeks with her rough, damp cloak.

Miles said, "I know."

"How can you know? You weren't even there!"

"The same thing happened to me on Othlore."

"What?" Hanna looked up at her brother.

"It's happening everywhere," Miles said. "The Way-trees in the old forests all across Noor are falling. And everywhere the trees die, children are Wind-taken."

Taunier crossed his arms and leaned against the counter. "But why?"

"We don't know why for sure, but the High Meer thinks there is a connection between the two. He said the children might have been taken to help the Waytrees in the east. We're heading there now to find out."

"Who would do that?" Hanna blurted. "It's horrible. And anyway, how could Tymm or Cilla or any of them be of help?"

Miles looked startled. "Cilla was taken, too? Mave's little girl who weaves so well?"

Hanna nodded. "She and some others were stolen from the market in Brim. Taunier and I were there when it happened." She realized Mother and Da must have been too overwrought about Tymm to tell Miles about Cilla. The pot boiled, and she removed it from the stove.

Miles said, "When the tempest came to Othlore, the boy beside me was taken up. I tried to keep hold of his ankle, but the gust smashed me against a wall and tore him from my grasp." He heaved a sigh. "As they spun higher I heard him and the others calling out in DragonTongue."

"What did they say?" asked Taunier.

"Words you wouldn't understand." Miles said this a bit too proudly, Hanna thought.

"But I've studied some DragonTongue myself," Miles added.

"Out with it," demanded Taunier. Hanna knew Taunier didn't like to be bettered any more than Miles did.

Miles pulled back his shoulders. "They called out 'Tesha yoven.' It's a binding spell."

Hanna dropped the rag she'd been drying her hands on. "Tymm said that before he was taken."

Miles leaned forward. "Are you sure?"

She nodded.

"It doesn't make sense. How would Tymm know those words?"

Hanna picked up the fallen rag and shook it out.

"He might have seen them in the Falconer's book," said Taunier.

"I've kept it locked away in the trunk. I'm sure Tymm never got a chance to read it." She turned to Miles. "What does it mean?"

"Bind the broken." He crossed his arms. "We use the spell in Restoration Magic class to mend broken pitchers or furniture or—"

"Like Tymm," said Taunier.

"Not like Tymm. He was . . . is," he corrected himself, "clever-handed, but we don't use glue pots at the meer's school."

"Bind the broken." Hanna tasted the words like a new flavor. This was what the Waytrees and the deyas inside them did. Bind the places where the worlds were breaking in two.

At the rough table, Taunier reached out and caught the candle's drip on his forefinger. Clear as rain at first falling, it hardened white on his fingertip. Hanna felt a flutter in her belly as he lifted the wax from his finger, formed a tiny boat, and put it on the table. This was the second time she'd seen his friendly way with fire, though the first time he'd moved flame.

Hanna found the thool can in the cupboard and stirred the brown powder into the pot. She needed to busy herself, to do something with her hands as she tried to take it all in.

Miles told them of another meer who'd sailed east early in the year. "She's a seer named Zabith who lived deep in Othlore Wood. She knew something was amiss before the rest of us. We hope to meet up with her, though we don't know if she reached Jarrosh."

Taunier spun the wax boat on the table. "If you meant to head east all along, why take the time to sail west to Enness?"

Waves beat against the hull. Hanna steadied herself and poured the thool for all of them. Miles stirred the hot drink in his mug. "The High Meer saw a face in the scrying stone," he said at last.

Taunier stopped spinning. "Whose face?" he asked, his voice faintly quavering.

Hanna looked at him. Was he wondering if the High Meer had seen him? Singled him out in his scrying stone for his power over fire?

"Hanna's."

Hanna's head felt suddenly light, as if she'd swallowed

the candle's glow. *The High Meer of Othlore sent them to Enness to find me!* She felt herself smiling. To be seen in a magical scrying stone. To be wanted . . .

Hiding her expression, she peered over the rim of her mug at Taunier. What did he think? Was he happy for her? Taunier met her gaze with silence. His head was tilted slightly, as if seeing her for the first time. She glanced away, suddenly uncomfortable.

Miles finished his thool in four gulps. "The High Meer said we were to bring the Dreamwalker with us." He wiped his mouth. "You know about her dreamwalks by now, don't you?" he asked Taunier.

"I know. I've followed her more than once to bring her home."

"Stop it," said Hanna, suddenly fuming. "Both of you are talking about me as if I'm not here."

"Sorry, sis." Miles put his empty mug in the washtub.

"Hanna?" Taunier scooted the wax boat across the table to her.

She picked it up. It felt warm. Weightless. The High Meer had sent them after her, a Dreamwalker. She'd not spoken to anyone about the things she'd seen in her latest dreamwalk. She was still trying to puzzle it out.

The door burst open. Meer Eason poked his head in. "We have brought your things aboard. Captain Kanoae said you are to bunk with her, Hanna. We slid your trunk under your berth." He seemed to catch the tension in the room. "Well, I have to get back on deck. Miles, will you show them to their quarters when you're done here?"

"I will, sir."

NINE

THE FALCONER'S BOOK

Wind erased their footprints,
And the people wandered lost.

—*The Book of eOwey*

Miles hurried them down the narrow passage to the captain's quarters, lit the oil lamp, and shut the door. Hanna sat on the bed, not seeming to want to look at him or Taunier. She tugged her fingers through her tangled hair. Taunier leaned against Captain Kanoae's map-covered table.

"Have you dreamwalked since Shalem Wood was destroyed?" Miles asked cautiously.

"Why do you want to know?" Hanna looked irritated. Or was that fear he was seeing?

"Something else the High Meer said. Wherever forests are falling, people are forgetting how to dream. We've seen a kind of hollow look on people's faces ever since we left Othlore, in places like Reon, and we saw it again in Brim."

"I know what you mean," Taunier said with interest. "The other morning when I came through Brim looking for Hanna, the townsfolk were acting strangely. Their faces had a grayish color, and the children just stood about. None of them were playing like they usually do."

Miles tried not to show the anxiety he was feeling. Losing dreams was a part of this all somehow, though he didn't know the connection yet. He'd been overjoyed to find Hanna safe tonight, but he couldn't forget the reason the meers had gone out of their way to find her. What good would it do to bring her east, where they'd be facing certain danger, if she could no longer dream?

Hanna went to the porthole window. "I dreamwalked after Tymm was stolen," she said. "A week after, if you want to know precisely when. All the elder trees in Shalem Wood had fallen by then." She peered outside at the lifting mist as she described the dreamwalk, the great black tree she'd seen, and the children climbing its branches.

"Tymm?" Miles asked, his mouth dry. "You saw him?"

Hanna nodded.

"A strange dream, for sure," said Taunier. "What do you think it means?"

"I don't know." She paced the tiny room, hugging her elbows. "I just remember what it was like seeing Tymm. I thought I'd found him, you know?" She stared at the uneven lamp's glow and shook her head. "Then I woke up, and he was gone again."

Miles looked into her eyes, one green and one blue. "We'll find him, Hanna. We have to find him." He was reassuring her, though his stomach churned, and it wasn't from seasickness. Before he'd left for the meer school, Tymm had helped him mend the fence with his small, clever hands. They'd laughed together, drinking from the water pouch, spitting arcs of silver water at the sheep on the far side of the fence. He clenched his jaw at the memory. "I've never seen nor heard of any black trees like you described in your dream."

"I hadn't, either. But before I left Enness, I searched through the Falconer's book and found something about a tree like that."

"Where's the book now?"

Hanna pointed to the trunk. Miles bent down and pulled it out.

"Let me," said Hanna. Opening the lid, she set the

heavy tome on the bunk and leafed through it until she reached a page about Kwen-Arnun.

"Listen," She traced her finger along the text and read the description: "'In the beginning when eOwey sang everything into being, Kwen-Arnun, the World Tree, held the world of NoorOth together. Kwen, white-barked and strong, embraced his tree-wife, Arnun, her branches black and shining. Male and female under the NoorOth sun, trunks and branches intertwining, together they were one.'"

She read the rest of the passage describing the great quake that shook NoorOth in the second age, breaking the worlds, splitting the World Tree in two, Kwen tumbling into Noor, Arnun crashing in the otherworld of Oth.

"'Storms blew over Oth, where Kwen's tree-wife, Arnun, was shattered on the ground. Her shining black trunk lay in pieces. Tempests swept through Noor, where Kwen fell, his branches twisted, his broken heart turning slowly to stone.'"

She looked up from the page. "Do you see?"

"Wait, look at this part." Miles read aloud the passage on the next page, part of the tale he'd never seen before: "'Some say that Kwen and Arnun died when they parted long ago, and Kwen's remains are buried in the eastern lands of Noor. But the great Mishtar, who fought alongside the dragons to protect the Waytrees, held that one day the heart of the World Tree might still be awakened, and Kwen and Arnun be rejoined.'"

Miles ran his hands along the script. In all the books he'd read at school, he didn't remember anything about the World Tree rejoining again someday.

Taunier said. "What does it have to do with the tree you saw in your dreamwalk?" Miles wasn't sure, either.

Hanna glared at them both. "Don't you understand?" she asked. "Tymm was in an enormous tree. It grew from the earth like a towering fortress, larger than any tree you can imagine. It was black and shining, too, and it says right here"—she jabbed the page with her finger—"that Kwen's tree-wife, Arnun, had black and shining branches."

Miles drew back. "But the female half of the World Tree is good, isn't she? She wouldn't take young children. Arnun wouldn't call an evil wind to steal our Tymm!"

"I'm not saying the World Tree is evil," Hanna argued. "Only that the tree is like the one I saw in my dream. It's the only mention of a black tree that size that I found in the book!"

"There must be other massive black-barked trees like that!"

"Nowhere in Noor that I know of."

"In Oth, then!"

Taunier put out his hand. "Stop it, both of you. Arguing like this won't help us at all."

Miles stood. "What do you say then, Taunier? Is there any sense in what she's saying?" He was sure Taunier would side with him.

Instead, Taunier looked from one to the other. "I say you're both missing something. There's a clue here that neither one of you seems to see."

"Aye? And what's that?" Miles asked, not even trying to hide his irritation.

Taunier read aloud: "'As NoorOth loosened into the seen and unseen worlds of Noor and Oth, the rift tore a black hole in the heart of the Old Magic, and a Wild Wind awakened with the breaking of the worlds.'"

"Wild Wind," Miles whispered. The boat creaked, and the acrid scent of burning lamp oil filled his nostrils.

"It's clear this wind has come again," said Taunier. "And this time it's sweeping up children."

TEN
CRACKED STONE

*The dragons have come to Othlore to hatch
their young in our mountain caves. Our
Waytrees are well guarded, and the meers
have welcomed our winged guests.*

—THE MISHTAR, *DRAGON'S WAY*, VOL. 1

Alone in the cabin, Hanna pulled on her nightdress. The small room had darkened when Miles and Taunier left with the oil lamp, but she did not want to light a candle when she had another light to read by. The stone she'd taken into Oth last year still glowed when she warmed it in her palm. Hanna pulled the lightstone from the trunk.

It was cold to the touch. She turned the gray-blue stone over and traced the jagged white line that ran down its side like captured lightning. Closing her hand, she waited for the familiar pale blue light to shine out between her fingers. Sitting cross-legged on the bunk, she opened *The Way Between Worlds* again. There would surely be more here to help them with their trouble now.

A golden ray rinsed the paper. Hanna raised the stone to eye level. The light used to shine blue. Had the color changed because she'd left the stone untouched for so long? Well, blue light or yellow, it was still bright enough to read by.

"Teacher," she whispered, "tell me what to do to help Tymm."

The book was as mysterious as the old man who'd written it. She imagined the Falconer, quill in hand, filling in the pages, remembering his house inside the hill, the way the herbs smelled the night he'd sung Miles's sacred name, his keth-kara, to heal him after the Shriker attacked.

When Miles was lost last year, the Falconer had said to her, "You will seek your brother in the Otherworld. For the boy who is bound must be freed by your hand." Back then he was talking of her older brother, not her younger one, yet the Falconer had shown more faith in her than anyone else ever had. Mother had feared her strange dreams and her sqyth-eyes; Da had thought of her only as a child, and worried she'd get lost on the mountainside while she looked for Miles. The villagers had called her a witch because of her strange eyes. And though Miles had been the Falconer's apprentice and had studied with him long before Hanna ever had the nerve to visit the old man's hermitage, the Falconer had valued her and had taken special time to prepare her for her journey into Oth.

The meer was gone now, but he'd left Miles his prized ervay and bequeathed her his handwritten book.

The Way Between Worlds was as much a journal as a book. It had its own kind of magic. Pages seemed to appear at one reading only to vanish later, as if freshly written text were brought forth to aid her each time she read it. Topics wandered from one to another, and she often found it hard to follow. At least the map pages stayed put and could always be found in the same place.

Closing her eyes, she let the book fall open again and again: a page on herbal salves, a description of Garth Lake in winter when snow crowned the Waytrees. She skimmed the pages faster, until she found the words *Wind Spirits*, and read about Noorushh, who rode a white cloud stallion above the sea, and Isparel, the wind dancer of the east. Would Noorushh or any other wind spirits be strong enough to carry her to the place where the Wild Wind had gone? She knew how to call Wild Esper but hadn't a clue about how to call the others. And nothing in these pages told her how.

The lightstone was warmer than ever. Her palm began to sweat as she flipped to the maps near the back of the book, passing the familiar drawings of Enness Isle and Othlore. There were several Oth maps. The Falconer had used the magic of the Waytrees to travel from world to world more than once. But the only Oth map from the east was of a place called All Souls Wood.

In tiny scrawled letters at the base of the map, she read, *The greatest forest of Oth.* Would the greatest forest in the Otherworld be the place where half of the World Tree, the black-barked Arnun, might have fallen?

Excited by the thought, she traced the edge of the map from a place called Taproot Hollow to All Souls Wood. Hanna looked up. Taproot Hollow? That place was mentioned in the game Blind Seer. What did it mean? She whispered the familiar rhyme.

> *"Children fly when worlds are shaken,*
> *Now the children are Wind-taken.*

Seek them there, seek them here,
  before the children disappear.
Dreamer, travel through the night,
Take Blind Seer robbed of sight.
Seek them there, seek them here,
  before the children disappear.
Bring the boy the torches follow
To the heart of Taproot Hollow.
Seek them there, seek them here,
  before the children disappear."

The verses had haunted her after the first children were Wind-taken, and she'd thought of them with foreboding again the day Tymm disappeared. But Blind Seer was only a kind of hide-and-seek game, wasn't it?

The clues went nowhere. How was she ever going to locate Tymm? She slammed the book shut, dropped the lightstone, and heard a crack.

There was a knock at the door. She plucked the lightstone off the floor, shoved it under the covers, and slipped on her cloak.

"Come in."

Taunier closed the door behind him. "Meer Kanoae

seems to think I should be dropped off at the next port to find my way home," he said heatedly.

"Why?"

"Not enough room for me on the ship, she says, and I've no reason to go east with the rest of you."

"Why don't you tell them?"

"Tell them what?"

"That you know magic. That you have a power that might help us."

He stood straight-backed as a soldier, his face hard and expressionless.

"You know what I'm talking about," Hanna said. "I saw you herd fire. It's a power few people have. I'm not even sure the meers themselves can do it." He still hadn't admitted his power to her, but she knew what she'd seen that day on the mountain. She peered at the burned corner of his green cloak. Evidence.

"I think they'll want you aboard if they know—" She faltered.

Taunier was pacing again. Suddenly, he turned and pulled up his sleeve. "Do you see this?" There was a brand on his upper arm—a circle with the letter *B* inside.

"That's . . . horrible. Who did that to you?"

"That's the wool merchant's work. The *B* is for black magic. He accused me of using black magic at his shop, when all I did was save his little girl's life in a fire and keep his filthy shop from burning to the ground!"

Hanna felt a drumming in her ears. Most folk on Enness Isle feared magic of any kind. It was one of the reasons they shunned her family. Hadn't the Sheens brought the monstrous Shriker to the isle long ago? Didn't they have a daughter who might hex you with her strange witch-eyes? A son who'd gone to Othlore, where folk were known to study magic?

It didn't matter that Mother told the town gossips Miles had sailed to Othlore to study music and medicine, or that he would return with skills to heal the islanders of all their sores and sicknesses.

She ran her hand along her own arm, sickened by Taunier's brand. If the wool merchant were here, she'd kick him in the gut and pelt him with stones for harming Taunier.

"Don't look at it like that," he snapped, quickly rolling down his sleeve.

He'd misread her. "The wool merchant should have been punished," she said.

"Aye, well, none in Brim thought so at the time."

She folded her arms and looked out the porthole. High above the sea, the mist had cleared and the moon was disappearing. "The meers aren't like the island folk. They wouldn't punish you for using magic."

He answered her with an abrupt turn of the heel and slam of the door. She put her forehead against the thick glass of the porthole. If she told the meers about Taunier's gift, she knew he'd hate her for it. She wanted to go after him, convince him to speak to Meer Eason and Meer Kanoae. A shadow crossed the water. Earlier this evening the moon had hung full over the sea. She shivered, trying to fight off the foreboding feeling as she watched the lunar eclipse. Should she take it as a sign, or was she reading too much into a natural event?

The next full moon would be Breal's Moon. Would she be home by then to make the round white candles and shape the fruited bread? Only if the two worlds held together. Only if she found Tymm and the other children and brought them safely back.

She kept her cloak on and sought her bunk for warmth. Pulling the lightstone free from the covers, she placed it in her lap. Too upset to sleep, she was about to pull *The Way Between Worlds* closer to her when she noticed the familiar jagged white line along one side of the stone. There was a deeper crack now along the white line. Had it broken when she'd dropped it? A stone was a solid thing, and she'd dropped it only on the floor before Taunier came in.

Hanna peered at the crack. Something was moving inside.

She wanted to scream and push it away. The crack widened and a tiny black claw poked out. Another crack. A second claw appeared, gripping and tearing away at the edge of the lightstone.

ELEVEN

THE PIP

*And they saw in this one moment
the promise of new life.*

—THE BOOK OF EOWEY

The stone wobbled in Hanna's lap as the life inside fought to get out. One last crack and the stone split open.

A featherless bird lay in Hanna's lap, its bulging eyes shut. The golden creature glowed like living embers. Its wings were folded fanlike across its back, each no more than two inches long. The thing had no beak, but a long snout. It was, she realized, not a bird.

Hanna blinked. Gingerly, she put out her finger, touched the soft skin of the wing. "Terrow dragon," she whispered.

The egg had seemed a stone when it washed up on the beach the year before, ordinary enough when she'd first picked it up. She'd liked its smoothness, its quiet blue color, and the jagged white line down one side that reminded her of lightning. Later, when she found her way to Oth, she'd been surprised when the stone began to glow.

Miles had called it a lightstone. But if it had been a terrow's egg all along, how could it have come to her from the sea? Terrow dragons laid their eggs in caves, or so Granda had always said. The sea would have been a cold place for an egg, but then the terrow's shell in her lap—the outside of what she'd thought had been a stone—was thicker than her finger, not at all flimsy like a bird's egg, and now she could see there was also a soft pinkish padding inside the shell.

She thought of the terrow she'd seen the day Tymm had been taken. She still didn't know if the dragon had come to help her and the Waytrees, or if she'd burned the thorns to keep Hanna away from the deyas.

A memory came. When they were in Oth, she'd offered her lightstone to the Sylth Queen to save Breal, but the queen had refused the gift. There'd been strange whispering sounds from the sylth folk and the sprites as Hanna held the lightstone in the air. "Lightstone," they'd said one to another. "Dragon's tear."

Dragon's tear. Could the terrow who came to Garth Lake that day have been the pip's mother, looking for her lost egg? She might have been, but by then Hanna had had the lightstone for a full year. That would be a long time to search for an egg.

The hatchling stirred and opened one eye, revealing a slit black pupil. Around that was an iris, blue as a mountain lake. This surprised Hanna. She'd thought dragons' eyes were yellow.

"Have you come to help us, little pip?" she asked. It seemed a lot to hope for, but she was in need of hope. Dragons lived in Noor now, but they were once creatures of Oth, and they still carried the magic of that world.

The pip began to stretch itself on her lap, pressing its four legs outward, arching its back like a cat, then slowly unfurling the tail that had been tucked up beside its belly and wrapped daintily about its neck. As the tail came away Hanna saw the purple ring around the terrow's throat. She'd read descriptions of dragons before—the purple-throated ones were female.

"So you're a girl," she whispered. It made her glad somehow, on a ship full of men, with the exception of Captain Kanoae. "You're a lovely birthday present, though you're a little early. I won't be fifteen for another two weeks."

The terrow opened her jaws in a yawn, emitting a tuneful squeak. A row of tooth buds made tiny mountain ridges along her orange gums. Would she need milk? Birds and lizards didn't suckle, but dragons might.

The ship rocked softly. Hanna felt happy with the wonder of this unexpected, shiny new life. "Are you hungry, little one?" Baby birds ate the spill of their mother's bellies. Hanna would be willing to chew a bit of bread or meat for the pip, but she would not go so far as to swallow it and vomit it back up. The very thought turned her stomach. Then again, the terrow was a small kind of dragon. Aside from the little wings, it looked more like a lizard than a bird, and lizards ate beetles and spiders and such.

"Wait here." She placed the pip and the broken shell on her bunk.

Hanna crept to the ship's galley and was soon back with a bit of meat. She hadn't run into Taunier and was glad of that. She didn't want to speak of the pip to him or anyone, not yet. Hanna chewed the beef until it was soft, then put the brown lump in her open palm.

The hatchling blinked, flicked out her long orange tongue, and took the meat. In a moment it was gone, and she licked Hanna's hand with her gritty orange tongue.

"Well," said Hanna, "that settles dinner."

She felt suddenly foolish talking to a pip who, no doubt, heard her words as so much babbling.

Captain Kanoae might come into the cabin any minute. Would she approve of a baby dragon on board?

"What am I to do with you?"

The pip stretched again, then stood up on trembling legs. Hanna held very still as the dragon made her way across her lap and began to crawl up her arm, much like a cat would climb a tree. Tiny sharp talons dug into her sleeve as she worked her way up to Hanna's shoulder.

"Ouch," complained Hanna, but it came out in a laugh. The terrow lifted her golden head and sniffed her cheek. "If you're looking for my cheek pouch, I haven't got one." Female dragons carried their young about in their dangling cheek pouches the first few months of life. The terrow gave up her search and hid under Hanna's nightdress instead, curling her slender tail loosely around Hanna's throat.

The glimmering tail looked like a golden necklace in the dark porthole window.

"You can't sleep there," scolded Hanna.

"Thrissss," hissed the pip.

"Thriss, is it?" said Hanna. Thriss—courage. Not a bad name for a dragon.

Hanna's neck grew warm. It felt like the touch of her granda's hand when she was very small and needed comforting on a dark night. She tucked *The Way Between Worlds* back in the trunk and closed the lid.

"Good night, Thriss."

Hanna lay down carefully on her side. The pip began to purr.

Captain Kanoae had used her powers to fill the sails and increase the *Leena's* speed in their hurry to reach Jarrosh. But eleven days after Hanna and Taunier boarded the ship, they rounded Cape Misfortune and sailed into heavy storms. The crew were called on deck and went to war with giant waves and heavy winds. Everyone joined the fight but Hanna, who was too seasick to do much more than lie on her bunk and retch into a pail.

Hanna's fifteenth birthday came and went during the miserable stormy days, with no time to acknowledge it or celebrate. She lay in the cabin, feeling guilty that she was of no use to the others battling up on deck. Falling in and out of sleep, she kept her eye on Thriss. No one else knew about the pip, and for some reason Hanna couldn't explain, she had decided to keep it that way. The hatchling didn't seem to want to be discovered, either. She hid under the bunk the moment anyone came to see how Hanna was doing, or slipped into Hanna's empty boot when Miles brought her a little food.

The pip was growing daily, shedding her tiny golden scales as she grew. Hanna swept them up from the floor and kept them in her pocket, like found treasure. Thriss ate eagerly from Hanna's dish—Hanna was too sick to eat any of it—and cheered Hanna a little as she played with paper and string in the cabin. But as the stormy days wore on, Hanna's empty, darkened sleep began to trouble her deeply. She was used to her dreams, which were colorful even when they were the ordinary kind that did not take her walking. *Maybe the seasickness has dulled my imagination,* she thought. But she couldn't help remembering what Miles had said, that everywhere the Waytrees fell, people were losing their dreams.

What if it's happened to me? What if I've lost my ability to dreamwalk? Hanna tossed and turned on her bunk, closing her eyes to sheer darkness, opening them again with a pounding heart. What use could she be to the meers, and how could she hope to find Tymm without her power?

They sailed nine more days and nights through heavy winds. On Hanna's twenty-first day on the *Leena*, they left the storms behind at last and sailed into the sun again.

The boat rocked drowsily on the ocean swells as Hanna clumped down the steps to the galley. Thriss clung to her shoulder beneath her cloak. Hanna's secret hatchling had grown over the last three weeks, but she was still small enough to flatten herself against Hanna's shoulder under the ample folds of her hood, though her endlessly twitching tail tickled Hanna's back.

Alone with her pip in the galley, Hanna chopped carrots for the bubbling stew while Thriss toyed with a piece of string at her feet. After a while, the terrow abandoned the string and climbed up the table leg. Letting out a victorious squeak, she leaped into the air, flapped her paper-thin wings, and fell onto the galley floor with a splat.

Hanna bent over her, crooning, "Oh, poor thing." Thriss lifted her head, licked under her wing, and hissed at Hanna.

"Don't hiss at me. I didn't drop you, did I?"

Thriss ignored her. Climbing up onto the table, she said, "Fy!"—her pippish pronunciation of *fly*—and boldly took off again. This time she made a haphazard flight across the small room before landing on Hanna's shoulder.

"Bravo, little one," Hanna whispered excitedly. Tossing peppercorns into the mortar, she ground them with the stone pestle. Taunier and Kanoae liked their stew spicy. She put a little dish of crushed pepper on the side for them.

There'd been no talk of dropping Taunier off at the next port once the storms hit. He'd spent months on his grandfather's fishing boat as a boy and had proven himself to be the best crewman on the *Leena.*

Thriss climbed back down to the floor and scurried into the corner to toy with the string again. A moment later, she took off, flapped her wings, and crashed headlong into the cupboard. Hanna bent down to help her up, but the pip scurried back up the table leg. She kept trying, landing awkwardly on a hanging pan or on the counter, but when she nearly plummeted into the boiling stewpot, Hanna blew up. "That's enough, now!"

She tucked Thriss into the cupboard with a dishcloth

to curl up on, and gave her a small slice of meat. "Time for you to take a rest," she said. "Come out only if I call."

The pip gave a happy squeak, "Meat," and went at her meal hungrily. Hanna gently closed the cupboard, only just in time. Thumping footfalls came from outside the galley door, then Meer Eason poked his head in to ask when the stew would be ready.

TWELVE

FIRE ON THE SEA

*In the days of the dragon wars,
many died by fire.*

—*A Meer's History of Noor*

Miles had left Taunier on deck steering the *Leena*. Downstairs in the galley Meers Eason and Kanoae were hunched over the table, where Hanna sat listening. The smell of stew mingled with that of the hanging spices as Miles took his seat across from Eason.

Meer Kanoae was saying, "And though these storms have swept us east faster than any meer power could, they've also blown us into these shipping lanes in the Boundary Waters." She traced the map with her finger. "The King of Kanayar has claimed these waters. We're in for trouble if his border patrol catches us."

Eason frowned. "If we turn north now, we might be able to sail free from the Boundary Waters and—"

124

"Straight into the heart of the Whirl Storms," said Kanoae.

"Well," snapped Eason, "what choice do we have?"

Miles eyed the map nervously. The thought of more storms turned his stomach. Whirl Storms mounted powerful swirling winds that destroyed villages and cities; they'd downed some of the greatest vessels in Noor, leaving neither sail thread nor deck splinter behind. Agitated, he jumped up and took out a knife to slice some bread.

He'd been struggling too long with his own bad mood. The High Meer had told them they were likely to face tempests, but he hated the foul weather for taking them off course, hated how helpless the raging winds made him feel. When they'd stopped in Emberlee for supplies, they found the great forest beyond the city walls had fallen. The people there looked listless; the children were as somber and hollow-eyed as they'd been back in Reon and Brim. Even in Emberlee, the City of Kings, people had forgotten their dreams.

Miles cut the bread unevenly, crumbs falling around his hands. If he'd used his shape-shifting power and turned into a seabird, he could have flown ahead to Jarrosh and reached there weeks ago! He might have discovered why the trees were falling and found Tymm by now! He felt his skin prick, thinking of his hidden power left unused so long. Maybe there was a reason he'd been given such power, more than just to break the Shriker's curse? What if the High Meer had known all along he was a shape-shifter, and that was why he'd chosen him, a second-year apprentice, to come on this journey in the first place?

Miles cut another slice, his heart beating wildly in his chest. Something in him wanted release. He looked down at the knife in his hands. It took focus to shift, a vision of the creature he'd shift into, along with a willful intention and strong emotion. His hand shook as he tried to control himself. *My hands are my hands,* he thought, keeping them in view. *My arms are my arms. I will not grow feathers, will not take wing and fly across the sea. I will stay on with the meers and see this out.*

"When . . . ," he said at last, twirling round with the knife in his left hand and bread in his right. "Exactly *when* will we reach Jarrosh?" He was shouting, and he didn't care. Hanna looked at him wide-eyed.

Meer Kanoae was putting down her cup and coming to a stand when a sudden explosion rocked the ship. The

Leena lurched violently to one side, knocking Miles to the floor. The knife slid from his hand, and dishes flew from the counter, breaking all around him. The others lurched forward and gripped the table, which was bolted to the floor.

Up on deck, Taunier was shouting.

Miles's mind raced. *Pirates? Boundary guards? Were they being attacked?*

"Look," cried Hanna. A strange yellow light poured into the cabin. Kanoae ran to the porthole, her large frame pushing Hanna aside.

"Fire on the sea!" she shouted. "Everyone· on deck! Now!"

They raced up the steps. Crossing to the side rail, Miles saw four islands of fire burning atop the water. A hot wind blew down from above. Shielding his eyes, he squinted upward at a flash of gold and spied the great underbelly of a male taberrell dragon. Miles held his breath. The dragon was enormous, stretching a good sixty feet long from snout to tail. Its undulating body was iridescent green, but for the golden belly and chest and the telltale red neck ring that showed it to be male.

Breal barked and ran in circles about the deck.

Another red-necked male soared overhead. Higher up, a larger female flew. Terror and joy washed through Miles. Her majestic wings were larger than the *Leena's* mainsail. Miles's eyes filled with the wonder, even as the dragons wheeled menacingly above the *Leena* like hawks over prey.

Kanoae shouted orders. Miles couldn't hear her over the dragons' pumping wings—a sound like distant thunder, driving warm winds across the deck. The winds smelled of fennel and bay and something else Miles couldn't name.

One by one the dragons spiraled down and settled on the water between the floating islands of fire. The she-dragon landed about twenty feet away from the *Leena's* prow, floating like a swan, her long, purple-ringed neck curving gracefully up to her enormous turquoise head. The cheek pouches where she carried her young hung empty by her elegant neck. She narrowed her orange eyes. "Turn this ship about, manlings of Noor."

She did not speak in DragonTongue, but in the common speech of Noor. Dragons were masters of many languages; still Miles's ears pricked. Her voice was new and strange. Her tone varied like many voices in a choir, and there was an undertone of deep, dry notes below the words. Miles heard it as music. The rapt expression on Meer Eason's face told Miles that the Music Master heard it that way, too. There was a clattering in the sound as well, like the beating of dry sticks.

Captain Kanoae answered bluntly, "We sail for Jarrosh."

This brought an angry rumble from the she-dragon's throat, and the males on either side of her unfurled their enormous wings and shook them menacingly. Miles wiped the sweat from his neck. Breal began to snarl, and Miles shushed his dog, though he didn't blame him. Miles also sensed the dragons' rising anger as one animal senses another.

Had the dragons turned against humans again? He didn't want to think so, but the rush of heat along his spine told him otherwise.

"Turn about or you will meet our fire!" said the one-eyed male.

"We will not turn back," called Kanoae. "We have—"

She might have said more if one of the males hadn't spewed flames at her. Kanoae leaped back to avoid a scorching, and fire lit the deck where she'd been standing.

Miles raced over with a tarp to smother it, but the wind whipped flames up to the mainsail.

"Save the sail!" ordered Kanoae.

Everyone ran for a bucket and tossed seawater on the fire; still flames licked up the mast, devouring the bottom corner of the cloth.

Taunier had stopped, staring.

"What are you doing?" shouted Miles. "Refill your bucket!" He ran for more water, flinging it at the burning sail.

Taunier hadn't budged. He dropped his bucket, raised his hand, and held his open palm upward. Gazing fixedly at the burning sail, he waved his arm over his head toward the sea, his hand falling slowly in a long farewell.

The crackling fire on the mast leaned seaward, hesitated, then leaped. Following the arc of Taunier's arm, it dove from sail to blue-black water. The flames sputtered and hissed as they died out, and steam rolled above the choppy water.

Miles stood wide-eyed with Hanna, their water buckets forgotten. Had Taunier really moved fire with the wave of his hand?

The burnt sail whistled softly as the wind slipped

through a blackened hole. Miles heard the rumbling breath of the dragons.

"Fire Herd," said the she-dragon, addressing Taunier with respect. "Why sail with these traitors?"

Traitors? A tremor ran down Miles's back.

Taunier didn't have the chance to answer, for Kanoae was shouting, "You've gone and damaged my *Leena!*" Eason tried to pull her back, but she wrestled away, shaking her fist at the she-dragon.

The taberrells spit more fire, forcing them all up against the stern. The air throbbed with heat. It washed over Miles, tightening the skin on his face, drawing the sweat from his body until his clothes were drenched and stinking. Already Taunier had jumped onto the cabin roof. He raised both arms and herded the dragon fire overboard.

From somewhere behind Miles, Hanna screamed. Miles pivoted. A golden brightness whirred past his right ear. At first he thought Taunier had missed a stray fireball, but this thing was more than shooting flame. It was alive.

A purple-throated baby terrow flitted down and settled on the prow. She was not much larger than a five-month-old kitten. The hatchling reared her head back and hissed at the she-dragon floating just beyond the prow.

The she-dragon's flames vanished as if the terrow's tiny breath had blown them out. She laughed suddenly at the audacity of the tiny pip.

Taunier lowered his arms and jumped down from the cabin roof.

The taberrells floated near the fire islands like moored vessels. Neck extended, the hatchling flapped her wings irritably as she fussed at the great dragons floating before her.

Where had this pip come from? The female's cheek pouches had been empty when she landed, Miles was sure, and anyway, this pip was a terrow, a smaller, golden-scaled breed, not iridescent green like a taberrell.

The she-dragon tipped her head. "Little one, where is your mother?"

The pip turned a moment, then lifted her foiled tail and pointed to Hanna.

Hanna? Harboring a terrow? They'd been on the *Leena* three weeks together. Why hadn't she told him?

"Step forward," the female said sternly.

"Wait, Hanna," warned Kanoae.

"I will address the terrow's meer," said the dragon.

Miles thought to say his sister wasn't a meer, that unlike himself, she'd never studied on Othlore, but Hanna was already at the prow. He came to her side, still grasping his water bucket. The dragons hadn't summoned him, but Hanna was his sister, after all, even if she *had* hidden a terrow from him. They'd been preoccupied day and night fighting heavy storms, but that was no excuse.

"What is your name, young pip?" asked the she-dragon.

"Thriss!"

"Courage." The dragon nodded approvingly. "And who named you?"

"Mama." The terrow's voice warbled like a robin's. She nuzzled Hanna's arm affectionately.

"You shouldn't have come out like this," Hanna scolded under her breath. "You've gotten us into more trouble." The pip wrapped her tail around Hanna's wrist. Hanna stroked her scaly back and scratched the purple patch under her uplifted chin, much as she might soothe a kitten.

"Why did you keep this secret from me?" Miles

managed to ask, but the one-eyed male dragon interrupted him in a rumbling voice. "Where did you get the terrow's egg?"

"It came to me from the sea," said Hanna. "It seemed to be an ordinary stone at first, but it was beautiful, and I kept it in my pocket."

Miles suddenly knew what she meant by the egg. "A lightstone," he blurted out. "We called it that. A blue light came out of it when—"

"Who asked you to speak?"

Miles clamped his mouth shut. Blood pounded in his ears.

The she-dragon lowered her head and peered into Hanna's face. The nearness of the great beast made Miles's heart race. Her orbed eyes glowed menacingly. Her scales mirrored blue and purple light like shards of twilight. But it was the rows of long, sharp teeth that made him steel himself, those and her muscled jaw, which was powerful enough to snap a horse in two, let alone a man.

Taunier appeared on his right, the meers to his left. He was grateful to have them close by.

The ruffled scales on the dragon's neck rose up. "The girl child is sqyth-born. A blue eye and a green."

"One eye to the earth and one to the sky," said the male on the left. "One so born can call on earth kith and sky kith to help in times of trouble."

"Aye, Hanna's sqyth-eyed," said Kanoae. "What of it?"

The taberrells ignored the comment.

The she-dragon said, "The pilgrims have come."

One-eye shook his great head. "This flimsy girl is not the Kanameer. She did not come to us on the wind."

"Do not ignore the signs," argued the female. "The girl is sqyth-eyed, and she has brought the Fire Herd. It is the prophecy." Her head swayed as she began to chant,

> *"When the Waytree bridges fall,*
> *Roots die binding all to all.*
> *Noor Winds bring to us the Dreamer.*
> *Eye of earth and eye of sky,*
> *Soaring on the wings of morning,*
> *Come to us, O Pilgrim.*
> *Dreamwalker, free the first ones taken.*
> *From dark dreams let day awaken.*
> *Kanameer, our Kanameer,*
> *Come to us, O Pilgrim."*

The male dragons joined in:

"Bring to us our heart's desire,
One with mastery over fire . . ."

The males had more to sing, but the she-dragon ended the song midverse, calling, "This is our Kanameer."

The males joined in, chanting, "Kanameer. Kanameer." The dragons seemed to have forgotten their anger.

As the dragons sang, Miles trembled. He knew some DragonTongue, but what did the word *Kanameer* mean? The second half of the word, *meer*, meant "one who wields magic," but the first half? He tried to think. Servant. That was it. So Kanameer was "servant and one who wields magic," or simply, "servant of magic." Did the dragons see a servant of magic as a peacemaker? Or someone to be sacrificed?

His thoughts were soon overpowered as the rhythmic chant encircled him, and he felt himself falling under the dragons' spell.

The voices were rich and wild, deep and hollow, and there were broken sounds within them, too: a syncopated drumming, a snapping of sharp teeth. He'd heard them speak, but now he felt their music resonating in his chest. If a storm sang, this would be its song, or if a mountain had a voice, it would summon wind and cloud this way.

"Kanameer. Kanameer."

Miles began to sway. The water bucket tumbled from his hand as his blood danced to the song. His mind fought against it, but he went on swaying, just as the dragons swayed, just as the meers behind him swayed. Only Hanna stood still, her hand resting on her terrow's back.

The floating isles of fire fell to a low, red burning. The chant grew louder until the Morrow Sea seemed to sing. Waves lapping up against the ship drummed the chanters' time. *Kanameer. Swish. Swish. Kanameer . . .*

The she-dragon swam in closer. In a flash she reached out her scaly forearms, catching Hanna and Thriss in her right talons and Taunier in her left. Hanna's sudden screams were drowned out by the dragon's loud victory cry as she flew skyward.

Miles shook himself from the song-spell. "Wait!" he screamed. The wind swirled with the beating of the taberrell's giant wings as Meers Kanoae and Eason woke from the enspelling chant and shouted, "Stop! Bring them back!"

The male dragons stroked the sea with their powerful wings, and heavy waves raced toward the ship. A wall of freezing water swept Miles off his feet, lifted him high into the air, and smashed him into the rigging.

THIRTEEN
SHAPE-SHIFTER

You will know both flight and falling.

—*THE OTHIC ART OF MEDITATION*

Chaos on deck, as everyone scrambled to get a foothold, and Meer Kanoae shouted orders. Another wave crashed overhead. Miles caught the base of the mast and clung to it to keep from being washed overboard. The ship tipped wildly before righting itself.

Coughing and sputtering, he pulled himself to a stand. A warm wind stirred by the dragons' fire blew against his wet clothes. The female circled in the twilight sky above with Hanna and Taunier in each claw. Her forearms were tucked against her belly, sheltering her prey. The male dragons stirred the ocean again and lifted skyward. Miles gritted his teeth and braced himself as seawater swirled around his legs and sloshed overboard again.

"My harpoon!" Kanoae shouted.

Meer Eason grabbed her arm and tried to pull her back. "No meer has ever turned against a dragon!"

"We have to do something!" she demanded.

Above the arguing, Miles's acute hearing picked up Hanna's distant screams. Breal was leaping into the air, barking wildly.

Already the she-dragon flew high above the sea, dipping in and out of clouds. Hanna's screams tore through his head, ripped down his neck, and knifed his heart. He had to go after her. The idea of shape-shifting again filled him with terror, but every moment of indecision put Hanna and Taunier in greater danger. Hanna's cries ripped away his doubts layer by layer, as a strong wind will steal a scarecrow's clothing.

He couldn't think, couldn't wait to think. Even now, the dragons were winging east. Miles freed himself from the mast and splashed through the knee-deep brine. He needed room. There were no spells to call on, only the heat found at his core, pouring outward from heart and lung to spine, to head, to hands. A giant falcon. He focused on the image. Lifting his arms, he stretched them farther and farther. He shut his eyes, pictured the great bird stretched out and out and . . . nothing! Why hadn't he changed?

The *Leena* tilted. A freezing wave receded around his ankles and swept over the deck. Hanna's screams were getting farther away. *Hurry. Try again. Focus.*

"Miles!" shouted Kanoae from behind. "Grab a bucket and bail! What are you doing?"

He spread out his fingers, stretched until he felt a sharp pain between his shoulder blades. He leaned into his instincts, felt his ferocious desire, let the energy scream up his spine and race through his body. His arms grew broader, flatter, the stinging pinions feathering outward. His chest rounded. His face narrowed. There was a stabbing pain along his nose and jaw as they sharpened to a beak. *Fly!*

Miles flapped his enormous falcon's wings. As he took off he heard cries and shouting from below, but he didn't bother looking down. He needed speed to catch the dragons. He was smaller than his opponents, but large enough to free Hanna and carry her on his back down to the *Leena*. How he'd rescue his sister and Taunier both from the dragons he didn't know. But he was a winged beast now. He was like them.

His fear had been stripped away along with his human

flesh. He'd left the boy behind on deck. Now he'd fight to the death with pleasure.

Pump. Pump. More speed. Clouds covered the new moon. Lightning flashed ahead, and he saw the dragons outlined in the sudden brightness. He pumped harder still, working against the brisk sea wind. As the clouds rolled across the twilight sky, strength poured through him as if he'd eaten lightning, drunk the thunder.

The fennel smell from the dragons' scales wafted through the air. The males flew ahead, the female behind. His only chance was to strike and strike quickly. Miles darted for the she-dragon's underbelly, where Hanna and Taunier were caged in her black talons.

Landing on the dragon's forearm just above Hanna, he pecked and tore the fleshy part above the claw. Wound the dragon there, and she'd have to loosen her grip. The female roared in alarm and tried to shake him off.

"Miles?" He caught sight of Hanna's frightened face. She'd seen him shift before, knew his power. Her cry of recognition was caught by the wind.

Miles speared the flesh above the she-dragon's claw again, using his beak the way a woodpecker stabs a rotten tree. He jabbed until the dragon's hold on Hanna began to weaken. One of her talons was broken, and the tip was missing. Hanna used the gap to free her arm. Miles flew beside her. She would have to push her way out and ride on his back. His bird-form was large enough to take her weight, though he'd have to fly back a second time to rescue Taunier. Hanna pushed harder to squeeze the rest of the way through, but the opening was still too narrow. Next she tried to push her pip through to Miles, but the hatchling refused to leave her and scrambled to safety under her cloak.

From the right claw, Taunier was shouting, not understanding what was happening.

Miles flew higher, just above the claw, and tried to pry the talons farther apart. He was circling again to get a better purchase when One-eye fell back and flew below the female. There was a sudden blast of heat. Shocking pain seared Miles's flesh as the dragon's fire lit his left wing. He beat his wings frantically, tried to press his burning feathers against the she-dragon's scales and smother the fire, but he soon lost his grip.

Wing still burning, he tumbled helplessly down and down until he broke the surface of the churning water below.

PART TWO: DRAGONLANDS

When NoorOth was young,
Two worlds were one.
Kwen-Arnun, the great World Tree,
Reached green arms east,
Reached green arms west,
And dragons all flew free.
Oh, elderling, remember,
And brave youngling, believe:
eOwey sung NoorOth as one,
Embraced by the great World Tree.

—Dragons' Song

FOURTEEN

The winds warred with one another, and the people could not run from them.

—*A Meer's History of Noor*

The she-dragon held her prisoners close to her belly as she flew east behind the males, her great golden chest breaking the wind's flow. Hanna braced herself and peered through the stiff talons. The warm night air wafting down from the dragon's scales chafed her cheeks and dried her tears as soon as they left her eyes.

How badly was Miles hurt? Was he even alive? He shouldn't have taken such a risk, shouldn't have shapeshifted. Still, she knew why he'd done it. She would have done the same for him if she'd had that kind of power. But if he were dead now . . .

She wept again. Her eyes burned.

Taunier shouted something, but the wind washed away

his words. He put his arm out to her through the talons. She pressed her arm through the gap left open by the she-dragon's severed talon. The dragon's claws were too far apart, and their hands did not meet. Still, they left them outstretched a long while, the slick air blowing between them.

Hiding under her shirt, Thriss wriggled closer to her side. The pip could have escaped if she'd obeyed her and flown to Miles. But then she, too, would have fallen burning into the sea.

Riding the swift air currents east, the taberrells flew tirelessly a full twelve hours, through night to the edge of morning. Red clouds rolled across the water stained by the sun's first light.

Taunier called out, pointing ahead to a place where the crimson clouds were spinning round and round. There was a great hole in the sky, and clouds whirled around it as if they were swirling down an enormous drain.

Kanoae had warned them about Whirl Storms.

To avoid the storm ahead, the male dragons quickly veered to the right, where stray purple clouds still drifted slowly west. The female followed, driving hard against the wind. The giant funnel tilted, changed directions, and raced closer. The sky filled with a deafening roar. Trembling, Thriss burrowed her snout under Hanna's arm. The dragons turned again, pumping wildly in the opposite direction. Hanna gripped the talons and pressed her face between her fists, a new terror seizing her as she saw the storm's enormous power. It would swallow every cloud in the sky, suck the dragons in, too, and swallow them all.

"Hurry," she screamed. But the storm had already corralled them into the red clouds, where the fierce winds whirled them around and around. It felt as if the gale would rip off Hanna's skin, strip the flesh from her bones. Only the dragon's chest, held out like a great golden shield, kept her and Taunier from being torn apart.

The male dragons just ahead were still trying to fly against the Whirl Storm, but the bone-breaking, skin-ripping wind was nearly tearing them apart, too. Strong as they were, the roaring wind was stronger. At last the males gave up and folded their wings against their sides.

The Whirl Storm spun them all across the sea toward a green, mountainous land. The sun showed but half her face at the far eastern horizon, as if she were hiding behind the blue-green ocean, waiting for the trouble to pass before she dared bring on the day.

Gripping the female's broken talon, Hanna screamed into the wind. Far below, giant trees were sucked up, roots and all, as the storm attacked the coast. The dragons swirled with the trees and bushes, the storm stealing them, roots and all, from the face of the land. A parade of strange wildlife flew past: a spinning mountain lion, a deer and two fauns, a badger. More trees. Bushes. A tent. A man.

eOwey! A man. The man sped away and was gone.

In the screams of the storm, Hanna thought she heard her own death-song. She sang a raw-throated song against it:

> "eOwey before me,
> eOwey behind,
> eOwey below me in the earth and sea,
> eOwey above me at nightfall and by day,
> Surround me and protect me, eOwey."

Hanna sang the words as she never had before, for herself, for Taunier, for Thriss, for the spinning man, and, stranger still, for the taberrells. The swirling clouds changed from red to purple-white. The sun rose far across the sea. Hanna glimpsed the yellow orb through the clouds as the storm sucked them toward the ground.

A shredded tent slapped up against the dragon's side, slid down her legs, and wrapped about her claws. Hanna couldn't see ahead. She grabbed the fluttering edges and tore it away bit by bit until the wind took it again.

A hawk tumbled helplessly through the air, followed by a canoe.

"Taunier!" she screamed. "Look!"

He couldn't hear her above the howling wind, but he must have seen it, too.

The storm was blowing them straight into the mountainside.

FIFTEEN

DRAGON'S CAVE

*Friend of the wind, you cannot know where it
will blow.*

—*The Othic Art of Meditation*

As the mountain loomed closer, the screaming wind
sucked the dragons down and smashed them into
the sea. Hanna held Thriss tight in the swirling salt water.
A moment later a wave pitched the drenched dragons
onto shore. They flew into a cave at the base of the cliff
before the storm wheeled back, sucking driftwood trunks
off the beach and up into the sky.

"You all right?" Taunier called, coughing up seawater. Hanna checked Thriss and saw with great relief
that her pip had made it through. "We're okay," she
shouted back.

Lifting higher in the half dark, the she-dragon landed
on a flat stone far above the cavern floor and opened her

right claw. Hanna fell exhausted onto the cold stone and heaved a ragged breath. Thriss wriggled out of her hand, hissed, and nipped her fingertip.

"Ouch." Hanna sucked her sore finger. "Plunging into the sea wasn't my idea."

On her knees, she glanced down, and the ravine below made her reel dizzily. She crawled back and looked over her shoulder at Taunier. Why was he still talon-bound? The female dragon shook out her wet wings. The males on either side did the same. The shaking caused a small rainstorm that ceased only when they folded their wings again. Hanna braced herself and came to a stand.

Light leaked in from the entrance far below. The dark pool at the base of the chasm gleamed. As Hanna's eyes adjusted to the gloom, she saw with dread that they were not alone. On the far side of the deep crevasse a crowd of twenty or more dragons were gathered on a second stone terrace. They began to make angry, rumbling sounds.

The largest male, with a gash on his flank, spoke up. "Do they send children now to come against us on Jarrosh?"

Jarrosh. She'd made it to the east at last. In a dragon's claw, but she'd made it. The passage to eastern Oth would be here somewhere, and Tymm was on the other side. She closed her eyes a moment, thinking of him, hoping that he was all right, that she could reach him in time. The thought made her body ache. How could she cross over and find him when she and Taunier were captives?

"Do you think I would bring these two here without reason, Kaleet?" The she-dragon's voice was rough and clattering with threat. "I am your queen, your Damusaun. I say the Kanameer, the one who serves the Old Magic, is here. She comes to dream for us, and she has brought the Fire Herd."

Hanna trembled. Kanameer—one who serves the Old Magic? They'd chanted the word again and again before they stole her from the ship. Enoch had mentioned that name when he gave her the glass vial full of tears. "The Kanameer will know what to do with them," he'd said. But the dragons had mistaken her for someone else.

The scarred male dragon, Kaleet, raised his head. The bright red patch on his neck puffed out. "Damusaun, Dragon Queen," he said, bowing his head to the she-dragon, "we cannot help but see these two you have brought us are manlings." He voiced "manling" as if it were a curse. The dragons to his left and right hissed.

The Damusaun flicked Hanna's back with her talon. Hanna flinched.

"Manlings are deceitful," the Dragon Queen agreed. "But the Mishtar was human like these two. Time is running out. We will not ignore our prophecies."

Hanna wondered what she meant by "time running out," and, even more startling, "our prophecies." She tried to catch Taunier's eye, but he was staring fixedly at the huge taberrells across the crevasse.

A smaller golden terrow stepped forward. "She's weak-bodied as a grass blade."

Dry laughter followed. Hanna squared her shoulders. She might be small for fifteen, but she was strong. Hadn't she worked on her da's land? Helped at all hours of the night in lambing season? Cleaned the animal stalls? Hauled well water? But that would be nothing to these dragons. Sweat poured down her neck. *Thriss. Courage.*

"This cannot be the Kanameer," a male hatchling added. "It is just a female."

The she-dragon's chest swelled. "A female?" she growled. "Where does it say the Kanameer must be a male, hatchling?" Across the gulf, the hatchling cowered back against the cave wall.

"Damusaun," said the one-eyed dragon on Taunier's right, "show them how the other manling wields fire."

Voices chorused from across the rift, singing a third verse to their dragon song.

> *"Bring to us our heart's desire,*
> *One with mastery over fire.*
> *From across the eastern sea,*
> *Come to us, O Pilgrim."*

Hanna trembled as the queen released Taunier and nudged him forward with the jagged end of her broken claw.

"Show them," she said.

"And what if I refuse?" It was the smallest of whispers, meant only for Hanna, but dragons have sharp ears.

The Damusaun answered with a roar, ringing them in fire. Screaming, Hanna grabbed Taunier. Thriss raced up her leg and hid under her cloak as the flames closed in. The fire pushed them closer to the edge. It was jump or burn.

Taunier stood rigid as a pillar until Hanna pleaded, "Do it!"

"Then let go of me!" he shouted.

Without realizing it, Hanna had pinned his arms to his sides. She stepped back a pace as the terrible encroaching heat enveloped her. She tried to breathe but only managed to suck in more heat. Taunier lifted his hand and swung it down, slicing the fire like a blade. His body shook with concentration as he moved his right arm, sweeping the flames closest to Hanna off the cliff. Hanna felt instant relief. He put out his left arm, herding the rest of the fire off the cliff, the flames sputtering out as they fell.

The dragons across the gap let out a communal sigh. The challenging male huffed out smoke, yet he bowed his head in deference to the she-dragon. "Still, oh Damusaun, how can we be sure this other one is the Kanameer?"

The Damusaun's talons extended like cat's claws. "I am your queen. I say she is the one. Test her and see."

Across the crevasse, a few dragons thwacked their long tails. The drumming grew louder as the rest joined in, slapping their tails against the floor and wall, chanting, "Test her. Test her. Test her. Test her."

SIXTEEN

FIERCE, UNBENDING TRUTH

Dreamwalker, free the first ones taken.
From dark dreams let day awaken.

—DRAGONS' SONG

There was no place to hide. Hanna stood on the very edge of the precipice with Taunier. The rock walls echoed with the sound of the dragons' throaty voices. A fire had been lit across the divide, and she could see the gathered dragons clearly now. Blue-green and golden scales all winked in the firelight as they flicked their tails in unison, chanting, "Test her. Test her. Test her."

Her throat went dry. She remembered the barn cat's tail twitching like that as he considered the fun he was about to have with a mouse. Across the rift, a large male addressed the Damusaun in a raspy voice. "Throw her down the mouth. It is said the Kanameer can fly."

Hanna peered into the deep crevasse and saw a dark

pool very far below. Terror tightened her gut. She knew well enough what he meant by throw her down the mouth.

"Where does the prophecy say the Kanameer can fly?" insisted the Damusaun.

"Noor Winds bring to us the Dreamer," he sang.

The rest joined in:

"Eye of earth and eye of sky,
Soaring on the wings of morning,
Come to us, O Pilgrim."

The Damusaun was right. The lines didn't have to mean the Kanameer could fly. But how could she convince them?

Dragon voices swept around her. She felt dizzy, but she also felt carried along by them as if she were swirling high above the land again. They were giving her a way to live within their words, if she was brave enough to grasp on.

"I came through the Whirl Storms," she said. "They are the greatest of the Noor Winds." Her knees shook, but she couldn't let them see her fear. Standing up to them, she'd claim her own life and Taunier's. They'd escape with Thriss. Find Tymm. Taunier stepped a little closer until they stood shoulder to shoulder.

She continued. "I am also sqyth-eyed. My green eye and my blue show I have kith in the earth and sky who will bring magic if I call." She thought of her sky kith Wild Esper when she said this, though the wind woman was far away in the west.

Hanna's answer barely carried through the enormous cave. A flimsy human voice, a bird twittering before a roaring waterfall, but her speech was heard.

A terrow pip flitted across the crevasse and hovered close to Hanna's face, inspecting her eyes. Darting back across, he squeaked excitedly, "She is sqyth-eyed."

The dragons talked in low voices, wings wavering at their sides.

"How can one so small dreamwalk for us?" she heard one asking. And this from a youngling, himself no larger than a newborn colt!

Tails curled. There was a low hiss.

Taunier gave her a "now what?" look. She clenched her teeth to keep her chin from quivering. She would die if she was thrown down the chasm, and if she died, he'd be next. All hope of finding Tymm, of helping the Waytrees here, would die with them. She couldn't let that happen, but she couldn't think of what to say or do next.

The hissing subsided as the dragons talked among themselves. Thriss crawled out from under Hanna's cloak, nudged her cheek, and purred in her ear. Surrounded by her kin, the pip was too young to understand that she should be afraid, but her purring encouraged Hanna. Her skin still ran with dewy sweat, but her mind sharpened. She might not be the Kanameer they'd waited for, but she *had* come on the wind. She *was* sqyth-eyed. And all her life (until the empty nights on the *Leena*) she'd dreamwalked.

Could she dreamwalk still? She didn't know, but she had to speak from strength, not from fear. Before the dragons added another challenge, she raised her chin and told the dragons about the unicorn dream she'd had long ago. There was magic in that dreamwalk, and dark portent. She'd foreseen two monsters slaying a sacred unicorn in the meadowlands of Oth where the great stone oak stood, the tree called Brodureth, the Oak King.

The dreamwalk had haunted her three times before it came to pass, before Hanna came face-to-face with the angry Sylth Queen, who'd loved the unicorn that was slain.

Taunier gave her a wide-eyed look as she spoke about Oth. She read surprise on his face and disappointment. She'd never told him about her journey to the Otherworld last year. He was hearing things about her now for the first time, in the company of dragons. She wished she could explain it all to him and change his hurt expression, but that would have to wait.

There was silence in the great red cave as she spoke and whispering among the dragons when she was done.

"I am Kaleet." The largest dragon with the glaring leg wound held his head high. His golden chest shone in the low firelight burning across the deep rift. "You say you have been to Oth. How do we know this is true?"

One-eye at the queen's side answered before Hanna could speak. "How else could a manling know the Oak King's name? Who but the sylth folk would have spoken the name of Brodureth, the Waytree that was our ancient western bridge to Oth, may all honor fill his roots and branches."

"All honor to Brodureth," sang the dragons. "Our ancient dragons' bridge." Hanna sensed deep sadness in the chant.

The male called Kaleet shook his head, the scales

across his cheekbones clattering. "Tell us how you reached the Otherworld," he said. There was a sense of awe in his voice.

Hanna blinked. She was too overwhelmed at first to answer, but the dragons were impatient, and soon the thrumming sound began to grow again across the black ravine.

Hanna knew without being told that these ancient creatures would not tolerate any kind of lie. The dragons expected fierce, unbending truth, as the law of the Old Magic demanded. At last she said, "The deyas in the Waytrees called Wild Esper, the wind woman. She flew me to Attenlore in western Oth."

Sweat trickled over her upper lip. She licked the salty drops and waited. The weaving of her words, the truth about herself and her past, all were forming an invisible safety net, which must be strong enough to catch her and Taunier.

Across the gap Kaleet raised his head and breathed blue fire. The others joined him until a burning dome dazzled above. It was brilliant blue as a summer sky, with smoke-white clouds drifting on the wind. Hanna watched, enthralled. The indigo sky was like the one she'd seen in

Oth, where the vivid colors are sharper than any in this world. Taunier tipped his head back as they looked on with wonder.

"Kanameer," sang a golden terrow at the edge of the crevasse.

"Kanameer, O Pilgrim," another sang.

Soon all were singing, male and female, large and small, taberrell and terrow. Tails drumming in rhythm, they voiced the tune the Damusaun had sung to Hanna from the sea.

The voices resounded in the cave, the sounds doubled and tripled like rising sea winds. Hanna swayed as the song and drumming filled the air. Thriss tipped her head and sang, "Kanameer. Kanameer," in a high, birdlike voice. The pip climbed up Hanna's hair and coiled herself atop her head like a golden crown.

SEVENTEEN

BURNED

He lived like a man lost inside his own tent.

—A DESERT SAYING OF KANAYAR

Miles's heart drummed in his ears, loud, louder, the
sound of dragon wings beating the sky. He awoke
and winced. Meer Eason was leaning over the cot, gently
coating the burn on his left arm with salve. Gritting his
teeth, he tried to sit up, groaned, and fell back on the
blanket. The burn ran from elbow to wrist. "How long
have I been out?" he croaked.

"All night and half the morning."

Breal's head popped out from under the bunk like a
furry jack-in-the-box. He panted and licked Miles's hand.
His tongue came close to the burn but did not touch it.

Miles vaguely remembered falling, returning to
human shape while he struggled in the chill water, too

weak to swim. Salt water had filled his mouth as he'd flailed, then Breal had leaped into the sea to rescue him. There'd been a sudden torturous sharp pain then. Breal must have accidentally clawed his burned arm with his toenails while paddling. Miles had blacked out after that.

He fingered the jagged tear in his shirt. Breal had probably torn it while dragging him through the water. It had seemed strange at first to find himself clothed again each time he returned to his body, his garments shifting in and out of animal form with him, but he'd gotten used to it.

Meer Eason capped the jar of salve and placed it on the small shelf.

"What about Hanna and Taunier?" Miles asked.

"We're chasing the dragons east. But they're swifter than the *Leena*."

Sweat pooled at the back of his neck. "Why did they take them? What will they do with them?"

Meer Eason wiped his hands on the towel. The strong ointment smell still pervaded the little room. "Who can know the ways of dragons? Their thoughts are shielded from us. But," he said, "the dragons' visit stripped secrets from all three of you." His dark face hovered over Miles like an eclipse, the light from the porthole making a thin glowing line about his curly hair.

Miles breathed unsteadily.

Eason continued. "Did you know your sister had a dragon pip?"

"No." He was still upset about that. How could she have hidden it from him? They used to share everything to do with magic. He frowned. "And I didn't know Taunier had power over fire."

"Another secret revealed," Eason said. "The power to herd fire is a rare gift. The ancient kings of Kanayar once knew how, but the way was lost to the royal line long ago. Yet this boy—" He paused, thinking.

"And then there's the matter of your secret." He poured Miles a cup of water, steadying himself against the table as the ship rolled. "Tell me what happened back there."

"What happened?"

Their eyes locked. "Who taught you shape-shifting power? You've known since you came to Othlore that the art was banned from the school years and years ago."

"I did not learn it at school, sir."

"Where then?"

Miles was silent.

"We haven't much chance of finding Hanna if we hold back from one another, Miles. There's hidden strength in truth. Without it . . ." Meer Eason let his unfinished sentence move through the dim air between them, as if the unsaid words were small ships set adrift.

Miles took the cup of water, its coolness cleansing his parched throat. "I'll tell you," he said at last. He knew he had to shift again to find Hanna and Taunier.

"Do you know of the beast called the Shriker?" It was a long story. As they headed east in the wake of the dragons, he left no part of his tale unsaid; there was no point now.

Meer Eason leaned in closer as Miles told of the magic shape-shifting power the Sylth Queen gave him, how he'd used it to shape-shift into the Shriker's form to protect Hanna from the beast. He spoke of tracking the Shriker into the Shadow Realm of Oth and their bloody battles there.

"Hanna crossed into Oth to find me," said Miles. "Without her I would have stayed inside the Shriker's form." He shuddered.

"So both of you have crossed over before." Meer

Eason's voice was low, but it held a tone of respect. Few meers knew how to use the Waytrees to cross world to world these days. Though there had been many Waytrees in Othlore Wood, the mysterious passage, what some called the dragons' bridge, moved about, tree to tree, deya to deya, and even the High Meer admitted he'd been unable to find a woodland passage to Oth in these past few years.

Meer Eason's face hardened. "You hid too much from us, Miles."

Miles felt the boat rocking in the water, its instability mirroring his own confusion. "I didn't mean any disrespect for the school or toward you, sir. After I came out of the Shriker's form, I promised Hanna and myself I wouldn't shape-shift again. Not until I had more control over the power."

"Did you keep that promise until this shift?"

"Knowing it was against the school rules made it easier not to shift on Othlore." Now that the truth was out, he wanted to say more, to explain. Maybe then he'd understand it all a little better himself. Grunting from the pain in his arm, he managed to sit up in his bunk.

"I knew I had to strengthen my understanding of magic, so I studied hard and waited. I would have been happy enough to be blue-palmed at the end of this year, to learn a deal more before I ever tried to shift again." He gazed down at his left hand. It still saddened him that he'd had to leave Othlore before being given his true meer sign. He wondered now if he would ever have an Othic symbol emblazoned on his palm. But there was something else he wanted to say.

"When I shifted into the Shriker's form, something was missing from my magic."

"What do you mean?"

Miles frowned. "I don't know."

Meer Eason looked doubtful.

Miles tried harder. He'd feared shifting since his experience last year. If he could better understand what happened back then, he'd be less afraid to use his power now. "I was taken into a dark, animal place by my Shriker's shift. I can't explain it better than that, but I didn't have control over the shape-shift, or not very much, anyway. It overpowered me."

"Turning more and more into the creature one changes into has always been the danger for any shape-shifter.

And you stayed a long while within the beast, as you said. It can also be a matter of resonance."

"Resonance?"

"How shall I put this?" Meer Eason paused a moment. "If there are similar tendencies between the shifter and the creature he shifts into, that is resonance. Let's say the shape-shifter has a great love for the sea, he or she might turn into a fish, stay too long in the shift, and remain a sea creature from then on."

Miles said nothing, understanding this better than he wanted to admit. The Shriker's raw rage had felt far too familiar. All his life, Miles had hated the villagers down in Brim who'd shunned him and his family. They'd turned their backs on the Sheen family, because it was a Sheen who'd brought the Shriker to Enness Isle long ago, when Rory Sheen offered his bearhound to Death in exchange for his own life. Seeing Rory betray his loyal companion, Death had cursed Rory and turned his dog into the Shriker. Rory's dog had done nothing to deserve such treatment from his master, but on that night, man's best friend became his worst enemy. After that, the Shriker appeared in the shape of an enormous demon hound, hunting and killing folk on Enness Isle.

Since the time of the curse, the Shriker was driven by hunger for revenge. Miles knew that hunger, and he'd wanted to punish those who'd belittled him, to taste revenge himself.

Resonance, he thought, shuddering. His anger and the Shriker's anger had become one. Taken into the beast's power, he'd wanted to stay there and use it for his own revenge. This was the reason he'd been afraid to shift again.

Meer Eason asked, "What happened to the Shriker when you fought him in Oth? Did you manage to kill him?"

Breal stepped closer and laid his soft head on Miles's lap, looking up at him with his big brown eyes. There was a secret between them, one he could not tell even now. "The Shriker's gone."

Miles shifted his weight on the hard bunk, his heart beating fast. "I have to shift again, sir. Fly after Hanna and Taunier, or we might never find them."

Meer Eason didn't answer him directly. Instead, he began to pace the length of the room. "Where might the dragons take them?" he mused.

Miles waited anxiously. Did his teacher agree? Did

he want him to shift? He stood up and steadied himself on the tilting floorboards. But just as Eason turned, mouth open, to make a pronouncement, Kanoae burst through the door. "The boundary guards have spotted us."

Eason spun around. "Can we outrun them?"

"Their ships are larger and faster," puffed Kanoae. "They're gaining on us."

EIGHTEEN

SEA CHANGE

Enter generously into the song.

—*A Meer's Music*

Hands tied behind his back, Miles stared down at the turbulent black mouth of the East Morrow Sea. Two steps more, and he'd reach the end of the plank. Behind him drummers pounded. Meers Eason and Kanoae would be next to walk the plank.

The boundary guards had searched the *Leena*, tossing everything but food, ale, and valuables into the sea.

"We're not your enemies," Miles had argued hotly. "The High Meer sent us here."

This had made things only worse. "Black magic," one shouted.

"You can't trust meers," called another. "Tie them up and gag them before they cast a spell on us."

Their "trial" had lasted less than an hour. They'd crossed the Boundary Waters without permission and broken the King of Kanayar's law. The ship's captain pronounced them "filthy wizards sneaking past the boundary to join the dragons of Jarrosh."

"Hurry up!" The crewman prodded his back with his sword. Miles flinched. He'd already been flogged in front of everyone, a punishment for screaming through his gag to protest the sentence. As they saw it, he was trying to cast spells. The whipping had left his back raw and blistered, and his burned arm still stung.

He took another step. Three inches of plank left. If he didn't jump soon, the guard would run him through. He was overwhelmed by sorrow, anger, fear. His hands were tied behind him, so he could not swim. In a moment's time the dark water would swallow him; he'd sink along with the Falconer's trunk, which had been tossed from the *Leena* like so much trash. His life would go down, together with his longing to find Hanna, to rescue Tymm, to save the Waytrees that held the worlds together.

So much was left unfinished. He wanted to learn how to control his passions and his power. And someday, if he proved himself worthy, he dreamed of being chosen to become the High Meer, one as famous as the founding meer of Othlore, the Mishtar. That was his secret, passionate wish.

He wanted all of it. To have the world and keep the world. Life's end was now only a few breaths away. Tears streamed down his cheeks and were lost in the sea below. Water to water. Salt to salt.

The drumming grew louder.

Eason was humming the song *"Quava-arii."* The Music Meer could not sing the words, gagged as he was; still, Miles knew the song and its meaning. *Quava-arii*—ever changing. Meer Eason was signaling him to shape-shift. He'd never shape-shifted with his hands tied. *Think! Concentrate!* He closed his eyes, tried to envision a great bird large enough to rescue his friends from . . .

Crack! A whip lashed his back. Miles tottered and fell into the ocean.

Water shot up his nose as he writhed against the ropes, sinking. The East Morrow Sea was warm here. He could survive in these waters if he could swim, but his hands were tied.

Miles thrashed wildly as he sank. He must kick his

way to the surface, but where was it? He had to untie the ropes now! He pulled at the knots behind his back, wrenching hard, harder.

A loud splash. Another meer forced off the plank at sword point? No time to think of that. He was sinking!

A dark figure swimming above. Not a man or a woman. Breal had jumped in after him. He was swimming above, searching for him. The dog's paddling legs told Miles where the surface was. He kicked his feet, but could not move upward fast enough with his hands tied. He needed air, or he would pass out! *Change! Shift!*

Quava-arii. In the dark water he imagined a seal's slick skin. He stopped kicking and held his legs together. Panic overtook him as he sank farther down. *Think.* He held his heels close together and spread his feet outward: a strong seal's tail; pressed his arms against his sides and flattened his hands: flippers. The ropes slipped away into the water.

Miles's body grew long and broad and sleek, his neck thickened, his nose protruded to a point, seal whiskers grew on his upper lip.

Flipping about, he swam through the warm salt water, broke the surface with his nose, and took a deep, sweet breath. He snorted and filled his lungs again as the waves played around him. Relief!

Breal swam up and licked his cheek. His bearhound knew him even in his seal's form; there was no disguising himself from his dog. "Breal," Miles said in a croaking seal voice, "let's go." The guards on deck would not care for a dog that leaped in the sea after his master, nor would they mistake a seal for the boy they'd just pushed off the plank.

Miles dove underwater and tumbled round and round. *Quava-arii*—ever changing. Bless Meer Eason. Surfacing again, he and Breal skimmed across the choppy surface. A rectangular shape floated toward them. Miles swam closer. The Falconer's trunk. He said a prayer of thanks that his first teacher on Enness had built it to be watertight. The books would be safe, and so would his precious ervay, which he'd tucked inside for safekeeping.

The trunk might be good for something else, for helping Meer Eason or Captain Kanoae float atop the water. Miles nosed it closer to the ship and swam beside the enormous hull. The vessel loomed over them like a floating fortress, its white sails gray in the slim starlight.

He and Breal would have to try to rescue Eason and

Kanoae as they plunged into the sea with their wrists bound. Miles was fairly sure he could bring one meer up to the surface in his seal's form, but two?

There was little time to think. High above them on the ship's deck, he spotted Eason stepping onto the plank. He wanted to call out, but even in his sealskin, he didn't dare. Breal seemed to understand the need to stay hidden from the crew above. He, too, was as black as the sea, and he was smart enough to tread water silently.

The drumroll sounded. No one sang for Meer Eason as he walked the plank and tumbled into the sea with a loud splash. Miles heard the crew laughing above as his teacher sank. He dove down, swimming deeper until he found the struggling old man and nosed him along. He had to get Eason to the surface in the shadow of the ship, out of the crew's sight. He realized he couldn't do this alone. As he swam with Eason under the inky surface, he called for help. Not in a human voice, but with the sonic sound of a seal.

The call traveled underwater as Miles pushed and pushed, bringing Eason up for air. He kept Meer Eason afloat as Breal nibbled the knots to free Eason's bound wrists and tore the gag from his mouth.

"Thank you," Eason sputtered. "I . . . I can't swim," he admitted. Miles swam him closer to the Falconer's trunk. Eason put his arms across it. The trunk was no help. It sank under his weight. Eason let go in a panic and hurriedly clasped Breal as the trunk floated back up beside them.

Miles knew Breal could hold Eason up a short while, but the dog couldn't swim far with a man on his back. He took Eason from Breal to give his dog a rest. They bobbed in the black water. High above them Kanoae walked the plank. If she, too, didn't know how to swim, how could he hope to save them both? He was trying to quell his panic when a slick black head appeared, then two, then three. The seals had heard his sonic call.

Miles darted alongside the pod. There were six seals, seven including Miles, and all were taking turns carrying Eason and Kanoae on their backs. Even Breal needed their help after paddling three hours at sea. A seventh seal pushed the Falconer's trunk along.

When it wasn't Miles's turn to help one of his friends, he dove into the rippling current to tumble, flip, and twirl. What a life seals had! Who needed fame or power or riches or any worldly thing when you had the ocean to play in and seal folk to play with. He came up for air and croaked a happy song. The seals all seemed to understand. They chorused back to him, their chaotic praise making the meers laugh.

Miles beat his tail harder and cut through the water. Swimming was like flying. The waves were like gusting wind. Never in his life had he been so happy. If this was what it was like to be a seal, why would he ever want to change back into a boy?

He slowed at the thought, remembering Meer Eason's warning. Resonance. He already felt a part of him wanting to stay here, abandon all the cares of his former life.

"Miles," he croaked. His name sounded ludicrous in his seal's voice, but it was a reminder of who he was and what he was here for. He swam up to the seal bearing Meer Eason, offering to take a turn carrying the Music Master.

After hours of swimming through the warm, eastern sea, Meer Kanoae waved her arm and shouted, "Land ahead!"

Miles slipped through the silky water, poked his head up, and saw the distant shore.

NINETEEN

DRAGON'S DREAMWALK

I saw a girl with sqyth-eyes.
She was walking in a dream.

—THE HIGH MEER OF OTHLORE

The Damusaun tugged a shimmering cloth from a cell in the wall overhead. Winging down, she draped it across Hanna's shoulders. Hanna fingered the silky golden cape, realizing it was made entirely of shed terrow scales.

The cape swished in the she-dragon's warm breath. "Kanameer. We have waited for your coming. You will dreamwalk for us now."

Hanna looked into her captor's face. Dreamwalk? Now? She'd had no dreams at all since she'd left Enness Isle. And even when she could dream, she'd never been able to dreamwalk on command. The walks had a will of their own. They took her from her bed, walked her where they willed her to go, left her with confusing visions she often didn't understand until much later, or sometimes not at all.

The Damusaun stared at Hanna, her unblinking eyes yellow gold as torches.

Hanna knew better than to admit she couldn't dreamwalk. *Say something.* "I . . . I will need the Fire Herd to help me." She was stalling for time, asking for Taunier.

Taunier leaned a little closer. "What now?" he whispered.

The dragons were waiting. Taunier was waiting. Enormous as it was, the high, walled cave seemed suddenly too small.

How could she free herself from her own trap? She'd told them she was the Dreamwalker, *their* Dreamwalker, but it seemed her story had added only minutes to her life. If she could not do what the Damusaun commanded, they would surely throw her and Taunier down the crevasse. The edge of the toothless black mouth waited hungrily below.

"We are ready, Kanameer." The Damusaun's voice was firm. Hanna took that as a cue. She must act the part and make her own demands.

"I will wait until midnight," she said. "I do not dream-walk in the day." This was true enough; her dreamwalks usually began around midnight. Only the very last one she'd had on Enness Isle had led her up Mount Shalem just before dawn.

"And," added Taunier, "she will need a safe place to walk, so she does not fall. A beach would do."

Hanna squeezed his arm. Asking for a beach would get them out of this cave. She was glad he'd thought of it.

The Damusaun and her two male companions beat their wings and flew across the crevasse to confer with the other taberrells and terrows in low tones, leaving Hanna and Taunier alone.

"I understand you need to play along and pretend you are the Kanameer," Taunier whispered, touching the edge of her golden cape. "But what's your next move? What have you got planned?"

"What?" she asked, shivering. "I'm not pretending about my travels to Oth or about my dreamwalks. I mean I *do* dreamwalk." *Only not on command, and I'm not sure if I can at all anymore,* she thought wretchedly. "Oh, I need time to think!" Thriss climbed down to her shoulder and nuzzled her cheek.

"Think escape. We'll have to—"

She should have heard him out, but she interrupted, "Wait. When we get to the beach, you can sneak away while I dreamwalk. The dragons will all be watching me."

"I won't go, Hanna. I'll stay with you."

"But you could find the deyas here and search for Tymm," she whispered furiously. She wanted to scream. One of them *had* to get away and do what they'd come here to do.

He rested his hand on her shoulder. "I'm not leaving without you."

Hanna glanced at his dark eyes, and felt herself falling into them, her heated anger from a moment ago cooling to gratitude and relief. He'd stay with her. She fought the sudden impulse to touch his jawline, tuck a strand of black hair behind his ear, or, even more boldly, go up on tiptoe to kiss him. But what if his protectiveness had nothing to do with the kind of love she was hoping for? Still, she hesitated, and the moment passed. How could she be so bold before the dragons only to melt before Taunier?

The Damusaun winged back over to the high stone terrace and settled beside them. Her cheek flaps swung as she turned her great head. "Your crown." She lifted a silver circlet in the air for all to see. A sigh passed through the cave. The deep blue sapphire and emerald set in the forefront of the crown exactly matched the colors of Hanna's sqyth-eyes.

Taunier looked bemused. The dragons watched with silent intensity as the Damusaun placed the crown on Hanna's head. It was too large and slipped down, awkwardly resting on her ears so the jewels sat in the middle of her brow.

Hanna tried to adjust it, but it was no use. Taunier gave a half smile.

"*Abathan*, Kanameer," sang the Damusaun.

"*Abathan*, Kanameer," sang the dragons across the ravine.

Abathan, the Othic word for "peace." Hanna hoped the dragons meant it—that she and Taunier wouldn't be killed if she failed them. But her heart still beat wildly in her chest. What she wished for now was Mother's kitchen and Taunier coming in with the milk pail. She wanted Da and Tymm out in the hills with the lambs, Miles exploring Shalem Wood with Breal, the simplicity of home. She'd give anything for that.

The Damusaun bowed her head, and all the dragons followed, red-throated males, purple-throated females.

Hanna held her breath.

"We will take you to the shore now," said the Damusaun. "Climb up on my back."

Midnight. The wind whistled down the rocky beach. At the base of the high cliffs, Hanna and Taunier faced the long row of dragons standing like sentinels before the rock wall.

Their captors had chosen the dreamwalking place with care. Lighting bonfires on the beach, they gathered between the sheer cliffs and the sea, where there would be no chance for escape.

"It's time, Kanameer." The Damusaun's voice was rasping and wild, but Hanna was growing used to the sound. Now she heard a reverence in the she-dragon's voice that startled her, telling her first that the dragons *needed* this dreamwalk, and second, that they hoped the Kanameer would give them some important knowledge.

The weight of the dragon's desire intensified her fear. If only she knew what they were looking for. She dug her boot into the sand. She would try to do as they asked, and if a dreamwalk did not come, she would have to act one out and make the dragons believe. She thought this even though she feared she could not fool them.

The Damusaun leaned closer, her long sickle teeth gleaming yellow-white in the firelight. Hanna stared, eyes wide. How easily that long orange tongue could flick out, wrap around her waist, draw her into that great dark mouth. She shuddered.

Taunier gave her a gentle nudge. "You'd best get started, Hanna."

"Here," she said. "Take Thriss, will you?" She held the pip out to Taunier. "She doesn't bite most of the time." Taunier set the hatchling on his shoulder. Thriss wrapped her tail around his neck and hissed at Hanna. "Don't worry, little one," Hanna said, then she turned to the Dragon Queen. "I need a soft place to lie down." She was still stalling, but the Damusaun directed the four younglings to make a bed of seaweed under a leafy sapling near the base of the cliff.

The pips dragged the seaweed into place and patted it down with their tails. One yawned before drawing back, as if he would have liked to try the bed himself.

Hanna stepped into the green nest, lay down, and spoke to Taunier as he knelt beside her.

"When I sit up, you need to take my hand and help me stand. Let me walk the way I want to go. Don't disturb me or shake me awake."

"I've followed your dreamwalks before," he reminded her. "I know not to startle you awake."

"Even if I scream," she said earnestly.

"Even if you scream."

She was still uncertain that she would be able to fall asleep, let alone dreamwalk, with so many anxious beasts glaring down at her. She wriggled in the weeds, and made some adjustments to cover the lumpy places where the sapling's roots snaked out of the ground.

Taunier drew the edges of her golden cape across her front. "I'll do it just as you say. I hope you find something for them, Hanna," he added with a worried look.

Hanna wanted to say, *How can I find something when I don't know what they're looking for?*

"Try and sleep now," he said, before pulling back.

Hanna blinked up at the stars glittering between the sapling's leaves. She *was* very tired, and she missed her dreams. It had been over a month since the ancient trees on Enness fell. The first week she'd paced with Mother, both of them too upset over Tymm to go to bed, then there was the wakeful time on Great-Uncle Enoch's boat, and later the long, stormy voyage on the *Leena* when she'd been too seasick to sleep much at all—too ill to dream— at least she *hoped* that was why her nights aboard the *Leena* had been completely dreamless.

The Dragon Queen hovered in very close, so Hanna could see hundreds of jagged bronze lines etched across her chest. The battle wounds looked like scrawls cut deep in tree bark, though this tree was a living dragon. The rest of the dragons shuffled in to watch. The great heads lowered. Heated breath poured across her body.

Hanna closed her eyes, reached in her pocket, and gripped Great-Uncle Enoch's vial of tears. *The Kanameer will know what to do with them.* Where was this Kanameer she was pretending to be?

Waves pounded the shore. Eyes still closed, she imag- ined the sound was the dragons' heartbeats as they glared at her, snouts down.

Hanna let go of the small brown bottle and sat up. "Please, can you back away a little?" she begged.

The Damusaun huffed out smoke, then ordered the

others to step away, though she did not move very far back herself.

Hanna tried again. She shut her eyes. *eOwey, help me sleep, help me dreamwalk.* She'd never asked for her power, but the Falconer had said she'd been born with the gift for a reason. If that were so, she needed her power back. Breathing deep, she tried to relax. She thought of Tymm, his contagious laugh as he repaired broken fences in the sheep pen for Da, his deep concentration as he pieced together broken dishes in Mother's kitchen. When nothing needed mending, Tymm's swift hands were usually making something new, weaving mouse cages or crafting little wooden toys with his friend Cilla.

She thought of the Othic words he'd said before he was Wind-taken. *Tesha yoven.* Bind the broken. Her eyes were full of Tymm running through the hills, his blond head bobbing above the tall grass. *Tesha yoven*: Tymm's words, the chant the High Meer had asked Miles to say in meditation. Breathe in Tesha. Breathe out Yoven. She did this five times, six. Breathe in Tesha, breathe out . . .

Roses, red and yellow, growing on a green hill. She was flying over a garden with the wind spirit, Wild Esper. Hanna looked down. Wild Esper's scales flashed as she pumped her wings. Not Wild Esper. She was on the Damusaun's back. They circled the roses that were wavering, growing higher. Taunier, on a dragon's back beside her, was shouting, waving his arms.

They flew closer in. Not roses. Fire! Islands of red and yellow fire, like the ones she'd seen floating on the sea. Not a green hill, but a mountain filled with towering blue-needled azure trees. People running below screaming, shouting. Some with bows, some with axes.

The Damusaun joined more dragons roaring fire. Taunier waved his arms and drew the flames into a wall. It grew along the mountainside, separating the men from the azure trees.

The dragon circled over the grove with Taunier astride, arms out, keeping the fire wall in place. No folk below were harmed. No trees burned. Still, the men ran screaming as they fired their crossbows at the dragons.

Thwack! The sudden sound came from below. A spiked ball hurtled past and struck the terrow dragon on Hanna's left. The dragon let out a high-pitched wail as the impact thrust her backward. She doubled over, spiraling down. Hanna cried out in her dream, but her mouth made no sound. She searched the smoky hills below. Where were the spiked balls coming from? In the undergrowth she spotted four men hefting another metal ball onto the long wooden arm of an enormous weapon. She tried to scream a warning; again no sound came.

Thwack! A second ball sped skyward. The Damusaun lurched back and crumpled inward. Blood spattered across Hanna's face. The sky spun. Smoke. Burning. Blood. She was falling, falling . . .

TWENTY

SEALSKIN

To swim is to fly.
To fly is to dream.
To dream is to live.

—SEAL SONG

The seals swam toward the tiny sparks of light glinting along the far shore. Bonfires to guide boats in, Miles guessed. But as they came nearer, the pod darted between dozens of sharp rock outcroppings, too treacherous for ships.

On the faraway beach, sheer cliffs rose up from the sand. No welcome place to land even if a ship made it that far. That meant the fires weren't beacon fires at all, unless they were the work of pirates who meant to cause shipwreck so they could go after the plunder.

Eason was cautious. "Take us to the rock there, will you?" The meers were cold and tired, but they'd have to find a safer cove if pirates were waiting on the beach.

Miles swam in a little closer with the pod until he saw who'd set the bonfires.

Dragons.

Nearly twenty taberrells and terrows were lined up along the base of the high cliffs. They were so still Miles thought they might be statues guarding an ancient dragon ruin. Then he saw a tail flip up. The turquoise scales along the tip gleamed.

The other seals began to swim away as fast as flippers and tail allowed.

Miles croaked, "Wait."

Black eyes and black noses turned toward him inquiringly. Then Meer Kanoae saw the two human forms Miles had spotted by the bonfires. "It's Hanna and Taunier," she gasped. "Alive!"

"We've found them," said Meer Eason in awe. "You brought us to them, Miles!"

Miles warmed to his teacher's praise. "We need to swim in closer," said Kanoae, "find out what's going on."

The group paddled through the bay. They were near enough to the beach to be seen now if they weren't careful, so the seals and riders kept their heads down, moving silently in rhythm with the water. At the next rock outcropping, the meers climbed onto the jutting stone and hid with Breal behind a rough barrier.

Miles swished his tail and kept to the water. He fixed his eyes on Hanna. She was speaking to the dragons. Her words were clear enough when he could hear them above the waves.

"I rode the wind, or so I thought." Hanna gripped Taunier's arm and leaned into him. "But when I looked down in my dreamwalk, I saw I was riding the Damusaun."

A wave tumbled in, covering her next words.

". . . fire," Hanna was saying. "The people below were running and screaming. Taunier was in the air, flying beside me on his dragon. He was herding fire to keep the men with axes away from the azure trees when—"

Another wave. Curse this tide!

Miles watched the she-dragon who'd carried Hanna and Taunier away from the *Leena* lower her head, her cheek flaps dangling from her jaws like long, ornamental purses. "You saw truth in your dreamwalk. We guard the Waytrees here near the place where the World Tree fell." The dragon's voice was louder than Hanna's and carried well over the water.

"All was safe in these ancient azure groves until last

year, when Whirl Storms destroyed the great city of Kanayar. The King of Kanayar hungered for the tallest timber in Noor to rebuild his city. He broke the age-old treaty between men and dragons, and sent his Cutters to our woods."

The other dragons made an angry, rumbling noise. Miles felt the sound cross his sealskin, as if his black hide were a drum.

The Damusaun raised her wing to quiet them. "The Kanayaran king did not want those in other lands to know he'd broken his treaty," said the she-dragon. "He sent his border guards to the Boundary Waters to keep other folk away."

And to kill them if they tried to cross, Miles thought bitterly.

The Damusaun stepped closer to Hanna. "The king's Cutters use saws and axes and root poison to fell azures and harvest the timber. There is only one grove left here on Mount Olone. We fight to save the Waytrees that bind the two worlds."

Meer Kanoae sucked in a loud breath. "So," she said, "the dragons are on our side. I'm glad now I didn't use my harpoon."

Miles tensed, wondering if the dragons had heard

the remark, but the waves seemed to have covered it. He sighed, relieved. He wasn't sure what his next move should be. He would wait a little longer here in the dark.

A wave hissed on shore and drew away. The Damusaun's large, triangular head hovered above Hanna and Taunier.

"We told the King of Kanayar and his manling Cutters that the ancient Waytrees are bound together. If they poisoned the azure roots and chopped them down, other Waytrees of Noor would fall. We warned him of the terrible damage that would come to both Noor and Oth. But the King and his Cutters are dragon-deaf!" She lifted her head and breathed red fire. The other dragons on the beach did the same, until the red flames nearly obscured the black cliffs behind them.

Miles felt the dragons' anger, remembered the Waytrees falling, the deyas dying in Othlore Wood, and made his decision. With a flick of his tail, he entered the next wave heading for shore.

"Miles?" called Eason. "What are you doing?"

He knew the meers would need the seals' help to swim in, but he gave no signal yet. He would see how safe it was first. Pulling himself from the pounding surf, he struggled along the wet sand. His seal's body that was so lithe and graceful in the sea felt heavy and unwieldy now, as if he were weighted down with stones and wrapped tightly in a wet cloak. He wriggled toward the gathering, the heat of the bonfires crossing his slick sealskin. He rested a moment behind a black boulder. The dragons hadn't noticed him yet, but they'd soon catch his scent. He focused on Hanna, working up his courage.

TWENTY-ONE

PILGRIM

In days long past when NoorOth was one,
both land and sea were full of magic.

—*THE WAY BETWEEN WORLDS*

The dragons' fiery breath heated the night air, tightening the skin on Hanna's cheeks. In spite of this, she felt chilled. They were of one mind about the Waytrees, but what about the Wind-taken? Had the dragons seen the stolen children in Jarrosh? Did they know where the east wind had taken them, and why? She had to approach the questions with care. The Damusaun expected the Kanameer to be knowledgeable, not uncertain.

Another thing troubled her. She hadn't found the courage to tell the dragons the rest of her dreamwalk, the terrible weapon she'd seen.

Thriss leaped from Taunier's shoulder to hers and

flicked her tail. Hanna stroked the hatchling under her chin. She would start by telling them the queen was in danger. She had to pass on the warning before she asked them to help her find Tymm and the others.

"There was more in my dreamwalk, Damusaun. The men had a weapon, a trebuchet, I think." She frowned, remembering the device. "They used it to shoot large spiked balls into the air."

Hanna stopped, took a breath. "One of the spiked balls knocked a terrow from the sky. And then—"

She paused a second time, wiping her cheek with her sleeve, as if the queen's blood were still there.

"Tell us the rest," said the Damusaun. The bonfires on the beach washed bronze light across the she-dragon's attentive eyes. Hanna saw herself reflected in the queen's slit pupils.

She dropped her gaze to the battle scars on the Dragon Queen's chest, like ancient script. "I was flying on your back, Damusaun. You were hit."

The dragons on the beach roared in protest. The queen wrapped her tail about her feet, and terrows stepped up on either side. The she-dragon shone between her sentries like an emerald in a golden crown.

Since the moment the dragons had stolen them from the ship, Hanna had been afraid of the Damusaun. But her dreamwalk had joined them in some way. Now she was afraid *for* her. If bloody death were waiting for the queen, and if this attack was waiting for her, too . . .

"Look." Taunier pointed at a seal making its way awkwardly toward the fire. It must be a very brave seal to leave the safety of the waves and approach so many dragons. Hanna was about to turn back to the Damusaun when the seal held up its flipper and waved. The seal's gesture was so comically human that Hanna laughed. But her laughter caught in her mouth when the seal began to change.

A low rumble came from the dragons' throats. Taunier gripped Hanna's arm as the seal's body grew long and lean, as the tail split into legs and the flippers thinned and lengthened into arms. Hanna held her breath. At last the boy rolled over, got onto his knees, and stood shakily before them.

"Miles!" Joy and fear combined in that one word, joy because her brother was alive, fear because the last time the dragons had seen him, they'd set his giant falcon's wing aflame. Did they know it was Miles who'd attacked them in falcon form?

Still, nothing could keep her from racing down the beach and throwing her arms around her brother. Taunier ran up and thumped Miles on the back. He was cold and wet, and his dripping clothes smelled of seaweed, but that didn't matter at all. He was alive. Hanna drew back and looked at her brother. How had he come here? Where were the others? What about Breal? Where was the *Leena*? She felt the dragons waiting behind her.

Face them. Speak.

But before she could say a word, Kaleet snarled, "Shape-shifter."

There was a rattle of displeasure in his voice, and she heard low-toned agreement from the one-eyed male and the rest of the elder dragons. *Why did Miles have to shape-shift here on the beach right in front of them?* Hanna wondered.

She cleared her throat. "This is my brother, Miles. He's on our side." The words dulled in the wind. *Our side.* Did the dragons understand what she meant by that?

A long silence followed. Miles shivered beside her. He stole a glance at the one-eyed male who'd burned his wing, shuddered, and looked away. The bonfire burned bright, but he did not step any closer to warm himself.

A thin line of smoke trailed from the Damusaun's nostrils. Hanna thought, *I should say something else. What?*

Miles took a deep breath, then walked forward. Touching his fingers to his forehead in a meer's greeting, he bowed from the waist to the Dragon Queen. The hiss of sweeping water was the only sound along the shore. Miles kept his head low as the wave drew back, leaving a line of foam along the sand.

"*Abathan*, Damusaun," said Miles. "I have come a long way with my sister and the meers to find the Wind-taken children and save the greatest Waytrees of Noor."

The one-eyed male stepped closer to the queen. "Our prophecy does not speak of a shape-shifter, Damusaun."

The Dragon Queen glanced down at her broken talon, then up again at the dripping boy. "I see the danger you see, Endour. A shifter can renew or destroy."

"Please, Damusaun," said Miles. "Give me the chance to prove myself to you."

His wet cloak clung to his back, and his hair stuck up wildly. He was still bowing. Hanna wanted to say something in his favor, but Taunier gently held her back.

It began to rain. The queen stared at Miles a long while, then shook the drops from her scales. "Rise, pilgrim."

Relief flooded through Hanna as the taberrells and terrows gently beat the sand with their tails. When the soft applause subsided, Miles trailed back down to the water. Standing ankle-deep in sea foam, he cupped his hands to his mouth and called, "Come in."

Hanna let out a squeal of delight as she spotted Breal paddling through the dark sea swells, flanked by seals carrying Meers Eason and Kanoae. They rode a cresting wave into the shallows, where the meers slid into the waist-high water and fought the pounding surf the last few feet to shore. Breal bounded up and shook the water from his fur as Kanoae and Eason dragged the Falconer's trunk onto the beach.

TWENTY-TWO

DRAGONS' COUNCIL

I came to the blue azure forest,
where the boughs held up the sky.

—THE MISHTAR, *DRAGON'S WAY*, VOL. I

The hard coastal rain swept up the beach, driving them all back into the dragon's cave. High above, Hanna saw the broad shelves extending from either side of the sheer walls, where she and Taunier had stood facing the dragons only hours before. Now she was walking with Miles and Taunier by the dark pool of freshwater at the bottom of the crevasse.

Her head spun. It had all changed so fast. Miles and the meers were in Jarrosh. The fearful dragons dragging their long tails just ahead of them were now their companions in the war against the Cutters.

A freshwater stream filled the pool. Hanna and her friends drank, and Breal lapped the water noisily as the dragons dipped their long orange tongues into the pool. The water tasted of the forest and good green things. *The dragons are fighting for the Waytrees. There must still be enough growing here to bridge the way to Oth, to Tymm.* She swallowed, tasting hope.

Behind a large rock, Hanna opened the Falconer's trunk and changed into clean clothes, soft gray pants and a top that wasn't stiffened with harsh weather and grime. It would have been blissful to bathe and wash her hair, but there was no private place for this. She felt the dry cover of *The Way Between Worlds*, grateful the Falconer had made the chest watertight. Before closing the lid, she pulled out a clean cloth and the wound-care tincture. Kaleet had a nasty cut on his shoulder.

"May I?" Hanna uncorked the tincture bottle and held it up. Kaleet narrowed his eyes, sniffed the bottle, and puffed indignantly. He'd been one of the most outspoken against her. She worked to hide her trembling, so near his muscular jaws, as he let her clean the gash. He smacked his heavy tail against the wall once as she wiped sand from the wound, but he gave a nod of thanks when she was done.

She would have liked to clean the ugly marks on the queen's right foreclaw. But it would draw attention to the puncture wounds Miles had made, trying to rescue her. The dragons had seen her brother shape-shift from seal to boy, but she was fairly sure they hadn't known it was Miles in falcon form who'd attacked them, and she didn't want to get them thinking. Hanna bit her lip. The Damusaun was a warrior. The puncture wounds were small compared to the many crisscrossed scars on her chest and her severed talon. Reluctantly, she put the medicine away.

At the pool, the younger dragons caught wriggling fish in their swift claws. A few terrows showed off, skewering a trout on each talon and roasting them with their fiery breath. Breal barked in appreciation of the show, and Miles and Taunier laughed at Thriss, who tried the trick and dropped her trout on the sandy stone floor.

Later, as Miles, Taunier, and the meers sat talking with the dragons around the central fire, Hanna finished her meal in silence by the wall and planned her next move. She'd seen what was left of the nearby forest as the Whirl Storm blew her to shore. Azure Waytrees grew up on the mountain slope a long way from this cave. She needed the dragons to fly her to the deyas in the azures, who could help her to Oth in search of Tymm and the other children. Miles and Taunier already seemed intent on joining

THE DRAGONS OF NOOR

in the dragons' fight against the Cutters. She hoped she wouldn't have to cross into the Otherworld alone.

The discussion on the far side of the cave centered on the trebuchet she'd seen.

"We will destroy the manlings' new weapons," said Kaleet.

"Weapons?" asked One-eye. "The Kanameer saw only one trebuchet in her dream."

"There may be more, Endour," argued Kaleet. "We should burn whatever we find."

It seemed a good idea to Hanna, but the Damusaun shook her head. "Do that, and the Cutters will come running to the telltale flames and douse the fire," she said. "Better to take the weapons out and drop them in the sea. We will use the covering of night for this."

"We?" asked Kaleet. "The Kanameer's dream was a warning, Damusaun. We do not want you near the trebuchets."

"A warning, I agree," said one-eyed Endour, backing up Kaleet.

The tip of the Damusaun's tail brushed the water. Ripples raced across the dark pool. The cave was all too silent.

Hanna fed Thriss a bite of fish.

At last the queen spoke. "Kanameer?"

Hanna tucked Thriss under her arm and approached the queen.

"Tell us, do your dreamwalks foreshadow what is to come or only what might come?"

Hanna frowned, thinking. "They do both, Damusaun. Some of my dreamwalks come true." She thought of the great black tree she'd seen. Would she find that tree in eastern Oth?

Kaleet slowly shook his head. "The Kanameer saw you shot down, Damusaun. She, too, was falling in her dream. You should not risk your lives. Stay clear of the Cutters' camps until the trebuchets are destroyed."

The Dragon Queen beat the water harder with her tail. Mighty splashes rained down. Breal, who got the most of it, shook his fur, sending a smaller shower over Meer Eason.

"Are you telling me what to do?" the Damusaun growled testily.

Kaleet did not back away. Their eyes met. "I am asking, Damusaun."

The dragons in the circle repeated in rumbling voices, "We are asking."

Then, in a softer voice Hanna barely heard, Kaleet said, "Think of the egg you carry, of the queen to come."

Hanna gripped Thriss a little tighter. An egg. Another queen. She'd sensed it in her dreamwalk as they'd plummeted down, though she'd not been able to put it into words. Three lives falling. The third, she knew now, was the tiny future queen.

She passed her eyes over the Damusaun and thought she detected a telltale rounding at the base of her belly. The Damusaun flashed her a look and covered her abdomen with her tail. "We leave tonight," she said. "The meers may ride with us if they dare."

"I'll go!" Miles said eagerly. He stepped up next to Hanna.

Hanna leaned close to whisper in his ear, "Let the others fight with the dragons, Miles. I need you in Oth."

"I'm needed here," he whispered.

She would have answered back, but Taunier was up and speaking. "I, too, will go," he said. "Though I am not a meer."

"Come forward."

Hanna tensed as Taunier rounded the fire.

The Damusaun lowered her head to his level. "You

are not a meer, but you are the Fire Herd. Before you came, we could only stand sentinel at the edge of the wood. Now with your help we can make a fire wall to bar the Cutters from the Waytrees. Do you think you can contain our wall and see that the azures do not catch fire?"

Taunier held out his cupped hands. "How can I herd a great wall, Damusaun?"

"The Kanameer has dreamed it. You will ride a dragon."

Hanna remembered the danger Taunier had faced in her dream. She wanted to grab his broad shoulders and convince him to come with her to Oth. But she knew it would only infuriate him. Though she could not see his face, she could tell by his stance that Taunier stood resolute, even proud.

"Now let the meers reveal their signs," said the Damusaun. Eason and Kanoae stood and held their hands out to the fire. Blazing blue Othic symbols appeared on their left palms; the meer sign was first worn by the Mishtar, the man most honored by the dragons. The she-dragon looked pleased. Her head began to sway.

Hanna had seen palm signs before, and she still

remembered the one on the Falconer's palm. Each meer bore a distinct symbol. Seeing them, she felt a kind of awe, not at their power, but at their lit beauty.

"Miles," said the Dragon Queen, "where is your sign?"

Miles stiffened. "I am an apprentice, Damusaun." The queen huffed gray smoke and clicked her talons against the stony floor.

Hanna wrapped her hand about his arm and whispered, "It doesn't matter."

"It does," Miles hissed under his breath. "I would have been blue-palmed in a few months' time if I'd stayed on at school."

"You don't have to join the raid," argued Hanna. "I need you to go with me. You promised to help me find Tymm."

"You won't be able to bring him back if the Waytrees are down. It's Tymm I'm thinking of."

"Who is this Tymm?" The Damusaun extended her long neck.

Hanna started. She'd not meant for their whispered debate to be overheard. "He's our little brother, Damusaun."

"He was Wind-taken after the Waytrees fell," Miles

added. "Many children were stolen that way, and we're sure they were blown east."

The queen flicked out her tongue. "I saw these children."

They all spoke at once—Hanna, Miles, Taunier, the meers—their questions tripping over one another.

"Where did you see them?"

"How long ago?"

"When?"

The queen shook her head irritably. She was used to being addressed singly and with respect. When they all fell silent, she said, "A few dragons from our company patrolled Noor to see where the ancient forests were falling, as we knew they would when our azures were cut. Land to land they saw children taken up by the wind. Weeks ago, we saw the children blowing over our Waytrees here. I winged after them to see if our Kanameer and Fire Herd had come, for we knew our pilgrims would arrive on the wind. When I reached the azure grove, they were gone."

"Gone?" Hanna choked on the word.

"What do you mean, gone?" asked Miles.

"They were taken into Oth," the Dragon Queen said.

The passage, thought Hanna. *It is here!* "Did you follow the children into Oth? Can you show us the Waytree passage?" She was asking too many questions at once, but she couldn't help it.

A low growling sound filled the cave, coming not only from the queen but from every dragon's throat. Hanna tried not to panic. What had she said to offend them?

"We could not follow them, Kanameer," the Damu-saun said briskly.

"But Oth is your home, isn't it?" blurted out Miles.

"We were banished from Oth long ago, manling."

Hanna looked down at the sandy floor. Banished? She'd not seen any dragons in Oth last year, but she'd only explored a single island in the west. The Otherworld had as many lands as Noor. She'd assumed the dragons lived in the sunny eastern lands of Oth.

She toed a pebble with her boot, thinking. If the dragons couldn't cross over, how could they guard the way between worlds, or help her find Tymm? She shot a quick glance at Miles, Taunier, and the meers. They, too, looked stunned.

"Sit now," snapped the queen. "All of you." Her voice was brittle. She was giving them an order.

TWENTY-THREE

THE LAW OF THE OLD MAGIC

*I have seen the dragons burn their dead and
save a single wing bone to bury back in Twarn-
Majas when they return home.*

—THE MISHTAR, *DRAGON'S WAY*, VOL. 3

Hanna settled by the fire next to Taunier. *What now?*
Thriss curled up in her lap but did not purr.

The Dragon Queen peered at each of the five companions in turn. Her yellow eyes landed last on Hanna.

"A Dreamwalker may step into the future," she said,
"but I see your powers are limited, Kanameer. You do
not see behind you far enough to step back into the past."

One of the hatchlings snickered, and the queen held
up her tail in warning.

Blushing, Hanna ran her finger down Thriss's scaly
back. She did not look at Taunier, though he was close
enough for her to feel the warmth coming off his skin.

"Still," said the queen, "I would not expect any

manlings to know our trouble. The Mishtar was true to his word. He pledged to keep our banishment from Oth secret, to pass on the guarded knowledge only from High Meer to High Meer. But all secrets pass away in time."

Who had the power to banish the dragons, Hanna wondered.

"Do you know why we dragons guard the Waytrees?"

Miles said, "The deep-rooted trees house deya spirits, and they bridge the way between the worlds."

"Rightly said, pilgrim."

Hanna noticed her brother's chest swell with pride. She could have given the same answer, but she was still feeling the sting of the Damusaun's comment about her limited powers.

"Watching over Waytrees runs in our blood," said the queen, "since the first age when dragons guarded the greatest tree of all, the World Tree, Kwen-Arnun."

At the mention of the World Tree, all the dragons sent green fire toward the ceiling. The fire combined into a single burning tree. The tree seemed alive, its branches laden with silver fruit so ripe Hanna felt as if she could smell its sweet, rich nectar, so real she wanted to pluck and taste it.

Hanna knew the dragons had guarded the World Tree

from the beginning of time. But the burning tree here in the cave was like a prayer, and more than any words it showed the love the dragons had for their Kwen-Arnun.

Slowly, the tree burned out. Smoke swirled about, clouding the high ceiling.

The Damusaun said, "When the great quake split the World Tree in the second age and drove a rent through NoorOth, tearing the worlds in two, we winged to Kwen-Arnun's children here in Noor. We knew the World Tree's offspring would have the power to hold the two worlds together if they were left alone to grow strong. When the manlings came to fell the Waytrees for timber, we did not let the worlds split apart. We fought with talons, teeth, and fire. Many manlings died."

Hanna had studied the dragon wars; every child in Noor knew their history. But she'd not learned the reason for the war, or why the dragons fought, only that they'd been fierce enemies of man until the treaties were signed. The books were likely different at the meers' school, and she was sure she would have learned the truth if she'd read all the pages in the Falconer's book, for he, at least, was never one to lie. Hanna was still thinking about this when she realized the Damusaun was speaking to her.

"You have been to Oth, Kanameer. You must know the law of the Old Magic."

Hanna slid her hand in her pocket and grasped Great-Uncle Enoch's gift. The bottle was cool in her sweaty hand. She knew that magical folk who broke the law of the Old Magic were exiled from the lit lands of Oth, imprisoned in the shadow lands behind the great wind-wall, or expelled from Oth entirely. It was the law of the Old Magic that prevented the Sylth Queen from killing Great-Uncle Enoch when he'd mistakenly released the Shriker from captivity behind her wind-wall. Instead, she'd punished him by enspelling him in the oak tree. The same law also prevented the Sylth Queen from killing the Shriker, so she'd drawn Miles into Oth to do the deed for her.

Hanna cleared her throat and looked up at the Damusaun. "I know that those who follow the law of the Old Magic are forbidden to kill."

The smoke rising from the she-dragon's nostrils drifted toward the entryway, joining the gray rain outside. "So you see the way of it, Kanameer. We broke the law when we went to war. For that, we were banished from Oth."

Meer Kanoae said, "So you can never go home again?"

Hanna cringed inside. Sometimes Meer Kanoae was too blunt, but the Damusaun didn't snap at her. Instead, she raised her head a little higher and curled her long, spiked tail about her feet like a gown. "When the dragon wars ended, we signed a treaty with all manlings. They would let us keep our forestlands, and there would be no more bloodshed. The Sylth King of Oth pledged to lift the banishment if we abided by our treaties and kept peace with manlings for seven hundred years."

"Seven hundred years? But that's too long!" Hanna blurted out.

The dragons flicked their tails irritably. She clamped her teeth. Who was being too blunt now? Dragons lived far longer than men, and she sensed that many dragons here were very old indeed. Still, the punishment seemed overly harsh.

A cooling green color came to the Damusaun's eyes, sorrow, but no tears, though it seemed all the deeper for that. Hanna could imagine how she felt. She loved her own home on Enness Isle. Loved Mount Shalem, Shalem Wood, her family's cottage, the green hills that rolled down to the sea. What if she were banished from Enness?

A hatchling said, "Tell us about Twarn-Majas, Damusaun."

"Twarn-Majas," said the queen. "You have never seen it, little Agreeya," she said tenderly. "I was born there. No land is more beautiful, no ground more richly colored. The mountains there are deep-blue stone. Sky and land look to be brother and sister on a clear day. I still remember the scent of the masayan trees in bloom."

"I, too, was born there," said Kaleet.

"As was I," said another and another.

"Twarn-Majas. Twarn-Majas." Whispers drifted through the cave like a sigh. And for a moment Hanna saw the mountains rising blue against a pale green dawn, blue above the eastern Othic sea.

The Damusaun said, "This month on the night of Breal's Moon our banishment will end."

"Breal's Moon," whispered Taunier. "It's less than a week from now."

Hanna remembered the eclipse she'd seen through the porthole her first night on the *Leena*. Breal's Moon, the first full moon after an eclipse, was the night when it was easiest to cross from Noor to Oth and back.

The queen said, "We will be allowed to cross over

that night. That is, if any Waytrees are left by then."

Hanna started. If all the Waytrees were felled, how could she hope to bring Tymm and the others home? "There must be enough left!" she argued. "There's still an azure grove higher up the mountain. I saw it when the storm blew us here."

"Kanameer! Speak with your mind and not just your heart. There is but one grove left, and it's vanishing under the Cutters' axes and root poison. We are losing this battle—one we could win with ease if we could kill."

Miles stood. "We can kill for you, Damusaun."

The Dragon Queen roared fire. Miles leaped back as the flames nearly singed his feet. "You would kill men for us? Tell me, foolish boy, how that is any different than killing them ourselves?"

Meer Eason stood and cleared his throat, but Miles was already answering, "It's not, I suppose." He was visibly shaking.

Hanna stood up beside him. "My brother means no harm, Damusaun."

"Harm is just what he means." She snapped her jaws. "If you wish to help us, you must fight our way. Kill a single man, and we will be exiled from our homeland forever."

Taunier said, "We'll take a vow. Whatever you want us to do to help you save the trees, we will do."

Meer Eason and Kanoae joined them in a row facing the dragons.

Smoke curled from the Damusaun's nostrils. "Will you vow by breath and fire to fight but not to kill?"

They all said, "I vow it."

The queen sealed the vow by sending her fire to each in turn. The intense heat was startling. Hanna gritted her teeth, waiting for it to be over. When the flame was extinguished, she was grateful for the rain outside that sent a cool, wet wind coursing through the cave.

"We accept your vow," replied the Damusaun, and she bowed her great head to the small band of humans who had come so far to aid them in their battle.

TWENTY-FOUR

NIGHT BATTLE

Clouds came with rain and snow,
and the people forgot the stars.

—*The Book of eOwey*

Cool droplets pricked Miles's arms as he left the dragon's cave and crossed the sand with Taunier and Hanna. Clouds shrouded the moon. The spare light would make it harder for the Cutters to see the dragons flying over their camps. It would also be more difficult to find the trebuchets hidden in the hills.

They headed for the high stone arch to get out of the wet, while they waited for the dragons to assemble on the beach.

Hanna tucked a strand of hair behind her ears. It fell across Thriss's back like a blanket. "If I find the passage into Oth . . ." She adjusted her rucksack, and the corner of the Falconer's book stuck out. Miles covered it to keep it dry. The Falconer's maps could not pinpoint the Waytree passage here in the east. The mysterious passage from Noor to Oth was never in one place for long but moved, from Waytree to Waytree. It would not be easy to find. Hanna buried the toe of her boot in the sand and seemed to lose the rest of her speech. Taunier, too, was silent.

Miles said, "If you think you can find Tymm, then you have to go, Hanna. As things are now, we haven't much time." He leaned against the cliff rock, feeling torn. Part of him wanted to go with her. He'd promised Da he'd find his little brother, but he and Taunier were both needed here. "We'll fight to keep the Waytrees standing long enough for you to get Tymm and the others out of Oth."

Hanna wrapped the cloak more tightly about herself, Thriss disappearing under the folds. "When the Damusaun said she'd seen the children blowing over Jarrosh, I thought she'd tell us where in Oth Tymm had gone."

"She wasn't holding back from us," said Taunier. "She just—"

"Couldn't go after them," said Miles. He, too, had

been sorely disappointed to discover the queen knew so little about the Wind-taken.

"Still," said Taunier, "the Damusaun saw them disappear into Oth. We're closer to finding Tymm now than we've ever been."

Hanna rocked on her feet. "But we're no closer to understanding why Tymm and the others were taken."

Just overhead a spider clung to her damp web. The high stone arch was keeping them dry, but it was cold and later would be colder still. Miles took his sister's hand. "You'll understand who took them and why when you find them. I'm sure of that. When we were back in western Noor on Othlore Isle, the High Meer told us what he'd seen in the scrying stone. He believed the Wind-taken children were brought here to help the Waytrees."

"How?" asked Hanna, irritably. "How can they help the Waytrees if they're in Oth?"

"If we're fighting to keep the worlds together here, there must be others in Oth who want the same."

Hanna watched the spider climb her web. "I hope you're right."

"You found me last year," said Miles. "And you *will* find Tymm. You have to." These last words came from his belly, from the ache that had been there since he'd seen the empty cot in Tymm's loft.

He reached up to straighten her windblown hair. She was taller than he remembered, not a child anymore. *She's beautiful*, he thought. The idea startled him.

Taunier was gazing at her. It was more than a brotherly look. Miles was taken aback. Hanna and Taunier? His best friend and his sister? He wasn't sure how he felt about that. Or was he just imagining it?

"You be careful in Oth," Taunier said. He looked down at her, for he was nearly a foot taller than she.

Hanna squared her shoulders, a determined look on her soft face. "I'll do what I have to."

Taunier frowned, but Miles understood. Hanna would not promise to keep herself safe. She'd do what must be done to bring their little brother home.

"You're a good sister," Miles said, and he caught the faintest smile from her.

Breal trotted down the beach. Behind him, terrows and taberrells exited the cave with Meers Eason and Kanoae.

Taunier patted Breal. "I have to go now. My dragon is waiting."

Hanna rubbed Breal where Taunier had just withdrawn his hand. "Please be careful." It was the same thing Taunier had said to her moments before, and he, too, did not make a promise.

"I'll join you soon." Miles tried to hide his irritation as he said this. He couldn't wait to go to battle, and the Damusaun *still* hadn't told him which dragon he was to ride.

Farther down the beach, Meers Eason and Kanoae were mounting their dragons. Taunier climbed over a driftwood log and headed for a golden terrow. The red-ringed neck showed it to be a male.

Miles fought jealousy as he and Hanna followed his friend. They came to a stop at the driftwood log. The Damusaun had honored Meers Eason and Kanoae when she'd seen the blue meer signs on their palms, so he understood why she would send them out in the first wave of fighters. *If I'd been blue-palmed before I left Othlore,* he thought, *she would have chosen a dragon for me by now.* Yet Taunier was going out. The dragons seemed to revere his power over fire, for they could not rein it in or make it move the way he could.

Miles kicked the wet seaweed. The Dragon Queen

didn't seem to value his shape-shifting gift. Instead, she seemed to view it as dangerous. Well, wasn't herding fire dangerous?

"Look," whispered Hanna.

Just down the beach, Taunier was bowing to his terrow. Miles heard his formal speech. "May I ride with you, Findarr?"

"We will greet the sky together, Fire Herd." Findarr knelt down, extending his long neck. His ridged tail, which ended in sharp spikes, curled about him like a spiraling staircase. Taunier paused a moment before stepping closer to the giant kneeling form. Putting his hand atop the base of the scaly neck, he climbed on.

Miles and Hanna followed Taunier and Findarr as they joined the first group of dragons parading down to the water's edge. Meers Kanoae and Eason both waited atop their taberrells. Meer Kanoae seemed as sure on dragon's back as she did captaining her vessel. Her thick hair was braided and tied back with a leather strap. Meer Eason wriggled on his perch, less confident than she. Still, he gave Miles and Hanna a nod from above. Breal wagged his tail and barked, which made the meer laugh and wave, and Hanna waved back.

Miles tried to look cheerful. *There are plenty of dragons left,* he told himself. But with every minute, his mood was darkening. When would the Damusaun choose his partner?

Hanna couldn't fly into battle after the warning in her dreamwalk. No one wanted to risk her and the Damusaun being shot down from the sky. And anyway, Hanna was bound for the Waytrees, higher up Mount Olone.

At some invisible signal, the dragons all unfurled their wings, some golden, some blue-green, and lifted over the water. Taunier, Meer Eason, and Kanoae glided higher and higher above the thin clouds. In the gentle rain, Miles watched Taunier and Findarr turn and disappear beyond Mishtar's Prow star as they headed for the glade in search of the hidden trebuchets.

Breal nudged his side.

"Come on," Miles said.

Hanna didn't budge. "I'll stay here a moment longer."

Miles took off up the beach. More dragons were lining up, and he was ready to fly. His heart raced. He wasn't going to miss the next departure. He crossed the beach to where the Damusaun waited. The queen's vast form glowed iridescent in the wet moonlight, the crosshatched scars on her breastplate lit up like lettered runes.

Bowing, he addressed her. "May I ride with you, Damusaun?"

It was the formal speech of the rider's ritual, delivered as perfectly as Taunier's request. The she-dragon spat a javelin of fire at Miles's feet. He jumped back, the toes of his boots smoking.

"Your ride is mine to choose, pilgrim," she growled.

"Forgive me," he said, trembling with fear and awe. Taberrell dragons were the largest living creatures in Noor, and their queen held enormous power. It would have been easy for her to spit her fire directly at him and burn him to a crisp. He saw again how forcefully she held back her great power.

On the rain-pocked sand the Dragon Queen flicked out her tongue.

Miles's eyes fell on the queen's broken talon, the saw mark just above it. He'd heard a Cutter had used his saw to sever the tip as she'd flown him away from the azures. The she-dragon did not speak of her talon or the man who'd severed it, but he'd overheard one of the terrows talking to another dragon in a hushed voice last night.

The Damusaun caught his gaze, buried the broken talon deeper in the sand, and gave her order. "You will greet the sky with Endour."

Miles felt a presence come up behind him, warm breath drifting through cold rain, the sound of a tail dragging in the sand. He pivoted, saw One-eye, and privately winced as he bowed.

"May I . . . ride with you, Endour?"

The dragon's long orange tongue flicked out. Knots of muscle rippled beneath his scales. The fiery burns along Miles's arm began to sting under his sleeve. Endour had scorched him in their brief battle, so why had the Damusaun picked One-eye, out of all the dragons on the beach?

Endour lowered his head. "One who fights is willing to risk all," he said in a husky voice.

"I will risk all." Miles wondered what his pledge meant and how he would be asked to fight when the dragons expected him to follow the law of the Old Magic. He and the meers had joined them without spears or swords, having no weapons at all but their hands and their wits. Still, Endour had claws, fangs, and fire. He found some comfort in that.

Endour said, "We will greet the sky together, pilgrim."

The rider's ritual was complete as Endour's voice washed over Miles, and the dragon knelt for Miles to climb on. They'd fought against each other, but that was in the past. They were out to protect the Waytrees. He would go anywhere with this dragon now.

Endour soared over the dark cliffs. Miles met the wind, feeling as if he were swimming in a great black sea. In that moment he found the gift the seal shape-shift had left him. Not a physical change of heightened hearing or keener vision like other shape-shifts, but a gift he'd abandoned long ago—a sense of playfulness he thought he'd never have again. He'd found it again when he tumbled in the sea in his seal's form, and that same sense of playfulness came back to him now as he greeted the sky with Endour.

The wind filled him like an empty flask. He drank.

They were still far away from the Cutters' camps. He let out a loud whoop as the land sped by below. The dragons before them seemed to swing from the very stars.

Turning east, terrows and taberrells rode the thermals high above Jarrosh, rising up and dropping down as the wind opened the way. They glided toward the base of Mount Olone, flying over mile upon mile of clear-cut forest. The Damusaun's words came back to him. *All the Waytrees were bound in their making, and the azures are the greatest of them all. When they fall, the others fall with them.* How many dead trees were below him?

Under the racing clouds, he stared down through the drizzle. Even with his heightened vision, it was hard to make out distinct shapes on the mountainside.

The dragons flew northeast of one of the lower work camps. As Endour swept soundlessly over the hills, Miles spied a long pole protruding from the bushes. And wasn't that the glint of metal?

"There." Miles pointed down to his right.

Endour spotted it with his single eye and swooped down. Two landed near the trebuchet, half hidden in a mix of saplings and boulders. Miles was surprised to find it unguarded. The Cutters must be too busy drinking ale or sleeping in their huts. He slid to the ground beside Meer Eason and looked up at it in wonder. The weapon on its wheeled stand was more than twelve feet tall, and the spiked iron balls piled beside it were each nearly a foot in diameter; he wondered how the men could even lift them.

Meer Eason's dragon helped Endour lift the weapon. Gripping the base in their strong talons, the dragons pumped their wings hard, sending up a pungent wind. It held the scent of fennel, of earth, and the sharp evergreen smell of azure needles, an odor Miles had not known before coming to Jarrosh.

Eason stepped closer and wiped the rain from his face. Together they watched the dragons struggling with the trebuchet. The great long-armed weapon of wood and iron was heavy, but they lifted it at last. Their flight seemed almost drunken as they dipped up and down with the weight; they flew over the hills to the deep, black water and dropped the trebuchet into the sea.

Miles was too far away to hear the splash even with his sharp ears. But he saw the weapon fall, and he raised his fist with Eason in a silent cheer as it sank out of sight.

"One down," said Endour triumphantly as the dragons returned. Miles could swear old One-eye was smiling. He laughed as he climbed on Endour's back and gripped the warm neck folds. Soon they were speeding through the night.

An hour passed as they crisscrossed the high hills,

and still no sign of a second weapon. Dawn would break in a few hours, removing the covering of night.

In the clearing just above the second camp, Taunier and his terrow wheeled down with the other dragons. Endour sped in. There! Another trebuchet. But unlike the first, this one was guarded. A shout came from below. "Dragons! Dragons overhead!"

TWENTY-FIVE

WING HOME SWIFTLY

Good friend, as you cross the sea,
Take your boat and sturdy oar.
Wait for me when you have crossed
Over to the farthest shore.

—Song "Good Friends Parting"

The camp exploded with screams and shouts as half-dressed men burst from their huts and plunged into the bushes.

"Load the ball!" one man shouted below. Endour winged down, claws extended to grip the trebuchet before the Cutters could use it.

Thwack! The first metal ball flew skyward, striking a rider-less terrow in the belly. She lurched back, screaming, wings flapping. Vicious roars came from the other circling dragons as her head drooped and she spiraled helplessly down.

Endour and Findarr flew in. Men panicked and ran. They were found out now. No need to haul the weapons secretly out to sea. They'd burn this one.

Cutters darted through the bushes below, shouting and scattering like rabbits. Still Miles spotted few manning the weapon. Two of the youngest terrow fighters, Agreeya and Yint, soared in, taunting the fleeing Cutters with squeals: "Jit! Jit! Jit!"

Endour circled the terrows. "Draw back, younglings!"

His call was answered by another spiked ball. Miles heard the telltale whistling through the night air before he saw it.

"Watch out!" he shouted. Endour doubled back and flew directly before Agreeya to shield her from the hit.

There was a horrendous jolt. Miles gripped Endour's neck, his feet flying upward with the impact. They spun back in the smoke, wings flapping, as Endour roared with rage and fire. Dragon's blood spattered over Miles's face and chest as they plummeted down and bashed into the treetops. The violent impact ripped Miles from Endour's back. He tumbled after the dragon, hurtling from branch to branch until he came to a sudden painful halt in an azure tree. Miles sucked in a sickened breath.

"Endour?" The dragon was somewhere on the ground below. Miles waited for the dizziness to subside, then carefully pulled himself closer to the thick trunk. His body throbbed with pain. The rough branches had left long bloody scrapes down his arms. The stinging cuts along his burned arm made him suck air between his teeth.

Screams and shouts from the continuing battle came from higher up the hill. Miles wiped the blood and snot from his face and peered down from his uneasy perch.

"Endour?" His eyes found the outline of the great, long body on the forest floor. Then he saw the gaping hole where Endour's belly had been ripped open by the spiked metal ball.

"No!" Miles jumped to the ground. At Endour's snout he waited to feel the dragon's warm breath, but there was none.

Dead. Miles drew back, shuddered, and looked away. It had all happened in a moment, the sound of the trebuchet, the ball careening upward.

He placed his hand on Endour's broad neck. Wind rustled the wet branches. Quietly at first, then louder, Miles sang the death knell for the great taberrell. *Kaynumba, eOwey, kaynumba.* The ending comes, O Maker, the ending comes.

In the time it had taken Miles to hear the spiked ball, Endour had flown between it and the young terrow. He'd given his life to save little Agreeya without a moment's thought.

Miles wept as he sang, though he'd flown with Endour only this one night. He sang the requiem they'd sung over Othlore Wood the night the great forest fell, and he felt as he did then that something very rare and very old had passed from the world.

Running his hand along Endour's neck, he wrote the Othic mark of passage in blood on his scales, *Walk home swiftly*; then, wiping the first word away, he changed the runes to *Wing home swiftly*.

When he cleaned his hands in the grass, the dragon's blood was still warm, and some of the stain remained on his skin.

Men's voices shouted down the hill. *Thwack!* They would kill another dragon tonight if they could.

Miles's legs shook. Endour had followed the law of the Old Magic; he hadn't killed a single Cutter. But the men did not follow such laws.

The King of Kanayar paid the Cutters to fell the finest timber in Noor, and neither the king nor his men seemed to care how many dragons they had to kill to get it. The wet wind had the metallic smell of dragon's blood on it. A fiery bolt shot up Miles's spine. He knew the danger of shifting in anger. He'd been sucked into the Shriker's form this way. But he let himself lose control. Let the rage over Endour's death pour through him and shape him with its fiery hands. Beneath the windblown trees his flesh began to stretch.

A scream ripped up his throat as the shift tore open his human form. The rapid change made him stagger. He fell onto all fours, his arms and legs growing, thickening; his fingers and toes sharpening into long, deadly talons. Heavy wings jutted from his splitting spine. Scales spread over his body like tarnished armor.

Roaring, he beat his wings, lifted higher, and soared over the clearing.

He was king of the air, masterful and mighty.

He was a dragon.

High above the mountainside, he inhaled the wet air like wine. Never before had he known such power, not even when he was the Shriker. He was ten times stronger than any beast alive, a hundred times stronger than a man. Taking on speed, he careened toward his enemies.

His nostrils caught the smell of the Cutters' fear-drenched sweat before he saw them. Their scent heightened his desire for revenge. Down below, two men grunted as they loaded a spiked ball onto the leather basket of the trebuchet. A third man helped them pivot the great weapon on its metal axis.

"There's one!" The men's backs were to Miles. The one who'd shouted was pointing at a soaring terrow. "Filthy dragon! This will down him soon enough. Release the—"

Miles's deafening roar overpowered his next word as he wheeled down, breathing molten fire to the earth. The men fled, screaming. Miles winged in closer and tore the garments off the back of one. The man lost his balance and fell headlong down the steep hill.

Spinning about, he captured another man and dropped him into the trees. He heard him scream as he tumbled down, cursing as he hit and broke the branches of the sapling in his fall. He'd fly back to kill him and the others later. First he had to destroy their despicable weapon.

Miles doubled back and lit the trebuchet. He circled overhead and watched the long launch arm burning. He could not burn the spiked balls, but he flew down, took several in each claw and hurled them down the mountainside.

He soared upward. Below him, men were running, shouting, terror sharpening the pitch of their voices. He dove down, letting the angry fire build up in his chest. He'd set the putrid men below alight. He'd kill them for killing Endour!

Two taberrells flew past on his right. Kanoae rode the second. Miles turned and dropped back out of sight. Dragons had a heightened sense of smell. What if the taberrells caught his scent and recognized he was not one of them but was a human in dragon's form? Would the Damusaun be angry if she knew? Uneasy with the thought, he headed toward the cliffs.

Thwack! A ball had been released. A third trebuchet? Where? He pivoted too late. The flying metal ball spun him sideways as the spikes tore through his scales and flesh. Searing pain swept through his body. He screamed fire as he plummeted down.

TWENTY-SIX

THE HOLLOW ONE

Can a sister find a brother?

—Wild Esper

The she-dragon bore Hanna above the sea cliffs to another beach on the west side of Mount Olone. The constellations shone through a rent in the clouds high overhead. The prow star of the Mishtar's Ship sparkled, and down below, Hanna saw herself and the Damusaun skimming across the starry reflection in the black mirror of the sea.

All the trees had been felled at the base of the mountain here along the shore. The Cutters were gone, and the camp amid the stumps stood empty. The queen landed on a wide strip of sand.

Hanna dismounted. "Why bring me here, Damusaun? You know I have to search for a way into Oth. My brother—"

"Come."

They crossed the deserted beach. The seaweed coiled in green piles like discarded gowns. Thriss wriggled in her sleep and nudged Hanna's neck with her cool snout as she rounded a driftwood pile. Up an incline, the Damusaun stopped where sand met brown, uneven earth: the edge of what had once been an azure grove. One towering tree remained amid the stumps. Even at night Hanna could see the giant tree was hollow, too damaged for the Cutters to harvest.

The Dragon Queen nodded. "It is like an open doorway, is it not?"

Hanna stepped closer. "Damusaun, if this is the way into Oth," she said breathlessly, "if you found it for me—" She hugged the queen's leg, thick and rough as a tree trunk. A little shy over what she'd done, she let go. "I wish you could come with me to look for Tymm."

"You know I cannot do that," the Dragon Queen said testily. Then, softening her voice, she added, "You will have to go without me, Hanna."

Hanna reveled in the sound of her name. The Damusaun had called her Kanameer, pilgrim, but this was the first time she'd called her Hanna.

The pain of being known bit into her heart, but it wasn't a bad sort of pain. There was joy behind it. She couldn't look into the queen's eyes just yet, still digesting the new fragile bond between them. She glanced at the rounding belly, where the new queen slept in her shell under the scales and skin, then lifted her eyes to the she-dragon's chest, to the war scars tracing darker bronze lines against the gold scales. Did they hurt at all? *I'm just getting used to living with dragons,* she thought. *Now I have to leave the Damusaun. I can't even bring Thriss with me.* She felt a lump growing in her throat. She'd have to reach Oth alone.

Gently pulling Thriss out from under her cloak, she handed the sleeping pip to the queen. Thriss awoke to find herself cradled in the Damusaun's arm, gave a squeak of pleasure, and went back to sleep.

Hanna adjusted her knapsack, mentally noting what she'd packed: the Falconer's book for its eastern Oth map showing the way from Taproot Hollow to All Souls Wood, where, she hoped, the black tree grew. She also had a knife, a full water pouch, a few herbal tinctures (though she'd left many of them back in the dragons' cave for Kanoae to heal war wounds), and, finally, Thriss's shell, which still glowed a little, even though it was broken.

Hanna spoke to the Waytree. "Is there a deya within?" No answer came. But the Cutters had devastated this fallen grove. The deya might be too afraid to come out. "I'm coming inside to greet you," she warned. "I hope you don't mind." She stepped through the grass, passed under the ten-foot-high arch, and entered the hollow tree.

She knew the deyas guarded the way, moving the mysterious passage to Oth from tree to tree. She hoped this was the one.

Feeling her way into the darkness, Hanna called, "Hello?"

She thought of an opening spell she'd memorized from the Falconer's book. It had not helped her into Oth when she'd tried it by herself last year, but the way had opened later when the wind woman used it in the old forest.

"*Open as you have before;*
Let the traveler through the door.
From this opening begin;
The only way out
Is in."

Hanna waited, holding her breath, then sighed. She'd never learned the proper way to say spells. Things might have been different if she'd been allowed to study on Othlore. The hollow vault smelled of earth, fungus, and rotting wood. Hands out in front, she made her way along. *So dark. So dead,* she thought. *It's like an open grave.*

She squared her shoulders. *Stop it! You're only imagining things.* Still, her gut told her otherwise, and she had to stop herself from racing back outside to the Damusaun. Through the entry, she saw the queen waiting in the rain. Thriss had awakened. She clung to the Damusaun's cheek flap, beating her small wings, using the flap to swing back and forth.

Hanna forced herself to turn away from her friends and step farther into the dark trunk. "Is there a deya here I can speak to?" The words sounded dull and lifeless. Biting her lip, she put out her hand, felt something soft and spongy on the wall, and hastily drew back. *Don't run. Stay here. Find the way in.*

"Tymm," she whispered. "Tymm." As if his name itself were an opening spell.

She inched along, feeling up and down so as not to

miss an entrance. Her arms and legs itched. The damp darkness inside the tree engulfed her. She stopped. Something was wrong, very wrong, with the Waytree.

"It's too dark," she called. "I can't find a way in."

The Damusaun could come no closer, but she breathed fire. A golden light filled the hollow tree. Hanna brushed at her prickling arms and legs. There was no passage, no opening other than the one she'd come through. And the rotting wood was moving, crawling with millions of red and black beetles. That meant the tickling she'd felt on her arms and legs . . .

Hanna rushed out, screaming, "Get them off me!" She jumped up and down in the rain, sweeping her hands down her sides. Thriss flitted over and clung to her, poking out her tongue and hungrily gulping down her favorite treat. The Damusaun lent her fire, the wave of warmth sending the rest of the beetles scuttling back into the cool, dark tree.

"Ugh!" cried Hanna, shuddering. "I should have known this azure couldn't lead me in. The tree is hollow," she said with disgust. "It is dead."

She ran her hand through her wet hair. She should have known it wouldn't be that simple. It was never easy to find the way in. And anyway, a dead tree without a deya couldn't open the way into Oth.

"Stupid," she muttered.

"What?" said the Damusaun.

"Nothing."

"Tell me, Hanna."

Hanna plucked the last few beetles from her arm and fed them to Thriss. How long did she have before the worlds split apart? A few days? Less, if the Cutters managed to log more Waytrees?

"I have to break through, Damusaun. I have to bring Tymm and the others home before the worlds split apart."

"You fear you will lose him."

Hanna nodded, holding back tears.

The Damusaun flattened her ears. "I lost my brother long ago." She pointed to her chest. "His name is written here."

Hanna stepped closer. So some of the scars were words.

"The names of the dragon dead were blood-written on my scales when I became Damusaun. Here is my brother."

Hanna couldn't read the words. "What was his name?"

"Therros. The name means 'wanderer.'"

Hanna traced the lettering with her fingertip. "I'm sorry, Damusaun."

"I promised Therros I would bring one of his wing bones across the dragons' bridge to Oth. He wanted me to bury it at the base of Shangor Mountain, where the sea meets the foothills. Where the waves speak."

The queen paused. "We were both hatched there." She no longer looked at her brother's name scar but at the small bulge of new life rising below her rib cage, where her golden chest scales subsided into green. She did not have to say that she was waiting to lay her hatchling in Oth, not here in exile. Hanna knew.

The rain came down harder, blowing sideways up the deserted beach. "You said you saw your brother in your dreamwalk," said the queen. "You know he lives. Keep searching."

"I will."

Hanna wiped the water from her face and shivered. Rain. Tears. It didn't matter which.

"Come." The Damusaun encircled her and Thriss with her tail. Drawing them close to her warm body, she sheltered them under her wing.

TWENTY-SEVEN

EVER CHANGING

Quava is loss. Arii is renewal. Together in the Othic Tongue, "quava-arii" means "ever changing."

—*THE WAY BETWEEN WORLDS*

They'd spent two nights in battle trying to destroy the trebuchets, and in the daylight hours, dragons flew out in teams with the Fire Herd to keep the fire wall protecting the last Waytrees on Mount Olone. The last grove was dwindling, mostly due to the Cutters' deadly root poison that spread invisibly underground and felled trees all too quickly without saw or ax.

While Taunier and his team worked at the fire wall, the Damusaun called the rest of the dragons to the great stone arch by the sea. A bright, midday sun lit the choppy water. Near the archway, Miles took his place by the youngling, Agreeya. Halfway down the circle, Hanna and Thriss stood in a small patch of shade under a lone sapling. Even from here, Miles detected the dark worry rings around his sister's eyes. She'd been dismayed when the hollow tree had not turned out to be a way into Oth. Yesterday, while he lay recovering from his wound, she'd searched the last grove atop Mount Olone, walking tree to tree beyond Taunier's fire wall. She'd found no entry to Oth there. Only at the Damusaun's insistence had she returned to eat and rest a little before going out again.

Miles turned his attention to the Dragon Queen. He'd missed the second night's battle, when two more trebuchets were found and destroyed, but he was fit enough to go out with the rest of the company tonight. If there were more weapons hidden on the mountainside, he wanted a part in their destruction.

Feeling along his side, he secretly checked his bandage. Kanoae had wrapped it a little too tightly. Yesterday Breal had found him in the hills, back in human form. Half crouched with pain and still bleeding, Miles had barely managed to dart from tree to tree before Breal came along. He might be out there still if his dog hadn't helped him home.

Meer Kanoae had skillfully stitched his gash yesterday, her gentle talk and soft touch surprising him. A fighter herself, the Sea Meer respected battle wounds. She'd nodded approvingly at the way he'd handled the sharp pains during the operation. The fadeweed hadn't numbed him completely. He'd bitten down hard on the leather strap and had cried out only once.

The queen addressed them. "Kaleet has located a few storage huts where the Cutters stow their saws, axes, and, we hope, hide their devastating root poison." She looked from face to face and flicked her tail at one of the less attentive pips. "We will mount an assault on the huts," she said. "But first, we will prepare for what's to come." Her eyes fell on Miles. "Approach, shape-shifter."

Miles flinched. Why was she singling him out? He'd not told them he'd shape-shifted into a dragon. Instead, he'd let them think the gash down his side was from the fall from the sky when Endour was shot. Had the dragons caught his scent when he was in dragon form and informed the queen?

Ignoring the shooting pains in his side, he walked as upright as he could, faced the Damusaun, and bowed. How many times he'd wanted her to call him out and recognize him for his gifts. But he wasn't the Kanameer or Fire Herd spoken of in the dragons' prophecy. The queen hadn't seemed to expect or even want a shape-shifter.

"Yesterday while you slept and let your wound heal, we burned Endour's body, saving a wing bone to bring with us to Oth."

Miles nodded. He'd told the dragons Endour had died to save a youngling. He hadn't named Agreeya, who was just old enough and large enough to join the battle. He had not wanted to shame her. "I sang *Kaynumba* over Endour's body," he said.

The Damusaun flicked her tongue. "You shape-shifted into our likeness."

So they *had* scented him. Miles's mouth went dry. "I . . . I had to shift to hunt down Endour's murderers and help destroy their trebuchet. I needed—"

"It would be better for you not to speak, pilgrim." The Damusaun whipped her tail. "You put us all in danger when you shifted. If you had killed a single man while in dragon skin, we would have been exiled from Oth forever."

A low growl swept through the crowd.

"I . . . I did not kill, Damusaun."

"You kept the vow you made by breath and fire?" she asked.

"I kept it," he whispered. He was grateful to chance or eOwey or the wound that downed him, all those things that had stopped him from going through with his plan to slay Endour's killers. He could never have forgiven himself if he had destroyed the dragons' one chance to go home.

"Meer Eason," said the Damusaun, "do you have the knife?"

"I do," said Eason.

Knife? Why a knife?

Eason and Kanoae joined Miles. The Music Meer pulled out the Falconer's knife. Miles would recognize the elk horn handle anywhere. He'd last seen it when Kanoae used the blade to cut his cloth bandage. In Eason's hand the flat side of the knife caught the sunlight.

Hanna rushed through the crowd to the Damusaun. Long neck arched and head low, the queen blinked as she listened to Hanna's hurried whispers. Was Hanna pleading for him? Miles's temples pounded. The Damusaun spoke in Hanna's ear. A look of surprise crossed his sister's face.

Miles said to Eason. "I don't understand what the Damusaun wants."

"Just do as I say."

The Music Meer was trembling, but whether it was

out of fear or excitement, Miles couldn't tell. Something in his dark brown eyes asked Miles to trust him, even though he gripped a knife.

Kanoae brought a bowl of seawater up the beach and placed it near Miles's feet. A knife. Seawater. Were they about to enact some ancient dragon rite?

"Roll up your sleeves," said Kanoae.

Meer Eason began to hum. Then he raised the knife and deftly cut a slit in Miles's left upper arm. Miles bit down on his tongue as he felt the stinging blade. Meer Eason continued to hum, as a tiny rivulet of blood ran down to Miles's elbow, over the burned patch from his earlier falcon shift, and dripped onto the sand. Kanoae pressed a clean cloth against his stinging flesh.

Miles took a sharp breath, as Meer Eason pulled a folded leather square from his pocket. He opened it and tossed twelve round seeds into the air.

The Damusaun breathed fire on them. The seeds turned from brown to bright orange as they flew up in the heat. They spun higher and higher like sparks from a fire before cascading down again. Eason caught them in his cloth and held them near Miles's chin.

"Breathe your keth-kara on them," he said softly.

Miles's head spun. His keth-kara was the sacred sound eOwey voiced to form him in the womb. The Falconer had sung it to him last year, but only when he was in great need of healing from the Shriker's wounds.

"Will you . . . Are you going to take it away from me?"

Eason's mouth twitched into the shadow of a smile. "No one can take your keth-kara from you, son."

Meer Eason waited, but how could his teacher ask him to intone his keth-kara in front of the dragons? In front of everyone present here? Eason held his gaze.

Kanoae said, "Your keth-kara will awaken them."

Miles looked from one face to another. He licked his lips and began to sing over the glowing seeds, softly at first, then louder. There was an answering in the wind, or seemed to be. The orange seeds began to unfurl. Tiny glowing worms wriggled on the leather cloth.

"That's it," encouraged Eason. "Now, this will burn."

The dragons gathered round with Hanna as Eason held the leather cloth beside Miles's left arm. The worms inched across the leather, entered the knife slit, and disappeared under his skin. Miles gritted his teeth to keep from screaming.

Glowing spots swam under his skin as the worms

traveled down his left arm to his hand. His palm burned as if placed on the stove. He crumpled to the sand to cool his burning hand in the water bowl.

"Wait," warned Kanoae.

Miles held his hand above the bowl. Surely, the ceremony was over. He'd given away his sacred name. They'd cut his arm, fed worms into his flesh. What more could they ask of him?

"Now," said Eason.

Miles plunged his hand in the water and felt relief. When the flesh was cool at last, he stood again. His legs felt weak, and he was cold and shivering now. Kanoae tied a cloth about his upper arm.

"That's better," Miles said through chattering teeth.

The Damusaun breathed fire. Taberrells and terrows parted so Miles could draw closer to the flames. When the worms had crawled into his arm, he'd wanted only water, only cold. Now he needed warmth again.

Miles held his hands toward the flames. His palm was no longer painful. He felt only the smallest tickle where the worms had gathered under the skin.

"Show us, Miles," called Hanna. She was beaming at him.

"He will be the first meer since the Mishtar to find his sign with dragon fire," said Eason proudly.

Suddenly Miles understood what the tingling in his palm meant. He'd not been singled out to be reprimanded for Endour's death or for shape-shifting. They'd initiated him as a meer. His heart raced. He'd never seen the ritual on Othlore. It was always done in secret. One apprentice at a time would enter the dome room, emerging later red-faced and sweating, proudly bearing a palm sign. No one ever divulged what happened inside.

Now he knew. He was smiling, brimming with excitement. He held the flat of his hand out a little longer until the Damusaun's flames died down. Then the she-dragon honored him by reading aloud the ancient Othic sign. *"Quava-arii."*

Miles recognized the words to the song Meer Eason offered on the ship the night he walked the plank.

"It is the right word for a shape-shifter," agreed Kanoae.

Miles bent his arm. The blue symbol on his palm seemed to glow with its own inner light. A spiral shape with a crescent in the middle. The crescent shape stood for loss, the spiral for renewal. He followed the spiral with his eyes. At first it seemed to be spinning outward, but as he looked more closely, it appeared to be spinning in. It was both, he knew suddenly; the symbol itself was ever changing. He laughed with relief and gratitude. He was a meer in his own right. A meer now and forever.

Waves drummed the sand as Miles bowed to the Dragon Queen. He stayed down, arms and knees trembling, collapsed with joy, exhaustion, and disbelief. He wanted to shout, laugh, dance, cry.

At last, the Damusaun said, "Rise, pilgrim. You are a meer now."

Miles's legs shook uncontrollably. He wasn't sure he could obey. But this was the Damusaun's first command to him as a meer. He got to his feet, wanting to thank her, thank them all. His heart was so full he couldn't speak.

"It was bold of you to shift to dragon's form," said the queen. "Only one meer before your time has done this."

"Mishtar," said the dragon to her left.

The cliff walls seemed to echo the name as all the dragons repeated it. Miles swayed. He knew the Mishtar had practiced the art of shifting. The first High Meer knew all the ways of magic, but he'd never heard of him or anyone else daring to change into a dragon.

"Now," said the Dragon Queen, "your meer sign pledges you to honor all your oaths."

Miles nodded, glimpsing for a moment a purpose for the ceremony here, before another battle.

"You understand me," she said. It was a private speech between the two of them. The Damusaun expected him to honor the pledge he'd made to her not to kill. She had a shape-shifter fighting alongside her. A help. A risk. A danger. If he killed in dragon's form, everything would be lost. The Dragon Queen's gift to him had also served her own purpose. She meant to bind him to his word through this meer sign.

"I understand," he said.

The Damusaun held him in her gaze a moment longer, then addressed the rest of the company. "Our patrols have not seen any more trebuchets. To the best of our knowledge, we have destroyed them all." The dragons beat their tails happily.

"Still, I warn all to fly with care," she added. "Now we fly to destroy the Cutters' cache of saws, axes, and root poison. The last Waytrees must stand!"

And they gathered beneath the trees to sing the death knell.

—THE MISHTAR, *DRAGON'S WAY, VOL. 3*

Miles clung to Dramui's neck ridge as she flew soundlessly over another Cutters' camp. Higher up the moonlit mountain, he caught sight of the Damusaun. Behind her, Hanna and Kanoae flew on their terrows. His sister had spent all afternoon and night searching the last remaining azure grove, looking for the right Waytree to usher her into Oth before it was too late. Miles's dry throat stung. He licked his chapped lips. *Find the way,* he thought. *Bring Tymm home.*

There were so few Waytrees left now. The dragons had fed the fire walls to keep the Cutters away, yet somehow a few men had managed to sneak past with more root poison. The dragons were betting the Cutters stored their cache of poison with the saws and axes in the huts they'd found, but they couldn't be sure.

Taunier rode Findarr over a burning storage hut. Miles felt the intense heat as Dramui dove down. Findarr soared to the left, and Taunier waved his arm to herd stray islands of fire back toward the hut. Dramui added her flames to the others', torching the walls and devouring the roof. Taunier brought his arms together. The roaring inferno engulfed the Cutters' saws and axes, turning them into molten puddles.

Men raced up from the camps, shouting and firing their crossbows. Through the heat and smoke, a dragon's piercing cry rang out. Miles looked up to the mountainside just as Kanoae's terrow lurched back, flapping her wings wildly. A second black whirring ball cut through the air. The Damusaun turned and sped toward Kanoae's terrow, but not before Hanna's terrow doubled over, plummeting toward the ground after Kanoae's.

"Anteebwey!" Miles screamed the devil's name. The Cutters must have found a way to hide another trebuchet!

"Turn about, Dramui! Hanna and Kanoae were hit!"

His dragon was dodging arrows and Miles was too impatient to wait for her to wing him up the mountainside.

Abandoning Dramui, he plunged into the air. His back split. The bones in his arms branched out, his skin stretching into wings. The sudden shape-shift knifed his hands, turned his fingers into sharp talons. His neck lengthened, snakelike. A long tail grew from the base of his spine. Sharp teeth jutted from his roaring jaws.

The word he roared was *"Hanna!"* But it came out as fire.

A group of taberrells found the newest trebuchet and set it aflame. More shouts. More screaming. Miles left the raw sounds of battle behind as he sped toward the high meadow where he'd seen the terrows fall.

In the windy meadow he alighted near the Damusaun. Kanoae and her dragon lay in the blowing grass along with Hanna's terrow. All three were torn open by the spiked balls, their blood black in the dim light. Antig, Shagin. He knew all the dragons' names now, from hatchling to elderling, for they'd spent long hours together in the cave, and those who fight together come to know each other well even in a short time. The smell of blood, dragon, and human filled the air. He did not need to come any closer to see that Kanone and the terrows were dead.

The Dragon Queen cradled Hanna. Miles tried to

speak as dragons do. No words came; instead, he made
a croaking noise. The Damusaun looked up, but it was
Hanna's face he sought. Her skin was pale; her eyelids
white. He leaned in closer and pricked his ears to listen
for a sign of breath. Wind in the grass, the clicking of
katydids, battle sounds in the hills far below. His dragon's
heart pounded as he waited for the quietest of sounds
that must be there, *had* to be there.

The Damusaun began to sing. Her dragon's voice
was deep and rough, but Miles understood what she was
offering. The Dragon Queen had found his sister's keth-
kara, just as the Falconer had found Miles's self-sound
last year, when he was at the point of death.

The she-dragon sang softly, searching for the right
intonation. She would not find it. It would take a human
voice to sing the sound. Hanna's face had a hollow look.
Shift back now, he thought. *Sing!* But fierce rage at the Cutters
still burned inside his chest. He'd have to let go of his
wild anger to return to his human shape. He strained to
quell the burning, and found the powerful dragon's form
lent him the strength he needed. For Hanna. Let go for
Hanna.

Miles focused to shut out the sounds of battle. A

playful breeze blew a strand of light brown hair across his sister's cheek. Her face was very still. Taking a deep breath, he filled his chest with the cool night air, the deep blue scent of azure needles, the salt smell of the sea. Even as Miles's chest expanded and the fire in him cooled, his body shrank, his wings and tail disappeared, sharp teeth and talons vanished.

Standing before the Damusaun, he sent the cool air he'd taken from the night back out again as pure sound. The keth-kara the queen was singing changed with his human pitch, the notes correcting themselves between the two of them. Hanna's keth-kara was earth and sky together, just as it should be for a sqyth-eyed girl.

He sang the song of Old Magic eOwey intoned at Hanna's beginning, and as the sounds blew out between them, he heard the wind sing them back and saw his sister's brows lift as if in question. She turned her head, put out her hands, and sat up. Miles wanted to rush over and throw his arms around her, but he recognized her strange inward look and held himself back. Hanna's face was awash in dream as she climbed out of the Damusaun's arms. Turning, she began to walk toward the azure trees growing at the far edge of the high meadow, the only untouched grove still standing on the mountain.

"My sister dreamwalks," he whispered. Relief flooded through him. She was all right. She would live.

He heard again the sounds of battle from the mountainside. "I have to go," he said suddenly. "But someone needs to follow Hanna when she dreamwalks. Could you do that please, Damusaun?"

"I will."

The queen opened her wings. "If you are thinking to shift again in this fight, Miles, remember your vow."

Miles's eyes fell on the bodies of his friends in the grass. Kanoae's arm was draped across Antig's golden neck. Her foot was wedged against Shagin's tail, as if the three of them were curled up in sleep.

He'd left Dramui fighting alongside Taunier and the other dragons farther down the mountainside. How many more would have to die? His throat constricted as he blinked back tears. "But they're killing us, Damusaun."

A low growl came from her throat. She wasn't forbidding him to shift, only to control his need for revenge. He bit his lip, tasting his salt tears for Kanoae, the dead terrows at her side, and, before that, for Endour.

The Damusaun's neck scales rippled as she waited for his answer.

Miles wiped his dripping nose. "Don't you want to kill the Cutters for what they've done?"

The Dragon Queen raised her tail and bashed the ground hard enough for Miles to feel the rumbling in his feet.

"I would crush them with my talons," she hissed. "Break their bones and burn them if I could. But kill one manling, just one, and we'll destroy the pardon seven hundred years of peace has earned us." The Damusaun coiled her tail about Miles's legs and drew him nearer. Her eyes were two suns in the morning twilight. "If you shift again, you have to promise me, pilgrim."

He felt the rippling muscles in her tail. She called him pilgrim, though he was not the Dreamwalker or the Fire Herd mentioned in the prophecy. *Bring to us our heart's desire, one with mastery over fire. From across the eastern sea, come to us, O Pilgrim.* The song line was for Taunier, but he'd gleaned something from his dragon-shifts, he realized. He could have mastery over fire. Not the visible kind that burned on the outside, but the rage that burned within. The dragon's form had empowered him to do it.

The queen released him and drew back. Miles hated the Cutters for what they'd done, but now he loved the Damusaun more. He would not come between her and her homeland in Oth.

"I promise, Damusaun," he said.

TWENTY-NINE

EVVER'S PLEA

Some call the azures Forest Fathers,
for they are the oldest Waytrees in Noor.

—*The Way Between Worlds*

It was snowing in her dreamwalk. Hanna opened her hands to catch the frail blue flakes. Thriss hummed in her ear as the snow twirled down. Each flake was long as a lady's finger, slender as a bone. They were warm and dry as they piled up on Hanna's upturned palm. Not snow, then. She drifted into the blue flurry of falling azure needles.

Low voices filled the predawn gloom. She was dream-walking—moving in easy strides up the mountainside. Thriss coiled about her neck and pressed the top of her head against Hanna's chin. Woodland giants took shape before Hanna in the dusk, azure trees stripped of their needles, the wind undressing them as it sang around their branches.

Root poison was killing them, stripping them of their needles. She walked closer to the ancient trees. Mist or smoke entwined their bare branches. Above the singing, the far-off sound of a babe's cry drifted through the woods. Hanna entered the old forest where the trunks quavered. Where was the child?

Naked branches knocked together like great hollow rattles as azure needles drifted down from the high canopy. Wind tugged at Hanna's cloak and hair, drawing her in with invisible hands.

Dawn's pale copper beams filled the glade. The wailing was quieter now, and as Hanna entered a small clearing on the hill, she saw it had not come from a babe at all but from an old, bony woman curled up on a log. Her dark-skinned face was pinched, and her eyes were closed.

"Hello?" At Hanna's soft greeting, the old woman stirred, opening her eyes. Both were milky-white. She was blind.

Reaching through the cascading needles, Hanna touched the woman tenderly on her shoulder. The green knit shawl came apart in her hand like spiderwebs.

Touching the shawl awakened Hanna. Such a light gesture, but she blinked and looked about, suddenly aware of her bruised thigh, her throbbing head. She only half remembered that she'd been shot down and fallen from the sky. The old woman was still on the log. The azure needles were still falling. They hadn't disappeared with her dreamwalk: something new. Was it the closeness of the azure trees that blended reality and dream? Down the hill beyond the little clearing, she caught a glimpse of the Dragon Queen pacing in the long grass. Hanna felt confused, the way she always felt after one of her dreamwalks.

She addressed the old woman. "I'm Hanna. What is your name?"

"Zabith."

Needles drifted onto Zabith's white hair, her dark, wrinkled neck. Her name whispered through Hanna's mind. Miles had told her of the Forest Meer from Othlore who'd sailed east last winter. But this blind old woman seemed powerless, not like any meer she'd ever met. Hanna helped her up from the log. Zabith had been tall once, but she was partly stooped now, and she looked frail. "Why were you crying?"

Zabith did not answer. She traced Hanna's cheek with her dry fingertips, then moved up and touched her eyelids. It felt as light as a moth landing on her skin.

"You are sqyth-eyed," she said.

"How could you know that?"

"A Forest Meer can also be a seer." Zabith let her hand drop.

A seer who's blind? thought Hanna.

"The trees are dying," Zabith said.

Hanna looked uphill. All the azures in her view were losing their needles. "But there must be a few healthy Waytrees hidden in the last grove up here," she argued, unwilling to give up hope just yet. "The dragons have been trying to protect them."

Zabith covered her mouth and spoke huskily through her parted fingers. "Too late. No one can save them now."

Hanna gripped the old woman's shoulders. "How can we help? Tell me what to do."

Zabith sniffed and tightened the wrap of her shawl. "You're late. Very late. We were not sure you would come. And where is the boy?"

The old woman talked of one thing, then another. She was a meer, but perhaps the illness that took her vision had also taken her mind. Hanna rubbed her throbbing temples. "What boy?"

The swirling blue needles were turning color. A thick

rust-colored carpet buried Zabith's feet and piled up around Hanna's ankles.

Bring the boy the torches follow to the heart of Taproot Hollow.

The answer had not come from Zabith; it had come from the Waytrees up the hill. The last stand of giant trees on the mountain looked skeletal without their needles.

Following the voices, Hanna climbed the hill with Zabith. The azure trunks creaked and moaned, a sound the *Leena* used to make on the ocean swells. The crunching needles underfoot added their dry sound to the deya voices. Just ahead, the tall deyas wavered flame-like as they emerged from their Waytrees. Male and female deyas, twelve to fifteen feet tall, stood before the mammoth azure trunks. Tendrils of mist coiled around their rooted feet, entwined their colorful robes, and shrouded their long, proud faces.

"Hannalyn." The voice came from one or all; she could not tell. The sound had the heaviness of earth about it, as if the deyas were speaking from their roots instead of their mouths. Hanna did not wonder how they knew her name. The deyas were ever watchful. They would have seen her arrive and would have witnessed all the changes going on about them. Silent and observant in their trees, they came out only when they wished to do so, or when the death of their Waytree forced them out.

It was alarming to see so many of them leave their trees at once. Deyas could not live apart from their grandtrees for long.

"Please," Hanna said, "go back inside your azures. The dragons still fight the Cutters. Try and keep your homes alive." The short speech awakened Thriss, who poked her snout out from under the cloak, rubbed the top of her head up against Hanna's chin, and purred.

One deya stood before the rest. His long face was as gray-white as his mossy hair and beard. He was not the largest spirit, but he looked to be the oldest of them all.

"I am Evver," he said. "We must go, Hannalyn. Our roots were weakened with poison. Now they are torn. Soon, there will be no Waytrees left to hold the worlds together."

Behind Evver, the deyas whispered, "Sqyth-born one. Sqyth-born."

Evver held up his broad hand to quiet them. He bent down to look at Hanna's sqyth-eyes.

"You are the Kanameer. Servant of the Old Magic."
The deya's deep voice poured over her like a waterfall.
But his next words surprised her.

"You will lead us through Taproot Hollow to All
Souls Wood."

Hanna tried to steady herself. She was supposed to
lead *them* to All Souls Wood? But she'd come here to ask
them for passage to Oth. Looking into Evver's deep green
eyes she wanted to say, *I'll take you to the wood.* Instead, she
said, "I'm not sure how to find the way."

A loud cracking sound came from the grove. Evver's
face darkened. "The breaking comes," he whispered. The
deyas behind Evver buried their faces in their hands. A
low creaking and groaning poured from the silhouetted
forest. The last giant trees on the mountain began to
sway, as if a great wind had come up from the sea, but the
air was all too still.

Hanna watched in horror as black lines shot up the
enormous trunks, followed by earsplitting cracks as the
trunks broke in two, and branches came raining down.
The deyas turned and fled down the hillside. Hanna
grabbed Zabith, but the old woman couldn't run fast
enough. Just as the nearest falling tree was about to crush

them both, Evver scooped them up in his great, long arms and carried them down the hill.

The deya set them down in the damp grass. Three more mammoth trees toppled down. Holding on to Zabith, Hanna felt the falling in her body, the riveting sounds as the trees struck the ground, hitting her bones like a hammer. She was breaking, falling, as she felt all the hope go out from under her. She cried until her throat felt swollen, her nose clogged, her eyes stung.

The last tree fell and the mountain stilled. Rust-colored azure needles swirled down. Hanna checked on Thriss hiding under her cloak.

"Evver," Hanna said in a shaky voice. He bent down to hear her better. "Thank you for saving us."

"You are welcome, Kanameer." He returned her gaze with piercing green eyes. "You are the Dreamer who will lead us to All Souls Wood," he said. "But where is the boy?"

She bit her lip, wishing that she could help this kind deya. "I'm sorry, Evver. I don't know who you mean."

"You do," he said. His confidence startled her. She stroked Thriss's slender tail. When she and Zabith had first followed the deyas' voices up the hill, they'd heard them softly calling, *Bring the boy the torches follow to the heart of Taproot Hollow.*

Words from the game Blind Seer. She went over the last verse in her mind:

> Dreamer, travel through the night,
> Take Blind Seer robbed of sight.
> Seek them there, seek them here,
>   before the children disappear.
> Bring the boy the torches follow
> To the heart of Taproot Hollow.

They wanted the boy who had power to herd torch-light. They wanted Taunier.

The Damusaun flew Taunier to the mountainside, a sleek blue flame guiding her way as she descended through the layered mist to the ridge of Mount Olone. She landed on a barren patch of rocky ground. Taunier dismounted near a jumbled pile of branches before the queen winged up again to disappear into the fog.

Hanna huddled with Zabith, waiting. Thriss had brought her message to the Damusaun. *Ask Taunier to join me in the high meadow and bring the Falconer's book.* Hanna could barely make out Taunier's small light in the fog as he made his way through the maze of tumbled logs.

She lost him for a few minutes until she saw his dark head appear again, gilded by the light burning just above his outstretched hand. The flame went out when he lowered his arm to climb over the last giant trunk between them.

"You've come," she said simply. It had seemed hours since she'd sent Thriss to the Damusaun with the message for Taunier. She clung to Zabith to keep herself from rushing over and throwing her arms around him.

Taunier dipped his hands in his pockets. Hanna followed his eyes as he squinted through the swirling mist. Here and there the deyas sat hunched over on their dead trees. They looked like giant marble statues of fallen gods, stonelike figures moving to lift a twig or to lean to the side. The picture was one of defeat. One deya seemed to be washing his face with handfuls of azure needles. He moaned quietly as the rust color dusted his nose and cheeks.

"Taunier," she said hoarsely, "this is Meer Zabith. The Forest Meer Miles told us about who sailed here from Othlore last winter."

Taunier put out his hand, saw that she was blind, and jammed it in his pocket again. "It's good to meet you," he said hesitantly. When Zabith did not answer, he added, "You'll both be hungry. Meer Eason sent this." He pulled some dried fish from his rucksack and broke off three pieces. They ate together and shared the water pouch. The liquid cooled Hanna's throat. She hadn't realized how thirsty she was.

"Some of the Cutters escaped in ships," Taunier said. "Others are hiding out somewhere on the mountain." He scuffed the needled ground with his muddy boot.

Hanna read the sorrow on his face. "Who died?"

"We lost four dragons last night," said Taunier. "The dragons were burned this morning in ritual fire." Taunier's voice was raw. "And we lost Kanoae."

"Kanoae?" A thickness came to her throat, saying it. They'd been hit together, fallen together, but she couldn't imagine Kanoae gone. She'd been so strong, so fearless. Hanna had few tears left; she'd spilled so many with Zabith as the forest fell, but hearing about Kanoae made the loss cut deeper, and more tears came.

"We brought Kanoae's body down the mountain," said Taunier. "She will be buried at sea."

Hanna nodded and wiped her eyes. The Sea Meer would have wanted that.

"The rest of us are all right," Taunier added, half-heartedly.

Hanna was fighting to breathe against the blade of sorrow that had slipped beneath her rib cage. She spoke, hoping to salve the wound with ordinary words. "Did you bring the book?"

Taunier pulled *The Way Between Worlds* from the rucksack and handed it to her.

"The mist is thick," said Zabith. "Give the girl a light to read by."

Taunier reared back a little, unused to Zabith's direct manner; then he clicked his fingers and sparked a small bright flame. It hovered an inch above his fingertips. Hanna flipped open the book to the Oth map showing the way from Taproot Hollow to All Souls Wood. The path was circuitous and not easy to follow; she adjusted her eyes to Taunier's small light, trying to trace it on the page.

The Falconer's map would help guide them once they were in Oth, but it did not show her where to find the Waytree passage here on Mount Olone, for the Falconer knew the mysterious passage never stayed in one place for long. She looked up. "How can we find the entrance with all the Waytrees down?"

Taunier's face shone in the beam of his bright flame. He crooked his neck and studied the map. "I haven't a clue."

Meer Zabith hobbled to Evver and leaned against the cracked log to speak to the hunched deya. There was a motherly manner in the way she held herself upright and touched the torn robes, though Zabith came up only to the giant deya's knee.

Taunier said, "The Damusaun can't help you find it. She said she could not come any closer than the cliff, you know, because of . . . them." He motioned to the deyas, still sitting here and there on the logs.

"The law of the Old Magic still keeps them apart," said Hanna.

"But the dragons fought to save the azure trees. The deyas should be grateful to them even if they . . . we lost," he said, including himself with the dragons. He snuffed out his finger flame so Hanna could not read his face. But that hardly mattered; his voice gave him away.

Hanna closed the book. "Don't blame them, Taunier. The trouble is an old one."

Taunier scanned the hill. "So many of them." He seemed to be speaking to himself.

Evver joined them. He was a good fourteen feet tall, but he stooped to bring his head down closer to their level. "We will leave now. Are you ready, Fire Herd?"

"Ready?" Taunier looked at Hanna.

"Didn't Thriss tell you? We need you to come with us to Oth."

"But why am I to come?"

Zabith grabbed the edge of his cloak. *"Bring the boy the torches follow to the heart of Taproot Hollow."*

Taunier frowned and gently shook her off. "That's from a game." He shot Hanna a puzzled look. Was the old woman crazy? Hanna wasn't sure if she could explain it herself, but she tried. "Evver has promised to try to hold the worlds together from the Oth side if they can find the Waytrees there. If the deyas can do that, we'll have time to bring Tymm and the other Wind-taken back across to Noor before it's too late."

"We must go now," said Evver. "We cannot live long without new trees to house us."

How long? Hanna wondered. She eyed the rest of the deyas sitting alone or in groups on the logs, sixteen of them. They were all tree-thin, and their once rich garments were threadbare. She scanned their noble faces, cracked now like old bark; they looked as if they'd aged a hundred years in the hours since their Waytrees fell. How far could they walk?

Taunier snapped his fingers, and the small bright flame appeared again. The deyas hated fire and were loath to burn the branches of their fallen azures, but they could not hope to find the entry to Oth in the thick mountain mist without torches. Evver took up a fallen branch and braved the first flame, then one by one the other deyas followed his example, stooping reluctantly to hold their cracked branches out to the Fire Herd.

Torches lit, the group made its way slowly through the felled forest. Giant logs littered the barren mountainside, making walking difficult as they headed up the slope. Every once in a while, Evver stopped to lift first Hanna, then Taunier and Zabith, over an enormous log.

Hanna and Taunier had protested at first, but Evver said it was only right that as he was so much taller, he should help them.

Placing Hanna back on her feet, he said, "You will find the way in, Kanameer."

"But what am I to look for?"

Evver did not answer her with words. Instead, he stopped now and again to touch the spidery roots at the base of a fallen azure. This grove, his grove, had contained the largest azures of all. When the trees fell, the enormous root balls had left great holes in the ground. Hanna joined him to peer down into the dark. One tree held the way. But how was she to tell which one in this mass of logs? She made her way from tree to tree, looking down the deep root holes, though the sight of the dark maws made her shudder.

It was nearly nightfall when Hanna stumbled upon a great root hole, and a voice inside her whispered softly, *Here.* Looking down, she felt both drawn in and repelled, but she stood there all the same and waited for Evver and the rest to join her. It was the largest root hole she'd found thus far, and she couldn't see the bottom. She would have to wait for more deyas to come up the hill with their torches.

A wind crossed the mountaintop, and Hanna pulled up her hood, missing the feel of Thriss underneath as she did so. She saw torches moving up the hill; she felt their warmth across her back as their light spilled down into the hole. Taunier's boots appeared. Next to them came larger deya feet with snakelike roots sprouting from the ankles. All were gathered in a circle now around the pit.

Hanna cautiously peered over the edge. They expected her to find the way to Taproot Hollow and All Souls Wood. Everything was supposed to be there: her lost brother, the rest of the Wind-taken, new Waytrees for the deyas. But something was wrong. How could this hole be the way? It looked like a bottomless grave.

THIRTY
ENTANGLED

Seek them there, seek them here,
before the children disappear.

—FROM THE GAME BLIND SEER

The underground cavern seemed endless. If it were day now up above, Hanna could not tell. Time was blind down here. The darkness would have been complete if Taunier hadn't used his skill to keep the torches alight. Hanna adjusted her damp cloak and tried to ignore the hollow fear cradled in her belly. She wasn't sure *where* they were going. Was this the right passage to All Souls Wood, or would the winding tunnel end in a high rock wall with no way out?

Evver stepped up beside her with his torch. In its light, she could see tree roots dangling from the rocky roof like matted troll hair. They were passing under the remains of the clear-cut forest, trees the Cutters had chopped down, leaving the stumps and roots behind. Overhead, bats opened their wings and closed them again in the torchlight, but none flew down. The rich smells coming from floor, roof, and walls reminded Hanna of Shalem Wood in winter, when the cold wind sharpened the earthy scents.

They caught up with Taunier. He'd belted his cloak; still, under the cloth, Hanna could see that his shoulders were hunched. He glanced back at Zabith walking with more deyas farther behind them, then spoke in a low tone. "I don't understand what Zabith meant about me being the boy the torches follow," he said. "They're just words from some old game."

The whispered comment was meant for Hanna, but Evver was close enough to catch it. "A game?" he said. "You can call it a game. But it's more than that. We deyas heeded the words. We waited long for the three of you to join us on the mountain before we tried to cross over. Meer Zabith, our Blind Seer, came to Mount Olone, then the Dreamer appeared, and last, you came, the—"

"I know, I'm the Fire Herd, but it doesn't make sense." Taunier drew his fingers through his tangled black hair.

"How can a game children have played for hundreds of years be a prophecy?"

A slow smile crossed Evver's face. "What better way than a game to pass a prophecy down through the ages? The deyas have watched playing children chant the words in every land in Noor."

"But that's the trouble," argued Taunier. "Only children play it."

Gentle laughter sounded behind them. The other deyas were listening in and seemed amused at Taunier's frustration.

Evver moved aside a dangling root. "And why do you think that is, Fire Herd?"

Taunier didn't answer. Hanna ventured, "Because . . . it's meant for children."

"Just so. The Otherworld is a place of magic and dreams. Many adults have forgotten Oth. If the worlds began to break apart again, we would need the children. The Old Magic tells us so."

Evver's words came over Hanna like a soft sea breeze that made her skin tingle. She wasn't sure why, but Taunier must have felt it, too, for he said, "How does the Old Magic tell you this? Does it speak to you?"

Evver laughed. "Not in the way you think."

As they turned another corner in the passage, Evver talked about the beginning of all things. His words were like ones she'd read in *The Book of eOwey*, but it was as if she were hearing them for the first time. In the dim passage she imagined eOwey singing the bright stars, the sky, and all the worlds into being. The song went from singing wind to silent air, filling all created things down to their very breath.

"eOwey's Old Magic is everywhere," said Evver. "We deyas know this in our roots. You let the Old Magic sing through you when you herd fire, Taunier, and the Kanameer lets it speak to her when she dreamwalks and when she listens closely to her heart."

Hanna thought of the whispering voice that had told her to stop and wait at the root hole. Was that the Old Magic working in her? She'd followed it, hoping it was the way to Taproot Hollow. Now she wasn't so sure. She feared now that there was nothing but a wall at the end of this long passage. They would have to turn back, defeated.

Would the deyas still follow me if they knew I wasn't sure of the way? If they didn't think I was their Kanameer?

She cupped Great-Uncle Enoch's brown bottle in

her hand, felt the stopper that held in the tears. The Kanameer will know what to do with them. *That's just it,* she thought. *I don't know.*

A buzzing sound drifted through the passage.

"What's that?" said Taunier.

"Bees?"

"Underground? It's not likely."

She pressed on. She'd come east to rescue her brother, to discover what was killing the ancient forests, and found more than she'd expected to find: dragons fighting to protect the Waytrees, the Damusaun and her clan needing a way home, deyas who must journey with her to Oth or die. She knew she would do everything in her power to help them, whether she was the Kanameer or not. Perhaps the title didn't matter so much as long as she was determined to give her all. This new thought filled her like good, warm bread and eased the fear that had been growing in her since the dragons first crowned her.

An hour later they reached a fork in the tunnel with a small entrance to the left and a larger one on the right. Taunier lifted his hand and turned his fingers. This small movement brightened all the deyas' torches, spilling light on the choices ahead.

Meer Zabith emerged from the crowd, hobbled up to the front, sniffed the hanging roots, and pointed left. "I see the way."

See? Hanna thought. *You're a blind old woman.* But she wasn't rude enough to say it aloud. "The passage is too small that way, Zabith," she corrected.

Evver bent down, and peered in one passage, then the other. "What do you say, Kanameer?"

Zabith kept her bony hand up, stubbornly pointing left. Hanna shifted from foot to foot. The left tunnel might lead to a dead end. If so, they would have to retrace their steps and try the other way. The deyas were tired, and she shouldn't overwork them. She could consult the map again, but she'd lost count of all the twists and turns they'd taken in the past few hours. She flushed. *Stupid! I can't believe I didn't keep better track. Now I have no idea which way to go.* "I'm . . . not sure," she admitted.

"We'll go this way then," Zabith insisted.

Evver nodded. At the same moment Taunier flashed her an exasperated look. "Are you sure, Hanna?"

His question echoed her own doubts, infuriating her all the more. "Come on," she said.

Hands out, Zabith stepped inside to lead the way.

The passage soon narrowed even more, and the abundant hanging roots lengthened. Zabith seemed unusually energized as she and Hanna pushed aside the tangles to make their way through.

Evver and the deyas had to crouch and lower their torches down around their knees to keep the roots from catching fire. No one complained, but the farther in they went, the more Hanna sensed Taunier's frustration, which only added to her own. He dragged his feet behind her, coughing now and again as the walkers stirred the dusty air.

Zabith was a meer of Othlore, Hanna reminded herself, even if she was old and blind. And hadn't Evver said the game Blind Seer was some kind of prophecy? That there was a reason all three of them were supposed to come? She struggled with her doubts as she pushed against the roots.

The buzzing they'd heard earlier had intensified. The deyas began to hum, harmonizing with the sound. Meer Zabith also began to hum. Hanna spied a clearing ahead where the root tendrils no longer hung so low. She raised her torch a little higher.

Evver hummed louder, and the other deyas followed

his lead. The rich sound filled the cavern until it seemed the very walls were singing back. Stepping around a rock, Hanna's torch spread a veil of light along the high ceiling. What she saw next made her stop cold. Beside a knot of black bats, the roots themselves were moving. There was no breeze blowing through the cave, none that she could feel, anyway; still, they wriggled like giant spider legs.

"Look," whispered Taunier.

Hanna craned her neck and saw the outlines of small human bodies: first one, then two, then more and more children entangled in the swaying roots above. They were lifeless. Their skin looked waxen . . . dead.

"Oh," she cried, leaping back against Taunier. "I shouldn't have brought you here!" She turned, dropped her torch, and covered her face with her hands. They'd trusted her, and she'd led them to this horrid burial ground.

"Stop hiding and look," scolded Zabith. "We've reached the heart of Taproot Hollow."

Evver said, "The Dreamers have been waiting." He stepped forward and jammed his torch into the ground. Light spilled across the rocky floor. Long arms outstretched, he began to untangle the roots wrapped about one child. The other deyas followed and did the same, their long, spry fingers parting roots as if they were untying ribbons around large Noorfest gifts.

"Come on, Hanna," said Taunier. "They're not dead. They're only asleep." Hanna wiped her eyes, then began to search the cave with Taunier. Most of the sleepers were too high for them to reach, but they found three cradled lower down. They gently pulled the roots away from a girl aged seven or eight, starting with her legs and moving toward her head. She yawned, climbed down, and joined the other children, who were gathering with the deyas. One child was whimpering. Zabith spoke to them all, saying, "Don't worry, dears. You've had a long sleep, and soon we'll take you home."

Hanna cringed at the boldness of her promise. The sleepers were so young. Where were all these children from? And anyway, they still hadn't reached Oth. She couldn't turn around now and take them home.

Taunier helped Hanna with another child. They freed the boy's muddy boots, untangled his short legs, and tenderly unwrapped his arms. Each sleeper had come awake when his head was freed from the roots' embrace. As they uncovered the boy's face, Hanna burst into happy tears. "Tymm?" she choked. "It's you! It's really you! I can't believe we found you!" The wind had blown them here? Why? Her head spun, but she was overjoyed. She hugged her little brother and caught the earthy scent in his curly blond hair.

"Is it morning already, Hanna? I had so many dreams!" he said groggily. Then he must have noticed the dark passage. "You woke me in the middle of the night."

"I had to." Hanna laughed though her tears. She was still holding him and didn't want to let go.

"You're squeezing too hard."

"Sorry." Hanna pulled back and began to wipe the dirt from his cheek. He turned his head before she was done and said, "Hey, Taunier."

Taunier chuckled and rubbed the top of his head.

"Leave off," protested Tymm. "I'm no baby."

"You did it, Hanna," said Taunier. "You found the Wind-taken, just as you said you would."

"I . . ." Hanna stuttered. "I just tried the way Meer Zabith wanted to go." She watched the old woman adjusting a child's wrinkled cloak. "The Blind Seer showed us the way," she added. "And now you won't be doubting the words from that old game," she teased.

"Aye, well." Taunier shrugged. "I can't say it isn't true, but give me some time to get used to it, will you?"

He flashed her a rare smile, and her heart felt light. She'd left off hugging Tymm and longed to throw her arms around Taunier. To curb the impulse, she pressed them tight against her sides. Taunier touched the base of her jaw, caught a tear on his fingertip, then playfully shook it off.

"No need for those now," he said.

The buzzing of the bees no longer puzzled her. The sound only added to the sense of light, of spring gardens and renewal. It meant there was a way out of this dark place somewhere ahead. If the bees were getting in, they must be getting out.

Tymm tugged her shirt. "I'm hungry, Hanna."

Hanna counted the other children huddled together under the sprawling roots. Tymm's friend, Cilla, stood near Evver, rocking back and forth on her feet. Including Tymm, there were sixteen children in all, as many children as deyas. Hanna wondered at that. Some of them rubbed their eyes, yawning, but a few of the youngest ones had begun to cry. The deyas knelt down and spoke to the little ones tenderly.

"Can we all sit here a moment?" Hanna asked gently.

The children gathered around the place where the torches were jammed in the ground, and the deyas settled in a circle behind them.

Hanna looked at the children's frightened, dirt-smeared faces. "We have a bit of food with us," she said. She asked Taunier to pass his rucksack and reached in for some of the dried fish. A small head poked up, blue eyes blinking.

"Thriss? What are you doing in there?" Hanna lifted the golden pip from the rucksack. The crying stopped as the children scooted closer.

"She is so small," Cilla said with a laugh. "I thought dragons were bigger than that."

"She's still a hatchling," Hanna explained. Some of the children extended grimy little hands to pet Thriss. A soft rumbling came from the dragon's throat.

"You're not supposed to be here, Thriss," Hanna scolded. "I'm supposed to take the deyas to All Souls Wood. And dragons are not allowed in Oth. What am I to do with you?"

Thriss poked her head in the rucksack, bit the end of a grass rope, and tugged it out.

"Hey," said Tymm. "That's mine. You should give it to me."

Hanna had asked Taunier to bring it along, and now she was glad he'd remembered. Thriss trotted about playfully with the rope until Tymm caught the other end and gave it a tug. She flitted up, spun around once, and let the rest of it fall on top of his head. Everyone laughed. Even the youngest ones were giggling as the baby dragon landed again and purred.

Cilla fingered Tymm's grass rope. She was a talented little weaver herself, and Hanna could tell she admired the handiwork. Tymm wrapped the rope about his narrow waist five times like a belt. It was a small thing that couldn't have saved him from the Wild Wind, but it was a thing he'd made all the same.

Taunier gave each child a bit of fish. There wasn't much, but they ate and passed around the water pouch.

"Do you know why you are here?" asked Hanna.

The children whispered among themselves. Tymm said, "A wind made me fly." He stretched his arms out and yawned.

"What do you remember?" asked Hanna.

Tymm sucked his lip, then said, "I had lots of dreams. You were in one dream riding on a dragon, Hanna, and the dragon fell from the sky and there was blood," he said excitedly. "You asked me to help you with that dream."

"What?" Hanna said, startled.

"You forgot how to dream because it had been all dark in your sleep, and so you asked me to help you dreamwalk. You were curled up in seaweed when I helped you." Tymm pointed to the ceiling. "Those roots helped me dream bright dreams."

"I dreamed, too," Cilla said. And the smaller children nodded, big-eyed.

"Was that why the Wind-taken were held in the roots?" Taunier said. "So they wouldn't lose their dreams?"

"Why else would they sleep in Taproot Hollow," said Zabith, as if the answer were as clear as day.

The oldest-looking boy stood and tightened his belt. He gazed across the circle at Hanna, his black skin shining in the torchlight. "I'm Kevin." He introduced another girl and boy. "The three of us were apprentices from the meer's school on Othlore," he said. "We were all at the top of our class in Restoration Magic." Kevin drew in the dust with his boot and squinted at Meer Zabith. "You used to live in the woods near the High Meer's river house, didn't you?"

"I'm Meer Zabith," she said simply. Kevin bowed to honor the meer, and though she could not see, Zabith nodded back in his direction.

The boy looked around. "The wind that blew us here called 'Tesha yoven.'"

Tymm and the other children nodded.

"Tesha yoven," said Evver. "Bind the broken."

Hanna remembered Tymm's cry, and talking about its meaning later with Miles on the *Leena*. She put her arm about her little brother, taking in the scent of his sweat and soiled clothes.

"Who wanted you to come here and bind the broken?" she asked.

"Who?" Kevin frowned. "I don't know. I thought you were here to tell us that."

Hanna stared back, incredulous. In the dancing torchlight, all eyes were suddenly on her; even the deyas searched her face, as if an answer lay there. She hadn't called them here. How was she supposed to know?

Hanna sputtered. "I . . . I . . ."

Stark silence. One child coughed.

Evver's long brown hand swept the air. "The Old Magic is at work, and the ways of this magic are beyond speech. The two worlds are breaking apart. Would the wind have brought you here without purpose?" he asked. "We will put our trust in the Old Magic and follow the way as it opens," he said quietly. It was not an answer, but the words seemed to calm the crowd. Evver's voice had a power in it, clear as rain, deep as a lake.

"But I'm still hungry," Tymm grumbled.

Taunier snorted a laugh.

"Well, I don't blame you," said Evver, bending low to pat Tymm's head. "*Essha*, boy," he said tenderly. "Do you hear those bees? There may be some honey farther along. Why don't we go and see?"

"All right." Tymm stood and wrapped his hand around Evver's smallest finger.

"Well, Kanameer," said Evver. "Lead on."

Taunier took up Hanna's torch, and they started off again. In the broad cavern the darkness was complete, and the torches gave no more light than they had an hour before, but Hanna gave silent thanks to Zabith for her stubborn insistence on this tunnel, and to Evver for his confidence in the power of the Old Magic.

The way felt open now.

PART THREE:
THE WORLD TREE

THIRTY-ONE

SONGS OF THE MISHTAR

*When the dragon wars ended, the Mishtar
turned his sword into an ervay to play his
Dragons' Requiem.*

—*A MEER'S HISTORY OF NOOR*

Rain spattered the dragons as they rode the storm's
chill drafts high above the East Morrow Sea. From
Kaleet's back, Miles could just make out the small sailing vessel the Cutters had abandoned in their harbor far
below. Meer Eason used it now to cross the miles of ocean
between Jarrosh and Yaniff.

There were no more living azures for the dragons to
guard, and knowing the Cutters would return to harvest
the fallen logs for the King of Kanayar to rebuild his city,
the Damusaun had withdrawn her forces. She would hold
her dragon council in Yaniff.

Miles shivered under his soaking cloak. Across the sea
he saw the jagged outline of the snowcapped mountains
beyond the expansive flatlands.

No man had set foot on Yaniff since the time of the great Mishtar. He would be the first. Miles hummed *"Avoun Darri,"* the song the Mishtar had played on his ervay when he sailed from Yaniff to his first dragon battle in Reon.

They crossed the shore and sped over the wide mouth of a river. A deep, shuddering sound filled the air, loud as thunder, though it had not come from the clouds. The land below them shook. To the north, great pieces of the mountainside broke off and tumbled down ravines. The foothills rolled like swelling waves, and in the flatlands below, Miles saw tall stone pillars topple over, breaking as they hit the earth.

"The split between the worlds grows wider!" the Damusaun called. "No one is to land!"

An hour after the quaking stopped, the dragons wheeled down and landed near the river's mouth. The wind picked up as Miles dismounted, sending a chill across his back. By the time Eason's ship arrived, they had set up camp along the river, well away from the remaining pillars that might be the next to fall if another tremor came.

The Damusaun left the rest of the group to walk toward the last remains of the ancient ruin. Miles knew he should leave her be, but he could not. He shivered as he followed her, his hair and cloak still sodden from the storm. It would be colder still when the sun set in this desert.

He walked in the undulating pattern her tail left on the damp sand. The patterns matched those the wind had made on the sand, like waves on a dry sea. Each swish of her tail erased her large footprints so it was as if no creature had walked there. She was making herself invisible. He wondered if she meant to do this.

As they came closer to the towers, he remembered how they'd looked from above. Before the quake he'd seen five or so ruins like this one across the landscape, with rows of enormous white pillars resembling jutting teeth in the desert's mouth. Many pillars in the ruin ahead had beams rising at an angle near the top—roof supports, Miles guessed, though the roof had crumbled long ago. What sort of building or temple had they once supported? He felt sure the monoliths were not the work of men, but dragon-made, a place of worship or sacrifice or both.

Had the queen come here to worship? He paused, waiting, and was nearly jolted from his spot by her sudden loud wail. There was fire in the scream. The piercing sound shook his bones and made his jaw ache. The bright hot fire burned his eyes. He covered his face with his hands, feeling this wasn't meant for his ears or anyone else's. This was why she had come away from the others.

They had lost.

The Waytrees and their deyas were gone.

She was the queen of a homeless clan.

He was not supposed to be witnessing this, but he felt the resonance of her angry cry in his bones.

When her screams were done, she wrapped her tail about a pillar and leaned her head against the white stone. Miles thought to turn back then, but she spotted him and motioned to him with her talon.

Miles bowed, then rose again. "How long do we have before the worlds split apart completely, Damusaun?"

"How long," the Damusaun repeated, her eyes half closed. It was not an answer, nor a question. The knowledge of the splitting worlds was beyond even the ken of dragons, the oldest living creatures in Noor.

The queen turned and surveyed the weary gathering

far away by the river. "Tell them to fish," she said. "We all need to eat."

"I have to ask you something. It's about Hanna and Taunier and—"

"Not now. I am weary. We will rest before we hold the council."

Miles saw she was in control again. She would hold whatever anger she felt about their defeat, keeping it to herself.

He was sure the queen had brought them here for a reason. The way between worlds was lost in Jarrosh. But there had to be another way to cross over. It would do him no good to argue with the Damusaun when he needed the dragon's help to find his sister, his best friend, and his little brother.

Bearing his disappointment and worry, Miles walked to the riverside to deliver the queen's message. Soon terrows and taberrells were catching fish in their great claws. Miles helped Eason make three tall brush piles. When the bonfires were lit, the dragons made ready to eat their meal.

Miles patted the ground at his side for Breal. He shared his dinner, carefully removing the tiny fish bones before feeding his dog. When both were satisfied, he adjusted his damp shirt and held his hands out to the popping fire.

"You don't want to do that," said Eason.

"Do what?"

"You'll want to keep your meer sign to yourself unless you're asked to show it."

Pulling his hands away from the fire, Miles inspected his left palm. The blue spiral had already begun to show. It slowly faded as it cooled.

"We are only two now," said Eason.

Miles looked down at his scuffed boots, remembering Kanoae's death. After the battle, they'd brought her wrapped body to the dock and placed her in one of the Cutters' abandoned boats. Meer Eason had buried her at sea on his way to Yaniff.

"She was a warrior," said Eason. "I sang *Kaynumba* on the ship's deck before her sea burial."

"She would have liked that." Miles didn't try to hide his tears, and the heat of the fire took them from his cheeks soon enough.

Eason said, "Kanoae would have wanted to die the way she did."

"She didn't want to die!"

"I did not say that, Miles. But all folk die sometime. Kanoae wouldn't have wanted to end her life old and feeble. As a warrior she chose to fight among dragons. Do you see?"

Miles frowned. He was about to say that she was as brave as a man, but he caught himself. The Damusaun was female, and she was the most courageous being he'd ever met. Like Kanoae, he'd been proud to fight alongside her and the other dragons, even though they'd met defeat.

"We lost everything," he said. "Kanoae's dead. The azures are gone."

Firelight bronzed Eason's thoughtful face. "It's true the battle is over," he said. "But eOwey's song is not over yet. We still have our parts to play."

Miles deepened the sandy rut around the fish bones. "What is my part?"

"It is not mine to say. But listen, and you will know when to join in."

"How can you still hold on to your belief now?"

"What else is there to hold on to?"

Anger, Miles thought. *Revenge*. But they wouldn't fix things, either. He knew the Damusaun felt the same when he'd witnessed her fiery scream, yet she wasn't giving in to it. What good was anger now? Where would it get them?

He tasted Eason's words. It was one thing to speak of eOwey's great song, another to live in this broken world. The earthquakes had come, as the High Meer warned they would near the end. Taunier and the deyas were somewhere in this world or in the other, following Hanna, looking for Tymm and the other children to bring them back before the worlds split completely.

Across the shooting flames, the Damusaun was eyeing him, her pupils glittering like black diamonds. He would ask her now to help him find Oth. There must still be a way.

But she spoke first. "The newest meer will help us now that the meal is done," she ordered. "Play your ervay to ease our company before I begin our council."

Miles stood unsteadily, feeling for his leather pouch. "It's been a while since I've played."

The Damusaun shook her head and snapped her teeth. She did not like to be kept waiting. Meer Eason gave him an encouraging nudge. The thought of playing before the Dragon Queen sent a jolt of fear down Miles's spine. No one but the great Mishtar himself had ever played before dragons.

Miles raised his ervay. The queen had promised to call the council soon. If his song pleased her, he could approach her again with confidence. His hands were stiff and awkward, and he felt like a beginner.

The ervay was cool against his fingertips as he began "*Avoun Darri.*" He'd hummed it flying here with Kaleet, but it was a difficult piece to play. The opening notes were not as perfect as he wanted them to be, but he kept going. He went on to play the sweet, deep melodies he'd heard in Othlore Wood. He'd thought the tunes were his own, composed on woodland walks during his first year as an apprentice, but he knew as he played them now that the melodies belonged to the ancient Waytrees on Othlore, to the deya spirits in the wood. He'd heard them from the singing boughs, the murmuring leaves, and translated them note by note.

The stone pillars, towering as high as Waytrees, cast long moonlit shadows across the ground. The tune spread out like invisible waters, encircling all, connecting everyone. The dragons joined in, singing, tails drumming on the sand.

The woodland requiem began to change from songs of loss to something almost joyful. The exhaustion Miles had carried from the arduous sea voyage and long battles with the Cutters lightened.

They were a small group here under the desert stars. Only two meers and a gathering of dragons, but they knew why they were here. They had not forgotten the great forests of old that once bound two worlds. Not yet.

The Old Magic has awakened.

—WILD ESPER

L ook!" Tymm pointed ahead. "Stars! Thousands of stars!"

Hanna had expected blue daylight, but the opening at the far end of the passage was black. Still, the fresh night air washing over her face held a woodland scent. At last! They must have reached the Valley of All Souls!

Hanna and Taunier raced toward the glittering stars, then came skidding to a sudden halt at the cavern's broad mouth.

"Stop, everyone!" warned Taunier. "Don't push. We're too high up." Sliding his arm through Hanna's, he peered down and gave a whistle. The moon hung nearly ripe over the valley floor a thousand feet below.

Hanna inched out a little farther to inspect the cliff. It appeared to be sheer on all sides. No jutting rocks to climb down.

A bat flitted past and flew down toward the valley floor.

"Now what?" Taunier whispered.

Hanna could feel the others waiting behind her. She didn't want to turn around, didn't want to meet their eyes.

Trees dotted the valley far below. At the base of the mountain, dark smudges gathered in larger clumps, joining to become a vast forest. The left side was too dark to see, but moonlight spread across the evergreens high up on the right side of the mountain. Here was the valley and the forest of Oth they'd come so far to find. She could see the trees the deyas needed to survive, but there was no way to reach them.

"We'll rest awhile," Hanna announced. Her throat ached with anger and disappointment. Behind her the deyas seated themselves on the dusty floor, and the children curled up in their laps in twos and threes like nestlings.

Hanna crouched against the jagged rock wall by the opening. Thriss crawled from the rucksack, perched on her knees, and licked her scaly forearm with her long, orange tongue.

"You shouldn't have stowed away like that," scolded Hanna a second time. "We're right on the edge of Oth, and dragons aren't allowed in." The pip ignored her as usual and began to clean the scales beneath her wing.

Hanna glanced at the weary company. Some deyas were singing the little ones to sleep, their own eyes drooping. One deya's head hung low, her long hair tickling Cilla's face. Cilla's nose twitched in her sleep. Hanna sighed. She was in charge of them all, from pip to child to deya. What did it matter that Thriss had come along? Oth was a thousand feet below. Impossible to reach.

Taunier squatted on his haunches and offered his water pouch. Hanna shook her head. There wasn't much left, and the children would need to drink again soon. Instead, she slipped a pebble into her mouth and sucked it to hold back her thirst. Evver's long-fingered hand lay across Tymm's back. The deya's garments were dirt-stained and his hair and beard tangled; even so, he had a kingly presence. *I can't let him die,* she thought. *There must be a way.*

"It's all right, Hanna," Taunier whispered beside her.

"It's not," she whispered back. "I wanted to help the deyas. To rescue Tymm and bring him and the other children safely home." It was hard to admit her failure aloud. She wished Taunier would put his arm about her. She wanted to feel his strength.

Taunier didn't hold her, but he did sit beside her, close enough for Thriss to playfully wrap her golden tail about his wrist. Close enough for Hanna to feel his breath tickle the hairs on her neck.

"Do you think Tymm wanted to be rescued?" he asked.

The question startled her. "What do you mean?"

"We used your great-uncle Enoch's boat to sail from Enness."

"So?"

"So listen, will you?"

"I'm listening," she whispered, though she didn't like his tone.

"We had to run off together because your mother and da wouldn't have let you come."

Hanna nodded. That was true enough, and she still felt some guilt over it.

"Would you have wanted your parents to rescue you?

To bring you safely back home before you made it to Jarrosh?"

"No, of course not."

"It might be the same for Tymm and the others."

"But they're only children," she protested.

"Some might call you a child."

"I'm fifteen. No one would say that." She was irritated at Taunier, but part of her was intrigued with his idea. What if by rescuing Tymm and the other children, she was preventing them from accomplishing what they'd come here to do? It was strange to think of it that way, yet the children hadn't seemed afraid once they'd fully awakened, seen Thriss pop out of the rucksack, and grown used to the deyas. While sleeping in Taproot Hollow, Tymm had somehow sent her the power to dreamwalk again when her own dreams had gone dark.

She guessed he'd sent the magic through the webbed roots in Mount Olone to the roots of the azure sapling where the dragons made her seaweed bed. Since that last dreamwalk, she'd returned to her vivid dreams and had dreamwalked without aid when she'd gone up the slope to find Meer Zabith. But Tymm's part in the adventure wasn't over. All the Wind-taken had agreed they'd been blown across the eastern sea to bind the broken, whatever that meant.

"If I didn't come here to rescue Tymm and the others, or to help the deyas find new Waytrees after their azures fell, what did I come here to do?"

"I can't tell you that, Hanna."

She was tired of being in charge. She leaned her head against the rock wall, exhausted, needing sleep, too worried to drop off.

Evver had said she let the Old Magic speak to her when she dreamwalked and when she listened closely to her heart. She'd felt a deep assurance when she'd left Enness with Taunier, after she'd dreamwalked for the dragons, and when she'd found Tymm and the others in the roots. Was that what Evver meant? It hadn't been so much like listening to a voice as a kind of quiet knowing. Still, if she were the Kanameer, wouldn't she have a clear, intelligent plan? A stronger sense of her own power?

Outside, the night was waning. Dawn brushed the valley in pale vermilion, and the trees were dipped in fruited light.

Taunier said, "If the dragons had come with us, they could have flown us down."

"You know they're not allowed back into Oth until Breal's Moon."

"I know."

Neither of them mentioned that Breal's Moon would rise tonight.

Taunier ran his finger down Thriss's back. "With the azures gone, I wonder if the dragons can get back at all now."

Hanna had wondered that, too. And behind that thought another, darker one hid. If she couldn't get the deyas to the trees in All Souls Wood, where Evver had promised to try and bridge the worlds from the Oth side, how could they bring the children home?

Turn back down the tunnel now, and the deyas would surely die. Stay too long away from Noor, and they might all end up in Oth forever. "There's no way out," she whispered.

Taunier leaned closer, his arm brushing against hers. "You'll have to use your powers to get us down," he whispered, "unless, of course, those deyas back there can fly."

Her powers . . . Hanna closed her eyes. There it was again. Was she supposed to dreamwalk them all down?

Fly? She couldn't fly, though she'd ridden with Wild Esper once or twice.

An idea began to form. "Taunier." She opened her eyes. "Come closer to the edge with me."

"Why? We've already looked down. There's nothing to grab on to."

"Please. Just do it."

Hanna tucked Thriss into the rucksack. "Stay in here until I say it's safe to come out." The hatchling gave a little hiss, but she crept back in.

The mouth of the cave was toothless, with no jutting stones to hold on to. Hanna stepped out as far as she dared, the toes of her scuffed boots only inches from the edge. Taunier gripped her arm; still, her stomach flipped as she looked down. *The wind spirits are my kith. I have the power to call upon the riders.* Wild Esper would not come this far east, but there were other sky spirits she'd read about in the Falconer's book that might come to her if she called.

"Hold me tight."

"What are you going to do?"

"Just hold me, Taunier."

Taunier wrapped his arms about her waist. Hanna held her breath a moment, feeling the warmth and strength flowing from his hands. She sighed, shivering a little at his touch, then spread her arms.

"Noorushh, rider of the sea winds, I am sqyth-eyed. My blue eye shows my friendship with the sky and marks me as your kith. Friend who rides the wind, blow to this mountainside. I call you here. I ask you to come."

Hanna called again, "Isparel, sky friend, one who dances with the east wind, I call you. I am your kith as you are mine. Dance on the wind above the valley. I wait here with the deyas. I wait for you to come!"

Hanna waved her arms up and down, as if already greeting the wind spirits. She had summoned both spirits, hoping at least one would blow to the high cave. The breeze picked up, whistling a stark tune as it swept up from the valley. Crisp air blew her hair and clothing back against Taunier, who was still holding her fast. Hanna caught the clean gusts and let them fill her.

"Wake up," she called to the deyas in the cave. "The great wind spirits are coming."

THIRTY-THREE

WIND RIDERS

*I saw Noorushh, the great wind spirit of the sea,
riding on a white cloud above the stormy water.*

—*The Way Between Worlds*

A giant wind rider galloped across the sky on his cloud stallion: the wind spirit Noorushh was racing straight for the mountainside.

"You did it," Taunier said, amazed.

"Get ready," Hanna shouted. She wanted to scream and scurry away from the opening, to hide from the powerful rider. But she spread her feet wider to brace herself. Taunier's long-fingered hands held her steady above the sheer drop.

"Look," he cried over her shoulder. "There's another one."

She saw a spray of colors flung across the morning sky: vibrant green, deep purple, burning orange. The swirl grew larger as Isparel the wind woman danced toward the cliff in her rainbow skirts.

Hanna tried to press down her growing terror. She'd done it, summoned two spirits, hoping at least one would come. Now both were here, blowing much too close together. It took only two spirits to begin a wind war, but there was no time to send one back.

"Come closer," Hanna called.

Noorushh swept up, his chalk-white hair and long beard blowing back from his stormy face. "I crossed land hearing your call, but I ride over the sea. I won't stay long."

"We have to reach the valley," said Hanna. "Will you fly us down?"

He rode his cloud stallion closer to the cliffside. "If you want a ride, leap on now."

Hanna peered at the valley, a quarter of a mile below. "Leap . . . now?"

Noorushh huffed at her indecision and tugged his silver reins to turn his storm steed about. There was no arguing with him. She had to leap now, show the others how to ride down, or lose her chance.

Don't look down. Just go! She wrenched forward. Taunier's hands tightened around her waist.

"Let go of me!"

"I won't."

"I said let go! I have to jump. It's the only way down."

"I can't let you do that."

"Mortals!" Noorushh spat cold raindrops that splattered her face and chest as he began to pull away. He was leaving! She had to jump. She stomped on Taunier's toes and elbowed him hard in the ribs. As he reeled back, sucking in air, she leaped for the racing cloud.

The sky billowed all around her as she tumbled down head over heels. She'd thrown herself off and missed! Where was Noorushh? The thick air jammed the screams back inside her mouth. Arms spread wide in the pummeling wind, she hurtled down, speeding closer and closer to the valley floor, then bright colors swept in from her left as Isparel caught her in her skirts and spun her round and round. Gasping wildly, heart in mouth, Hanna swam in the wind woman's twirling skirts.

"Can you fly in lower and put me down?" puffed Hanna.

Isparel laughed. "Why not dance higher?" She tossed her upward. Hanna flailed, stomach clenching, her limbs jerking as earth and sky roiled all about her. She knew wind spirits were tricksters, but she was not a toy.

"Stop it, Isparel! Take me down!"

It was the wrong thing to say. Isparel sped for the valley in a fury, her gown darkening with storm as she dumped Hanna onto the grass. Hanna pitched forward and caught herself with her hands. Palms scraped, knees throbbing, she turned over, reeling from flight. "Th-Thank you, Isparel," she stuttered, "for the wonderful dance." She had to make it up to the wind woman; if she lost both spirits, the others would be trapped in the cave with no way down.

Isparel twirled overhead, hesitating. She sent another angry gust toward Hanna, then laughed. "You were a pitiful partner."

Hanna stood dizzily. "I know. I'm sorry. Please, could you dance the others down? They would love to dance with you. I know they would." Hanna knew the children and the deyas might well scream in their mad descent, but it was the only way to reach the valley.

Isparel flashed upward and blew singing toward the cliff. Not to be outdone, Noorushh thundered by, his stallion darkening brown with rain. Hanna held her breath. Would they fight to take the others down? What had she done?

"Taunier!" she screamed. "I'm here!" She waved her arms in the desperate hope that he could see her from the tunnel opening. "Come down! Bring the rest with you!" She pressed her nails into her palms as she watched first one wind spirit, then the other blow past the dark opening in the high cliff.

Get on. Ride down. Easy. Easy.

At last Noorushh gusted down and gave a mighty shout as he came to a halt just above the floor of the valley. A handful of screaming children tumbled from his cloudy mount. Tymm and Cilla were the first to roll across the grass.

"Tymm!" Hanna rushed over to help him up. She was ready to comfort her little brother and was surprised to find his screams were not from fear. Wrenching away from her grasp, he took Cilla's hand and joined a circle of children shrieking with delight. "Wind-riders! Wind-riders!" they chanted as they spun around. The children fell again, laughing, too dizzy to stand.

More children tumbled off the stallion with the deyas. A few of the youngest ones hadn't enjoyed the ride. The two in Evver's arms were bawling. He rocked them, saying, "It is all right now." He lifted his head to admire the broad valley, his roots undulating in the rich green grass.

Tymm bounded back to Hanna. "We're going there for a drink," he said, pointing to a stream at the edge of the wood. Tipping her head back, Hanna cupped her hands around her mouth. "Thank you, Noorushh."

"The sea calls!" he shouted back. With a great gust, the wind spirit swept over the mountain forest toward the Othic Sea beyond. Hanna was thirsty, too, but she kept her place, head up, still waiting anxiously for the rest of her friends to land.

Taunier and Zabith were the last to spin down with Isparel. Meer Zabith was old and frail, but it turned out theirs was a graceful landing. Taunier braced himself, somewhat unsteady on his feet. He made a princely bow to the wind woman and said, "Thank you for the dance, Isparel."

Isparel swirled her skirts about him, covering him in rainbows.

Blood rushed to Hanna's cheeks. How dare she caress him that way?

"You will dance with me again," insisted Isparel.

"Another time," said Taunier.

Laughing, the spirit mussed his dark hair before she spun away. Taunier turned, passed Hanna without a glance, and headed for the stream where the children were splashing and drinking.

He's angry with me for kicking him away so I could jump, she thought. She wanted to stay where she was and let her jealous heat simmer a little longer, but they didn't have much time. Tonight was Breal's Moon; she had only one day to find trees for the deyas and bring the children back home to Noor. At the brook she drank greedily from the bank. The deyas waded in, drinking through their rooted feet.

On the far side of the stream, slender birches and willows were leafed in autumnal gold. Farther up the mountain, Hanna spied a swath of evergreens. None looked large enough to house deyas. There must be an ancient grove somewhere in All Souls Wood.

Taunier splashed water on his face and stood, hands dripping.

Hanna cleared her throat. "Sorry for stomping on your foot and—"

"You really gouged me in the gut." He rubbed just below his ribs.

"I had to. It was the only way to—"

Taunier turned from her, gazing over the valley. The cliff they'd flown down from looked so far away now, with the broad vale spreading out green before them. The back of his hand lightly brushed against hers, setting off small fireworks in her chest. She glanced at his profile, his slightly crooked nose, wide mouth, and high forehead. She knew every inch of his face. She'd absorbed it during innumerable stolen glances over the past year, drinking his features in small sips before looking away. She swiftly turned her head before he caught her.

Half the valley was still covered in predawn gloom. But where the morning sunlight touched the vale, she saw grasslands dotted with bushes and trees, and the creatures on the ground and in the air looked drenched in fairy light. The light here was so much brighter than any she'd ever seen in Noor. This was the Oth she remembered, a place brimming over with magic. The sun sweetened the air like honey, sharpened every wing, twig, and blade of grass. The air here thrummed with vibrant life.

"We must hurry." Evver pointed to the edge of shadow still covering half the valley. "The waking wood is growing smaller."

"Won't that part of the forest be lit up as the sun gets higher?" Hanna asked.

"The sun is up," said Taunier. "It must be something else causing the dark."

"Come on, everyone," Evver said. The brook looked deep in the middle. He scooped up Tymm and two other children to ford it. The deyas helped the rest of them across, and they made their way toward the patches of sunlight in All Souls Wood.

A mile farther on, they reached the foothills of the craggy mountain Hanna had seen from the cliff. The nameless shadow rising less than a hundred yards to the left of the trail disturbed Hanna. What was it? She tried to see inside, but couldn't make out any shapes in the dark. Shivering, she paused to soak in the golden shafts of light falling through the white-barked birches on this part of the path, thankful for the warmth.

The trail grew steeper as they left the valley. There were some taller pines here, but none large or old enough to house deyas. Taunier took the lead, walking with a sure stride, and Hanna strained her muscles, trying to keep up with him. Why was he walking so fast? Did he want to be alone?

Her boots scuffed through maple and willow leaves. They were far ahead of the rest now. She could make out Tymm's and Cilla's chattering voices down below. Evver and the deyas had chosen to walk apace with Zabith and the children. Or were they too weak to move any faster? She stopped to glance back. How thin they seemed. Evver hadn't told her how long they could live without their Waytrees. Was it because he didn't want her to worry or feel responsible if she failed him?

She turned, heart pounding, just as Taunier disappeared around another bend. "Taunier," she called, "could you slow down a little?"

Taunier paused near a mossy boulder and peered over the side of the trail. He appeared to be waiting for her to catch up, but she didn't much like the place he'd chosen. The trail had veered left, and the deep shadow was fewer than twenty feet away.

Taunier raised his arm and snapped his fingers. A flame grew above his outstretched hand. He held it higher, leaned over, then suddenly pitched the fireball toward the blanket of dark to the left of the trail and scurried down between the trees.

"Taunier? What are you doing?" She raced after him.

The ground leveled again below the trail. In the darkness, he stood among the logs holding his burning light aloft, his skin pale orange from its glow.

Taunier moved his hand and guided the light across the ground. No trees grew in this gloom, only dead logs lying every which way, like the devastated Noor forests they'd left behind.

"Why did you come down here?" Hanna demanded. The air tasted thick, as if they'd entered a pool of stagnant water. Taunier pointed. As her eyes adjusted to the dim light, she saw that just three feet away, a faun lay beside a fox. As Taunier moved the light she saw more bodies; sylth fairies still as stone, wolves, two bearded trolls with their knees bent, as if they'd fallen midstride. There were snakes draped belly up over logs, a family of great horned elk, and everywhere the ground was littered with sprites and birds, hundreds of them, all on their backs, their wings spread wide.

Hanna hugged herself, shivering.

Taunier knelt beside a sylth, whose yellow hair spread across the dark ground. He touched her cheek. "She's asleep." He began to shake her gently.

They'd awakened the children in the roots. Could

they bring these Oth folk out of their deep sleep? It would be cruel to leave them this way, cruel not to try to help them. Stepping cautiously around a troll, Hanna chose a young sylth who looked about Tymm's age. The boy's smooth face was lost in dream. She bent to shake his shoulder. He didn't awaken, even when she shook him harder. The fine dust that coated the boy's soft bark jerkin came off on her hand. She stood with effort, suddenly overcome with exhaustion.

"What's . . . wrong . . . with . . . them?" Her words came slowly, as the dark pressed down on her. Her body felt as if invisible weights hung from her shoulders. Alarmed, she looked at Taunier, who was struggling to walk toward her.

A booming voice came somewhere from her right.

"Eldessur kimbardaa!" Evver's warning voice rolled through the dark. "You are called. Come out before it is too late."

Hanna saw the deya in a spill of light on the trail above. A red-haired sylth in a sparkling gown stood on Evver's left. More sylths, some fauns, and a large bedraggled troll had joined them on the trail. The troll held Tymm by the collar.

"Let me go!" Tymm was shouting, arms flailing.

The troll held on. "I said stay back, boy. Ye can't go in there! Would ye end up like them?" He pointed to the bodies sprawled on the woodland floor.

Evver extended his hand, his long fingers going dark as they dipped in the thick shadow. "Taunier," he said, "Hannalyn, come out."

She lifted her foot, tried to move. Her legs were too heavy. She just needed to lie down and rest a moment before she went on. She crumbled to her knees.

Taunier's light burned out as he lunged forward to catch her. He wrapped his arm about her and slowly pulled her to a stand.

"Don't give in to it," he said.

Leaning closer to the edge, Evver sang:

"Esh ell ne da.

Ne da rumm pe."

Listen to my heart.

My heart beats for you.

The deyas, sylths, and troll joined in. Streaming voices met and harmonized into a river. The song drifted over the fallen trees and sleeping bodies, sending a fresh current through the dead air. Hanna felt the stirring against her cheek, cool as water, warm as breath.

"Come on." Taunier took her arm, and together they pushed their way through the thickened air.

Tymm wrestled free from the Troll.

The troll reached out. "I'm warnin' ye!"

"Here." Tymm loosened his belt, unfurled his grass rope, and tossed one end into the dark. He handed the other end to Evver. Trailing from Evver's large hand, the rope fluttered like a thin green flag in the warm wind of the song. Hanna and Taunier reached for it.

THIRTY-FOUR

THE HAND

eOwey sung NoorOth as one,
Embraced by the great World Tree.

—Dragons' Song

Miles awoke at dawn. Last night's bonfires were red coals. Meer Eason slept with his head on Breal's side. The rest of the dragons were curled snout to tail and snoring, but the Damusaun was missing.

The queen had begun the Dragon Council late last night. Miles had tried to stay awake, but exhaustion had won out, and he'd drifted off by the fire. He stood and scanned the desert, furious with himself. What vital plans had he missed? Had they talked about Hanna and Taunier and Tymm? Did the Damusaun still think there would be a way to bring her clan home? Sleep had stolen him when he'd most needed to be awake.

Miles searched the sand, found the Damusaun's tail

340

marks, and followed them into the desert. She'd disappeared again to some solitary place. He drank from the river, shook the droplets from his head, and continued trailing the serpentine patterns.

Near the temple ruin, stone spires cast long shadows in the pale, morning light. He followed a single shadow all the way to the pillars where the she-dragon had stopped sometime before dawn. The deep claw prints revealed that she'd paced back and forth before moving on.

Miles looked up. Some pillars in the long row still had roof beams stretching out like branches toward the far side. He imagined a dome spread overhead like a great forest canopy. There was nothing left of it now, but he sensed the dome had once been green, and so had the arid dragonlands. How long ago that must have been.

Dawn painted the clouds tangerine; the sky loomed pale purple. In the nearby bushes, insects began to click. Wind stirred the clouds above, and their twin shadows on the sand moved toward the mountain range.

Circling a pillar, he rested his palm on the cool stone. There were darker circles higher up along the pillar's sides, like knotholes in a tree. Miles leaned closer and whispered his deya name, "Mileseryl."

Silence. But then what did he expect? This was not a tree trunk. No deya dwelled inside.

Abandoning the ruin, he trailed through patches of dry grass bent low by the Dragon Queen's tail. Yaniff was strange and beautiful. Someday he'd explore the other dragon temples he'd seen from the air, climb the far mountains, and view what lay beyond.

A low rumbling sound crossed the desert. Miles spread his legs and adjusted his stance. The ground shuddered. The next mighty tremor knocked him flat on his back. Stone towers swayed left and right. Two crashed down fewer than ten feet away. Miles rolled on his side, tried to get up and run, but the molten sand pitched and rolled like a yellow sea. From the far-off camp, Breal was racing toward him.

"Breal! Lie down, boy!"

Meer Eason leaped onto a terrow, and the dragons all took to the air.

The desert shook. Miles got up and stumbled forward, shouting. Clouds of choking dust surrounded him, cutting off his view. How could the dragons fly over and sweep him up off the shuddering ground if they couldn't see him? He screamed louder and tried to stand, then fell back on all fours. In the next violent tremor the desert cracked. Before he could leap back, the split tore into a great fissure, and Miles plummeted down.

A narrow beam of sunlight poured into the crevasse. Miles slowly came to and saw a crack of blue above the high, earthen walls. His head pounded, and his chest and back felt badly bruised. He crooked his neck, peered down the deep crevasse, and gasped. He would have fallen to his death if he hadn't been caught here, but he was not on a ledge. He squinted at the dirt wall and let out a hoarse scream. A giant's skeletal hand thrust from the raw earth and clutched him with long, bony fingers.

"Help, someone!" No sounds of movement from above. Couldn't they hear him? He called again, his voice cracking with strain.

The bony hand seemed to grip him even tighter. Was the skeleton alive? Would the giant draw him back inside the earth? Sweat soaked his shirt. He should shape-shift smaller, free himself, but he'd never shifted to a smaller animal before, and the idea terrified him. What if he were trapped in a helpless little form, condemned to live out his life as a lizard or a mouse? It was unthinkable.

His rib cage ached, and his legs were numb. His flesh twitched with fear, indecision, anger. "Help!" he called again. "I'm trapped down here!"

Loud barking from above. "Breal! Get one of the dragons!" Breal lifted his muzzle and howled. It wasn't long before Miles saw the Damusaun flying overhead, before she carefully winged down into the wide rift.

"Don't move," she ordered. No trouble there. He hadn't been able to do anything so far but turn his head.

Flapping her wings to stay in place, the Dragon Queen used her sharp talons to free Miles from the skeleton hand. Once she had him securely in her claw, she flew up and placed him gently on the sand.

Miles sat up dizzily and spat. "Thank you," he wheezed. Every breath sent sharp pains across his chest and back. Had that hideous thing broken one of his ribs? Meer Eason leaped down from a terrow and ran toward him.

"Miles! We thought . . . Are you all right?"

"My ribs are a little sore."

The Damusaun left them together, and Meer Eason knelt and ran his hand along Miles's ribs. It was a gentle touch; still, Miles sucked air between his clenched teeth.

"Some bruising, but I'm fairly sure the bones are not broken." He wiped the dust from his hands. "Are you thirsty?" Eason pulled out his water pouch, found it empty, and headed for the river.

Miles rested his head against Breal's furry neck. The Dragon Queen flew back and settled on the sand before him.

Miles looked up. "What was that horrible skeleton hand that caught me?"

The Damusaun tipped her head. Her cheek flaps wobbled. "What hand?"

"The hand. The . . . giant bony thing back there in the chasm!"

Breal whimpered. Miles hadn't meant to raise his voice to the Dragon Queen, but surely she'd seen it? She'd freed him from it, after all.

"That was no hand, Miles. You were caught in Kwen's roots."

"Kwen? The World Tree?" He squinted up at her. The sun haloed her head in blazing white. "Did Kwen fall . . . here?" he asked.

The Dragon Queen drew a rune in the sand with her claw. "Since the breaking, we have guarded Kwen's remains and watched over his offspring. The greatest descendants grew here in Yaniff, their younger brother and sister Waytrees grew in Jarrosh."

It was hard to imagine a forest here, where miles and miles of barren desert blotched with dry grass led to the rocky foothills. Even the mountainsides were bare.

"I don't see the remains of any trees at all, let alone the remains of a giant one."

The Damusaun nodded toward the pillars.

Miles blinked. "But that's an ancient ruin. Those pillars are made of stone." He'd touched one less than an hour ago. Marble, he was sure of it.

"After Kwen was buried under the earth, a vast forest sprang up here in Yaniff," said the Dragon Queen. "It looked to be many thousands of tall white trees, but we dragons knew they were all shoots growing from Kwen's trunk, still partly living underground. These 'pillars,' as you call them, were once a vast green forest before they were covered in volcanic ash long ago. When they died, their siblings, the azures of Jarrosh, became the oldest living Waytrees of Noor."

She twitched her ears. "The quake awakened our hope, pilgrim. We saw the World Tree move. Kwen cared enough to catch you in his roots. Why do you think he did this?"

"Wh-Why?" Miles repeated. He was lucky to have fallen into the tree's thick white roots, but it didn't mean the World Tree had reached out and caught him. "I don't know why," he admitted.

The Damusaun thrust forward and snapped her jaws, as if to bite off his head. It's one thing to have a master crack a switch across your palms in school and quite another to have a dragon snap her long teeth at you. Breal yelped and fled a few feet back. Miles would have jumped up, too, but his legs were still asleep. He rubbed them hard. Thousands of needles pricked his skin from thigh to heel.

Meer Eason returned with the water. Grateful for the interruption, Miles drank thirstily, emptying the entire pouch. His teacher was prepared to stay, but the Damusaun tipped her head and flicked out her slit tongue. "You will leave us for now, Meer Eason." The Music Master glanced at Miles, then bowed and said, "Come on, Breal."

When they were alone, Miles said, "Damusaun, my mind still isn't clear."

She nodded in agreement.

"And the reason is," he went on more bravely, "I'm worried about Hanna and Taunier. And my little brother still needs to be rescued. I promised my da I'd find him, so I can't be sitting about here in Yaniff. I need you to show me where I can cross over." He stopped, knowing he was babbling. There had to be a way in still.

"You think we abandoned the Kanameer?"

"Not abandoned her, just, well . . ." He gazed up at the Dragon Queen's blazing, yellow eyes. In the stark sunlight, her scales sparkled like gemstones. Whatever came out of his mouth seemed to anger her. "I just think we have to go back after her and the others. I mean, I have to go," he corrected. "Because Hanna's my sister and—"

"We cannot go where she has gone, pilgrim."

"I know you can't go before Breal's Moon night, but I can go."

She shook her head.

A bolt of fear shot up his back. "What do you mean? I've been to Oth before. There must be a—"

"Where were you when we held the Dragon Council?" Smoke huffed from her nostrils.

He was too ashamed to say he'd fallen asleep.

She made a clicking sound with her tongue. "The dragon bridges from Noor to Oth are fallen now."

Heat raced across the desert in waves. Miles's head spun, and he tried not to be sick.

"I have ordered the clan to dig," said the Damusaun.

Miles looked over his shoulder and saw terrows and taberrells flying in and out of the rift he'd been caught in, like bees busy with their hive.

The queen's head swayed. "It will take them some time. Can you walk?"

The nausea he'd felt a moment ago had passed. Miles managed to stand upright, though his knees wobbled. He took shallow breaths to keep his ribs from screaming.

"When youth fails us, we return to ancient things." The Damusaun turned about. "Come, if you wish to see the cave of bones."

The Damusaun called me the Mishtar, friend of dragons, but it will take a lifetime to grow into the name.

—THE MISHTAR, *DRAGON'S WAY*, VOL. I

They hiked another hour on the trail through All Souls Wood, trying to run ahead of the shadow spreading from the deep rift where the worlds were torn. For that was what it was, Hanna learned: a creeping dark growing from that rift. According to the sylth, Yona, the darkness had swallowed all the other lands of Oth, and everyone but a few like herself who'd managed to escape had been caught in a deadly sleep.

Yona was strong of build, with red hair and brows that tilted over deep green eyes. She'd led a handful of sylths, forest creatures, and Othic folk on an arduous journey toward the light. But she eyed the shadow that was moving now across the face of the mountain. "This is all that is left," she said. "We'd thought Mount Esseley and All Souls Wood would be safe, but darkness comes even here."

Hanna shuddered, remembering the sylth boy she'd tried to awaken. He was still asleep, still caught in the dark. She knew it wouldn't be long before the rest of Mount Esseley blackened into endless night. If they were caught, they'd fall into dreamless sleep like the others, lying as still as the dead in the encroaching dark.

"Yona, how long have the lit lands been disappearing?"

"Two moon cycles now."

Two months. Hanna's mind went back to late August, when Tymm was Wind-taken and the Waytrees of Shalem Wood thundered down. On that day she'd not yet known that the Waytrees of Othlore Wood had fallen, too. "It's when the Waytrees in our world began to fall," she said. "Not just in my forest home on Enness Isle, but everywhere."

She tried to imagine the dark wave swallowing the magical sylth kingdom of Attenlore she'd seen last year in western Oth. Her heart raced and her hands went cold as she thought of the darkness engulfing the glimmer cities in all the Othic kingdoms, cities whose very walls shone with light. She imagined the deep shadow blotting out prairie, mountain, and valley in every land, even in the dragonlands of Twarn-Majas, where the Damusaun said the beautiful mountains were made of deep-blue stone.

There were so many places in Oth she'd never had a chance to see, so many magical beings felled and lost.

Carrying Zabith piggyback, Taunier passed a mossy boulder and caught up with Hanna. They were all overcome with exhaustion and hunger, the trail crowded with fauns and sylth folk hefting the youngest children up the path. Tymm rode on Grunn the Troll's left shoulder, and Cilla perched on his right. Both clutched the troll's beard, parting the hairy mass in the middle. Cilla was braiding her half. Her rugs were prized at home, but she wouldn't be able to do much with Grunn's tangled beard.

Farther back, Kevin and a few of the older children hiked soberly alongside the deyas. Evver dragged his large, rooted feet. His head was down, his shoulders hunched. Behind him, deyas leaned against one another, swinging their empty hands as they strained to keep up.

Stopping at a vantage point, Hanna spied a black

void looming over the high mountain ridge, and pointed to it.

Yona shivered. "The Outer Darkness," she said.

Hanna felt chilled looking at it. It was more ominous than the thick shadow creeping along the mountainside. "Why so much worse up there?" she asked.

"The darkness deepens closer to the center of the rift," Yona said. The tallest trees, the ones they needed desperately to reach, were just below that dark-rimmed peak. They talked of turning back, but there was nowhere else to go.

The snowy mountaintop stood white against the weight of blackened space as they hiked closer to it.

"Why do the splitting worlds send this horrid darkness?" Taunier asked. "Why does it put everything in its path to sleep?"

"The two worlds were bound in their making," Yona said. "Even now, what happens in one will affect the other."

"It's not going dark in Noor," he argued.

Zabith tapped him on the head. "There is more than one kind of dark," she said. "It's the loss of magic in Noor that casts a shadow here."

"Ah," said Grunn. "What's bound is bound." He crashed his meaty fists together. "We trolls knew the dark was comin' afore it began."

Yona scoffed, "We sylth surely would ken this loss before you."

"We'd a song my lady." He drew his shoulders back, Tymm and Cilla rising higher as he did so. He sang gruffly in Trollish. Yona translated for him:

> *"Darkness grow and darkness take,*
> *Till none in Oth are left awake.*
> *Ending worlds can nigh begin,*
> *Till Arnun tree entwines with Kwen."*

"The World Tree?" Taunier looked unconvinced.

Hanna recalled the lines Miles had pointed to in the Falconer's book: *The great Mishtar held that one day the heart of the World Tree might still be awakened, and Kwen and Arnun be rejoined.* Still, would that work with a long-dead tree split for thousands of years? How could it come alive and join again?

She'd rather rely on Evver. She knew him. Trusted him. Still, she wasn't sure the deyas, weak as they were now, could root down deep and help the Waytrees bridge the worlds long enough for her to bring the children back to Noor. Her head began to ache again. Since the Damusaun had named her Kanameer, everyone had counted on her: dragons, deyas, the Wind-taken children. Even the few Othic folk who'd managed to escape the growing dark seemed to be expecting her to help them.

Half an hour later, they reached a small grassy clearing and waited for the deyas to catch up. Evver crested the hill. His feet barely touched the clearing when he turned off the path and walked out among a stand of redwoods. Evver had been hunched over, pressing himself hard to make the climb. Now he drew up tall before the stately trees like a plant unfurling in the sun. Hanna held her breath.

Spreading his arms wide, Evver gave an ancient call, a sound like river water.

He paused, listening to the silent mountain, then said, "No deyas in this ancient grove. We will enter here."

Hanna wanted to grip Taunier's arm. She tugged a long blade of grass.

A sigh moved through the deyas.

"Yes, here." Another deya held up her hands.

The whispering branches seemed to welcome the deyas in one by one. Hanna watched, needing them to go, not wanting them to leave.

Evver waited for all to be safely housed before turning to a grand redwood that looked tall enough to have reached its two-thousandth year. He gestured to Hanna. "Come with me to the door."

She left the others in the clearing. Evver took her hand, or, rather, she wrapped hers about his smallest finger. His skin was cool as winter leaves when the snow dresses the branches. When they reached the redwood, no door was visible.

Under the blowing boughs, Evver let go of her hand and said, "We will root down here as long as we can, but we both know we cannot do this long."

Hanna nodded. She knew the rift was too great now for such a small grove to bind it.

Evver said, "If the worlds can be rejoined, you must find the way to do it in the time you have left, Kanameer."

His stern look passed through the brave guise she'd been wearing to hide her deep misgivings underneath. *She* must find the way? How could he expect her to do that? She wasn't even sure she was the Kanameer. She'd accepted the name only because so many of them had seemed to want her to.

"How can I? I don't know what to do or how to get back across myself with so much of Oth already gone."

"Say it, Kanameer. Tell yourself who you are."

"But," she whispered, "what if I'm not?"

"Do you believe in the power of the Old Magic?"

"The Old Magic." Hanna tasted the words, the magic that eOwey had sent out in song at the making of the worlds.

"It is all around you, and it is in you—small as breath and great as mountain wind. Do you feel it?"

"Aye," said Hanna. When she was with Evver, she felt the magic near.

"And you wish to serve?"

"I've never minded that."

"Then what troubles you?"

"I'm not . . . a leader. I'm not sure I have this . . . power everyone thinks I have." She felt herself blushing.

"*Essha*," said Evver. "You flew to Jarrosh in the Whirl Storm, dreamwalked for us and the dragons, brought us through the caverns of Mount Olone, rescued the

Wind-taken, called the great wind spirits to blow us down to All Souls Wood, and now you have helped us find our new grandtrees. Who but the Kanameer could have done all this?"

Hanna thought a moment. It did sound remarkable when he put it that way. "But I don't have the power to . . . I didn't always know what I was doing," she admitted. "And I didn't do it alone."

"I am the Azure King, yet you helped me along the way as I aided you."

Hanna saw Evver asking her to lead the deyas to All Souls Wood; she saw him rescuing her and Zabith from the falling azure, humming to his folk when they were weary, bringing the Wind-taken children down from the roots, comforting the youngest ones when they were afraid.

"Aye," whispered Hanna. "You were always quick to help all of us."

"This is what a Deya King does, Hannalyn. But I did not act alone. Why do you think the Kanameer must act alone? You needed Taunier's light, Zabith's vision, and I suspect you will need the youngest child who was Wind-taken before you are through. Indeed your 'power,' as you call it, is nothing more than the Old Magic. You could not have led us if you had not welcomed it and let it flow through you like the wind."

The breeze of All Souls Wood whispered between them. Everything she'd done as the Kanameer had felt so much like guesswork. But all along as she had found herself relying on her friends, her sense of direction, and her desire to help the ones she loved, the way she was meant to take seemed to open before her again and again. Was this what Evver meant?

The deya gave her a piercing look. "*Essha*, Kanameer. I must leave." He gestured toward the others in the clearing. "They need you. You will need to know who you are to go where you are going."

She knew Evver had to leave her, but she didn't want him to go.

"Kanameer. Say it with your mouth," he said. "Listen and allow it to settle deeper in your roots. Let the knowing of it feed you."

Hanna knew he was right. She couldn't let her uncertainty hold her down anymore. She would need to believe she was the Kanameer to let the Old Magic continue to flow through her and guide her. All Evver was asking her to do now was say the word aloud, to *essha* it, the deya word for "listen and understand."

She looked into his shining eyes, green as forest pools.

"I am the Kanameer," she said. It was a quiet pronouncement, but the word came smooth and sounded like a song inside her. She said it again, a little louder this time.

More than the dragons' crown, more than the golden terrow cape, the word wrapped its sound around her. And for the first time since she'd heard the title from the Damusaun, Hanna let herself believe it. The belief was as fleeting as the glint of sunlight in Evver's eyes, but a spark had come and, with it, the promise of some future warmth.

"Hannalyn," he said. "Kanameer. *Essha* now. You have far and far to go to find the light beyond the dark. But feel the ground beneath your feet as you walk. Heart to root, remember the ones who hold you up."

"I will remember." She wanted to say more to him, but already Evver was fading from his long journey. He'd stayed too long outside his tree.

"Go now." She motioned to the redwood.

He spoke no more before entering the trunk. Hanna

thought she heard a sigh as he disappeared, though it might have been the wind whispering through the branches. She did not turn back yet, but stared a long while at the rust-red bark dressed in pale sunlight. *You are home now,* she thought. Her heart ached with joy for him, sorrow for herself—one pain that branched in two directions. She would miss the deya and the courage he gave her.

Hanna rejoined Taunier and Meer Zabith. Together they made their way toward the little grassy clearing where the Wind-taken and Oth folk waited. Evver's words echoed in her heart as she walked. She didn't know how she was supposed to bridge the worlds or how she would overcome the darkness in the place where Noor and Oth were torn. But she sensed she must climb higher up the mountain, to the place the Oth folk feared most, the peak where the last lit land of Oth here in All Souls Wood met the deepest part of the Outer Darkness.

THIRTY-SIX

SHARDS

*You have far and far to go to find the light
beyond the dark.*

—Evver, the Azure King

Hanna led the party to a rocky plateau, near the highest peak on Mount Esseley, where the cliff touched the sheer black edge of the Outer Darkness. Stepping near, she felt its dying breath all around her, in the earth and dust, and the faintest smell of sea, drowned in a dark without wave or shore. She wanted to run as soon as she saw the night that was not night, the starless, moonless edge of dark. But her inner sense had led her to this hard ground littered with shiny, black, sharp-edged stones.

The moment she set foot on the cliff, she heard the stones speaking. Words whispered one upon the other, stacked words, strewn words, flowing wild and disjointed into her ears. She passed through the scattered rocks, listening, trying to make sense of them.

Pieces my again gather lover Kwen me build reach my help roots bring Oth broken Noor to Tesha from broken the Yoven bind world to again world join.

Each stone spoke a single word, so all the words came in a jumble. Hanna paced back and forth, trying to make sense of it, until she gave up and shouted, "Slow down. What are you trying to say?"

Her strained voice silenced the stones and startled Yona, who stood, arms crossed, watching her. Hanna looked at the stones on the ground. Where were the words now? Taunier crested the steep trail, panting as he carried Zabith. He placed her on the plateau, and she dusted off her clothes. Her shawl had nearly vanished; a few green threads remained draped across her bony shoulders. The children huddled around her and Taunier, looking about them.

Taunier brushed off his hands. "What are we doing here, Hanna?"

Hanna read the frightened faces, sylth and troll and human. The Outer Darkness was too close, the emptiness too frightening for them to stay here. She pointed at the ground and said, "The stones were talking."

It sounded very strange, but she didn't try to soften it with explanation—she didn't even understand it herself.

Meer Zabith and the children fanned out across the plateau, stopping here and there to pick up a sharp stone. She could hear them talking excitedly, their words overlapping as they interrupted one another.

"Over here," Tymm called to Cilla.

"This is a gathering place," said Hanna. It was, after all, what Zabith and the children were doing. Tymm had picked up a glassy black shard and was showing it to Cilla. She pulled another, smaller one from her pocket and cradled it in her palms. They exchanged the stones and scanned the ground for more.

Taunier passed them by, heading for the dark wall.

What was he up to? Hanna ran after him, calling, "Watch out." She caught the edge of his cloak, trying to draw him back. Taunier snapped his fingers, and a flame hovered just above his fingertip, as yellow as a honeybee. He raised his arm near the edge as if to see beyond, but the little fire did not lessen the dark, nor was there a reflection as there might be against a shining black wall, only emptiness.

Frowning, he turned to Yona. "You said the foothills

below this ridge met the shoreline of the Yannara Sea. But there's nothing here."

"The Outer Darkness grows," said Yona. "All of Oth disappears." Beside her, Grunn let out a groan. The sound seemed to propel Yona forward; either that or Grunn had given her a push.

"It's not safe this close to the edge of the rift," Yona said. "We should go back now while we can."

She spoke with authority, and Hanna fought the urge to agree. She was afraid. She wanted to get away from the dark wall, too, but she'd felt drawn up the mountain to this spot. And Evver had said to pay attention to that inner sense of direction she'd been following, to lean into the Old Magic that whispered quietly inside her.

"I am the Kanameer," she said. "We will wait here a little longer."

eOwey, please let my sense be right, she prayed. There was a soft *click-clack* behind her, like children playing marbles. She turned around to see Tymm, near the edge of the Outer Darkness, placing his shard beside Cilla's. *"Tesha yoven,"* he whispered.

"Tesha yoven," Cilla repeated, placing another shard on top.

They giggled, heads bowed close together. They were making something, though Hanna couldn't tell yet what it was. Watching Tymm's swift hands reminded her of the pieces he'd glued together the day she'd broken Mother's platter, of other times when he'd mended fences, woven rope from grass, fixed the leaky water bucket, or used Da's tools to make toys and gifts for the family.

The other children joined Tymm and Cilla, stacking stone on stone. They were moving quickly, hands dancing, talking to one another.

"Here."

"No, this one. That's right."

"Oh, give me that one."

They all seemed to know where to put the shards, not helter-skelter in a pile, but fitting them just so like puzzle pieces. And they *were* fitting them together, with no space in between, so perfectly it seemed that they were joined. A tower was growing taller and broader before her eyes. Soon it formed into a black trunk with branches growing from the sides.

"What is it?" whispered Taunier.

Hanna picked up a shard. It was cool and hard in her hand, but it was wood, not stone at all. She held it out to him. "Remember the dreamwalk I told you and Miles about on the *Leena*?"

"The black tree." Taunier looked both startled and excited.

"Thank you," said Hanna.

"For what?" He frowned, surprised.

"You said I shouldn't get in the way of what Tymm came here to do."

Taunier wasn't used to compliments. He gave her a single nod and looked away.

She caught Yona's questioning expression and tried to explain. "I had a dreamwalk after my little brother was Wind-taken. I saw him climbing a great black tree with other children; he was shaping a face in the giant trunk."

Yona went on tiptoe to whisper in Grunn's ear. He leaned down to listen before pointing over Hanna's shoulder. Tymm and Kevin were climbing up the thick low branches. More children followed, building the tree higher and higher.

There must have been magic in their hands, for the tree seemed to be filling out quickly. It grew from five feet to ten and more. When it reached twenty feet, the children were still adding to the trunk and building more and more branches. They whooped with excitement, passing shards up the trunk, climbing higher to fit them into place. Hanna had to crook her neck to watch them.

Tymm clung to a bough with one hand as he ran his other hand along the smooth black trunk. His fingers moved, pressing, shaping—a face began to form.

"Watch out up there!" Hanna called nervously. She was answered with the sound of her brother's laughter. She spotted Cilla shaping what appeared to be a mouth in the broad trunk.

Overhead, Kevin was building an eyelid over the second large eye.

A beautiful giantess began to appear. Hanna held her breath. The woman's features were soft and strong, her eyes set wide apart, her nose broad and flat, her lips full. The tree woman, all of shining black, was coming slowly into view.

The Wind-taken had come a long way to build her.

Hanna had discounted Tymm's gift back home on Enness Isle. Her little brother was handy, that was all. She'd never counted it as magic. She saw the wrongness of that now. If she'd looked a little closer at Tymm and the others earlier, she might have been able to see why they were chosen. By age six, Cilla had become a gifted weaver, selling small rugs and blankets for a goodly price at the Brim market. And hadn't Kevin said the three children from Othlore were at the top of their class in Restoration Magic?

Making, mending, restoring; from the littlest to the largest, they were all doing that now. But who had chosen them from every land, brought them on the east wind? Hanna still didn't know.

The large head was fully formed now, with long, silky hair that flowed down her neck and back.

"Arnun. World Tree," Yona said, gazing into its branches with awe. The other Othic folk were murmuring among themselves, so the name came across the air in small waves. "Arnun, wife of Kwen of old."

They all went down on their knees before Arnun.

Tasting the mountain dust in her mouth, Hanna rose again with the rest. The branches were moving now. Arnun gazed down at the hollow places still in her trunk and said, "Gather the rest of me."

The children worked even faster. Hanna and Taunier collected more black wood fragments and gave them to the Wind-taken, who nimbly climbed about her branches, adding pieces here and there. Arnun sighed contentedly while they worked, as if she were being bathed and dressed by many attendants and liked the feel of it quite well. She now stood more than forty feet tall, and still she was growing, her shining black figure very much alive against the darkness behind.

"Who among you heard my fragments calling?"

Hanna stepped forward and bowed. "I heard them speaking, Arnun."

"You are the Kanameer."

"I am." Hanna marveled at how easily she said this now.

"So it was you who led the clever-handed ones here. The ones the Old Magic blew east from your world to ours," said Arnun.

"The Old Magic was the one who sent the great wind?"

"None else would have the power to gather the ones who could restore me. The Old Magic works to keep things whole. How can you not know this, Kanameer?"

"It's just that when the east wind came, I thought it was evil. It took the children from us. We were afraid." Hanna remembered her terror when the wind stole

Tymm, the gust that had blown her down when she had tried to stop it. She was just getting used to the idea that the wind was a part of the Old Magic. It had carefully chosen children from many lands of Noor to help rebuild this half of the World Tree.

None of the Wind-taken had been harmed; they seemed, in fact, quite happy to be doing the task they'd come here to do. One boy was whistling as he pieced together long black roots at the base of Arnun's trunk.

Arnun said, "Tell me how it went in your world." She said this as if she expected a story to entertain her while she was being groomed. Hanna spoke of the long journey that had brought them here, of everyone in Oth and Noor who'd done their part to bring the Wind-taken to Arnun. She told Arnun about Miles and the meers who'd sailed from Othlore, and the dragons who'd brought her to the azure deyas of Jarrosh.

"I *essha* this," said Arnun at last. "The dragons guard Kwen far away in Noor."

"The dragons can return home to Oth if we find a way to join the worlds again."

"Join." Arnun said this wistfully, as if she were considering the word for the first time. "I reach for Kwen, and he is lost to me. We are the same World Tree. I in him and he in me. But our time has long been over."

She blinked her large, dark eyes at Hanna. "It is the age of the azure trees. They bridge Noor and Oth together now. But you would not have come here if they were strong."

Hanna covered her mouth and glanced at Taunier's troubled face. She'd left that part out, not knowing how to tell Arnun.

She summoned her courage to say the rest. "The azures are all dead. The Cutters poisoned them and chopped them down. They didn't know the azures were the greatest trees in Noor." That wasn't completely true. They'd wanted the best and largest trees for timber. The Damusaun had warned them what would happen, and the Cutters hadn't listened. She corrected herself. "They didn't understand or believe that cutting them down would make all the other Waytrees fall."

"Have humans lost all contact with the Old Magic?" said Arnun. "Do they not see how we all touch one another?" Lines stemmed across Arnun's face. Hanna was afraid to answer, worried Arnun might crack and break apart again. But the tree was waiting.

"They . . . wanted the best timber."

"Timber." Arnun shuddered. Her trunk shook, and pieces began to fall.

Hanna put out her hands. "Don't let yourself break again, Arnun."

The children climbed down the branches and scattered. Gathering the newly fallen wood, they scaled the lower branches and began to patch the hollow places in the tree.

"It was not yet time for the azures' age to end," said Arnun. "There are no trees with roots deep enough to replace them. And so the breaking of the worlds."

"If the children build you, Arnun, will you be able to bring the worlds together again?"

"*Tesha yoven.* This is what the children came to do." Arnun's voice was soft and proud as a mother's when she spoke of the Wind-taken. "But the magic weakens with the worlds so far apart. Even the Old Magic needed the help of the azure roots to cradle the Wind-taken, until the Kanameer could come and bring them the rest of the way here."

Hanna trembled, thinking of how delicate the balance was, how easily she could have failed her quest. It had taken all her courage to leap down into the black hole on Mount Olone. If Evver had not encouraged her, she would have turned away. Tymm and the other Wind-taken would have remained forever cradled in the azure roots, waiting for the one who would not come.

"We are here now, Arnun," she said. "We can help you bind the worlds."

"I cannot bind the broken alone. Kwen's heart has hardened into stone."

"Are you sure?" asked Taunier.

Arnun peered down at him a moment. "You are the Fire Herd," she said.

Taunier bowed.

"You can warm a heart of stone, Fire Herd, but you cannot bring it back to life once it is dead. The future grows behind me, and it is Darkness Come."

Hanna's throat ached. They'd come too late. She tried to hold back her tears. Was it all to end here, with a dark wave taking everything and everyone she loved? A sob was building in her chest, but she would not let it break. Evver's last words rode atop the wave instead. They came out unsteadily, but loudly enough for Arnun. "The Azure King told me, *Feel the ground beneath your feet as you walk. Heart to root, remember the ones who hold you up."*

Arnun sighed. "I cannot find Kwen's roots, Kanameer. He is in Noor. My own roots will not reach that far across the dark."

Hanna turned. Even as she and Taunier were addressing Arnun, the Oth folk, Zabith, and the Wind-taken were collecting more shining black wood pieces behind them. "The Old Magic called the children here to build you again, Arnun. They can extend your roots."

Taunier tugged her shoulder. "No," he whispered. "Don't ask the children to go out there." His eyes darted briefly toward the Outer Darkness looming behind Arnun.

"It's our only way home," said Hanna. "Evver and the deyas can't hold the worlds together for long. Oth will darken, and we'll all disappear with it, unless the World Tree joins again."

"The wind spirits could take us home," he whispered.

"Can you see the coastline? It should be just down there at the base of the mountain." She pointed to the wall of dark. "Yannara Sea is lost. Where is Noorushh blowing now?"

Hanna realized as she said this why it was so still and

silent here on the cliff. In the coming dark, even the wind had died. Taunier seemed to read the frightened look in her eyes. He clenched the muscles in his jaw and drew his shoulders back.

"Too late to reach out," Arnun said above them. "The darkness moves against my back. I lose all feeling where it touches me."

Hanna heard scrabbling sounds coming from her rucksack. Thriss wriggled out and flew up to a high, black branch.

"Thriss, come back here, now!"

"What is that pip doing here?" demanded Yona.

"Nothing. I didn't mean to bring her, only—"

Yona's eyes narrowed as she pointed at Thriss. Hanna caught the sylth's menacing look and jumped in front of her. "Please don't hurt her. She's just a hatchling."

Arnun brought the branch with Thriss up to her eyes for a closer look. "Little terrow," she said with a chuckle, "have you come to guard me?"

"Yessss," Thriss answered. She took off and circled the enormous tree, blowing a long, blue flame before her.

"Thriss!" Tymm shouted.

His friends joined in, "Thriss! Thriss!"

The tiny dragon flitted higher and flipped over in the air. A deep, rich laugh poured from Arnun's mouth.

Hanna went down on her knees, jamming shard after shard into her pockets. "Quick!" she called. "Bring those pieces here. Arnun needs roots. Longer roots!"

At the base of Arnun's smooth trunk, Hanna passed Tymm the black wood fragments and went for more as his small hands feverishly built long, spiraling roots into the dark.

THIRTY-SEVEN
THE HEART OF THE WORLD TREE

After Kwen was buried under earth,
a vast forest sprang up here in Yaniff.

—THE DAMUSAUN

I t had taken many hours to dig into the side of the
crevasse. The dragons followed the coiled white roots
deep into the earth. Young and old, large and small,
all claws were put to work delving out a great cave that
cradled the base of an enormous tree trunk.

The Damusaun flew Miles, Eason, and Breal through
the gaping hole and into the cavern. Sunlight slowly
seeped into the opening, and the wind blew in, as the
dragons came in ones and twos. Wings rustled as taberrells and terrows folded them against their sides. The
younglings backed away from the trunk and huddled by
the adults along the rocky walls, all taking in the World
Tree. Silence filled the cave.

The massive bone-white trunk lay on its side. Most of the felled tree was still buried in the earth, but the part they'd uncovered was imposing enough, broad and heavy as a toppled fortress. Gigantic coiling roots plunged sideways and down, and one stretched out the open mouth of the cave. Miles noticed the pale light bathing the root that fanned out like a giant skeletal hand. He rubbed his sore back where the white wood had pinched him too tightly.

Day was ebbing. The shaft of sunlight that entered the cave caught the dancing dust motes about the base of the trunk. How tall it would be standing on end, he could not imagine. The mammoth base was magnificent. Breal nudged his hand, his tail wagging slowly. Miles glanced at the dragons lining the walls of the cave. They seemed to need to hold their distance from the male half of the World Tree, part of the living tree their ancestors had guarded from the beginning.

Miles kept his right hand on Breal's soft head and waited. Tonight the moon would rise full: Breal's Moon. It was the night of crossing for the dragons, but how could a dead tree, however grand, offer a way to Oth? A tiny red beetle crawled along the patterned bark, like a brave explorer in a new world. Did Kwen's bark feel warm as wood or cold as stone? He'd like to know the answer to that, but no one, not even the Damusaun, had dared touch the mighty trunk.

Sunlight abandoned part of the cave mouth, and shadows shifted in the cavern. The change seemed to signal the queen, who bowed near the roots. "Dragon Bridge, great World Tree. We have brought the one you saved."

Miles tensed. Why was she speaking about him like this? He'd been ready to fight, to do anything and everything to prove himself to the Damusaun. But falling into those jutting roots had been sheer accident. And anyway, what did she think he could do with the tree now?

The she-dragon brushed her wing against the trunk. "Kwen," she whispered. "Noor and Oth are split in two. We need you to awaken and bind the worlds again."

"NoorOth. NoorOth. Bridge the worlds," the dragons chanted softly, their voices rough yet smooth as rapids.

Miles thought of what the queen had said: *When youth fails, we return to ancient things.*

"Kwen," said the Damusaun. "*Abb nayn kwii onan. Zuss.* We gift you with our warmth. Awaken."

"*Abb nayn kwii onan. Zuss,*" chanted the rest, and they sent blue flames all around the great trunk to warm the tree to life. Miles ran his hand along Breal's neck and watched the shining blue against the white surface of the bark.

"Awaken," he whispered. Their flames might still warm the tree to wakefulness. Surely, this magnificent tree could bind the worlds.

Some of the taberrells began to sing, while the rest went on sending out streams of fire. The Damusaun ran the backside of her claw along Kwen's white trunk, waiting as a healer waits to sense a change in a patient, as the dragons sang their song again and again. At last the queen shook her head. "He is cold."

Eason spoke. "Damusaun." She did not look his way, but she was listening.

"There is a line from an old desert song I learned as a boy. It says, '*The heart awakens from within.*'"

"We know this song," said the Dragon Queen, "but we would only damage Kwen if we cut into his center ring to find his heart."

Miles's flesh prickled as he watched the red beetle disappear into a small crack. A strange idea was forming in his mind. "I'll go in, Damusaun," he said impulsively.

"How would you do that?"

"There was a student at the meers' school on Oth thirty years ago, a girl named Yarta who could shape-shift into smaller and smaller things, birds, mice, and insects." Miles turned to Eason for support and met a frown of concern. He pressed on.

"Once," he continued, "she shifted smaller still into the song lines of eOwey, the vibrations all of us are made of." Surely, the dragons and his teacher knew far more about eOwey's life-song than he? Hadn't the Damusaun spoken of the Old Magic that connected all things? "I could do that myself. Shape-shift very small. Form into vibration and go into the heart of the tree."

The queen lowered her head. "This human girl, this Yarta. She saw with dragon's eyes."

"What do you mean, Damusaun?"

"We dragons see this vibration. I see you now that way, Miles, and though you stand very still, the millions upon millions of glittering motes that gather to be you are dancing." Her eyes were bright as she looked about the cave. "We are all this, my brother and sister dragons, this cave, the great World Tree. All dance within vibration in the song and breath of eOwey."

She tipped her head and peered down at Miles. "Do you see this?"

Miles frowned, thinking. He'd felt a kind of tingling when he played his ervay, as if every part of himself were coming awake, but he didn't see it—he felt it. Once when his breathing stilled in meditation he thought he'd caught a glimpse of movement, specks of glitter swirling, but the vision had vanished in three breaths. It was only when he'd entered the lit lands of Oth that he'd seen everything around him sparkling, thrumming. The very air had seemed to dance with life.

The Dragon Queen was waiting for his answer, and, with her, Meer Eason and all the dragons by the white World Tree.

"I saw this dance once in Oth, but I cannot see it now, Damusaun," he confessed.

"Your eyes are too small," she said. "But this learned meer you called Yarta had vision. What became of her?"

Miles wiped his sweaty palms on his shirt. Yarta had been a student, not a meer, but he didn't correct the Damusaun. There was more to Yarta's story, parts he'd rather not tell. The second time Yarta had tried the experiment she'd vanished into thin air and never returned.

Meer Eason knew the truth, for Yarta's disappearance was told as a cautionary tale to all the first-year students. Since that time the art of shape-shifting was considered much too dangerous to teach to apprentices.

Eason crossed his arms. "You should not do this, Miles."

"You are my Music Master," answered Miles. "But I'm a meer in my own right now."

Meer Eason looked alarmed. He turned to the queen. "It is a difficult shift, and surely the most dangerous kind."

"Damusaun," Miles said hesitantly. "Yarta vanished the second time she tried the shift. She never came back."

There was an uncomfortable rustling in the cave as Meer Eason spoke, casting more doubt. "Even Wielder Meers who have practiced Othic meditation years and years to understand what Yarta did have not dared to follow where she went."

Miles hadn't done his regular meditation practice since they'd left Othlore. If the Wielder Meers who were skilled shape-shifters couldn't make the change . . .

"Are you sure you wish to try this?" asked the Damusaun.

"Yes, Damusaun." Blood sang in his ears. "Hanna, Tymm, and Taunier are in Oth with the other Wind-taken." He glanced at Meer Eason. "If this is the only way to rebuild the bridge that binds the worlds and bring them back to Noor, I have to try."

His heart wanted it. His body did not. He was terrified at the thought of shrinking down smaller and smaller.

The Damusaun stepped closer. He caught the mixture of fennel, wet stones, and azure needles that was her familiar dragon scent. She had not stopped him when he wanted to shift into a dragon's form and fight. He knew she would not stop him now. She would let him choose the part he was to play.

Miles slipped the leather strap of his ervay pouch over his neck and handed it to Meer Eason.

Meer Eason touched his brow and dipped his head, acknowledging a fellow meer. He, too, would let him go.

The Music Master held the ervay over his head. "For Miles to shift into pure sound, we will have to play and sing from the time that he departs until his return. That was the way Yarta found her way from formlessness to form again the first time she shifted. The song cannot stop, not even for a moment, or he will be lost."

Miles was wracked with wave upon wave of fear. Every shift he'd made thus far was to a larger, stronger animal, and he'd relished the feeling of growing power. It went against everything in him to consider becoming a weak creature or, worse, to slip into nothingness. Yet here he was volunteering to do just that, and the lives of those he loved, maybe even the binding of the worlds, depended on it.

I have to make this work, he thought, but he feared this shift more than he'd ever feared anything. What if he vanished? Was lost forever? Miles stiffened his jaw, hoping Meer Eason and the dragons wouldn't detect the naked terror coursing through his body.

The Music Master put a comforting arm about his shoulder. Miles had one more thing to say before the shift, something for Eason's ears alone. "Sir," he whispered, "I've not kept up my meditation practice," he confessed.

"I know this," said Eason. "But you have played your music. It's that you can rely on."

Miles nodded, unconvinced. He whispered, "I've never shifted into anything smaller than myself before." He couldn't hide that from his teacher. "I need to . . . try that first," he admitted, motioning toward the tiny red beetle scuttling along the trunk.

"All right," whispered Eason. "Go on. I'll protect you."

The insect looked ugly. Repugnant. Miles swallowed. He used to think the stories about Yarta's shifts were stupid, the pointless games of a naïve girl, whose senseless death had left a legacy of fear and ignorance behind. Now he had to rely on Yarta's experiments, and on the one time she'd managed to return. He had to stake his life on it.

His heart drummed and, strangely, the one person he wanted to see now was Hanna. She'd seen him shift last year from boy to beast to boy again. She knew him better than anyone and still thought him brave. They all needed him to awaken the tree, to hold the worlds together, but the reason he must go, even if it meant his life, was because of her. Not because she was the Kanameer, but because she was his sister.

"Are you ready?" asked Meer Eason.

"Wait." Miles looked up at the Damusaun. "If I do find the World Tree's heart, what am I supposed to do to awaken him?"

"No one can tell you that, pilgrim."

The dragons' blue flames had died down, and the cave

was cold and quiet. Miles could see the breath misting from his mouth. He ran his hand along Breal's soft fur, letting his fingers say good-bye, before he addressed the Damusaun again.

"I'll go now."

Meer Eason began to play a simple childlike tune called "Merry-Go-Round" that made Miles smile. He'd need an easy melody to shift to something small, and Eason knew that. Eyes on the red beetle, Miles imagined himself shrinking down, envisioning a small, rounded back, hard and shell-like, tiny legs crawling up a great white tree. He let the tune take him even as he felt himself shrinking.

He closed his eyes. Panic swept through him as he grew smaller and smaller. Eyes open. He saw Meer Eason's feet. They were mountainous. He spread his tiny insect wings, flitted to the tree, and landed near his fellow beetle. The ridges in the white bark were hill-like. The beetle was traversing along a sharp-edged crevice just ahead of him. Folding his wings, he listened again to the song Meer Eason was playing and let his thoughts flow.

Quava-arii. Ever changing. You shifted smaller to make sure you could do it without losing yourself. You've done that, and you're all here, even in this tiny shape. Nothing's missing.

The thought soothed him. If he could shift so small and still be Miles, then he could go smaller, down to a flea or even . . . sound waves.

eOwey, help me. I don't want to lose myself.

He had no picture in his mind to shift to. No animal or insect. He had to let the song itself take him. The tune began to change as Eason slid into the dragon song they'd offered Kwen in the hollow cave. And now the voices that rose with the ervay were rumbling dragon voices. *Abb nayn kwii onan. Zuss. Tesha yoven.*

Awaken. Bind the Broken. Miles let the chant flow all around him in a river that carried him along in a warm current. It was like the time he'd played as a seal in the Morrow Sea, only more so. He left the body of the beetle and slowly let go. He was sound and wave, and still he was Miles. The surprise thrilled him.

Voices carried him, rising, falling. Miles willed himself to move faster within the song and found he could do that. From high notes to low, he did one flip and two and three. He was completely free. The happiness he'd felt swimming in his seal form and later flying on a dragon's back was nothing next to this.

The song mellowed, and he fell into its easy rhythm.

It was a new tune he'd not heard before, but that didn't matter; he could play and move within the sound as he circled his way around the rings, deeper and deeper into the heart of the tree.

The journey was near and far, and he knew straightaway when he'd reached the center ring.

> *Show me your heart, Kwen,*
> *Show your heart to me.*
> *Show me your heart, Kwen,*
> *And I will set you free.*
> *Show me your heart, Kwen,*
> *Show your heart to me.*
> *Show me your heart, Kwen,*
> *Life in the great World Tree.*

This was the song the dragons sang and the sound Miles rode as he searched. With the surrounding song, he lost himself inside the music, lost his worry, his loneliness, his need to prove himself, lost everything, yet he was not lost.

Miles didn't know how this was so, but it was so. The tune carried him and was him, and he belonged.

I in you and you in me, the dragons were singing in tune with the ervay. They were all inside the song of eOwey. He knew it now as he rode the sound waves. He would find the heart of the tree and awaken him for Hanna, for Tymm, for Taunier, for the dragons, the deyas, and the sylth folk of Oth, for all of them and everyone who lived and longed for both worlds to be gathered in.

THIRTY-EIGHT
ROOTS

*Feel the ground beneath your feet as
you walk. Heart to root, remember
the ones who hold you up.*

—EVVER, THE AZURE KING

The starless black was dead silent. The air felt so
thick it was hard to move hand or foot, hard at
times even to breathe. Hanna clung to Arnun's roots; all
that held her up in the vast, unending void. The only way
she could keep herself from retreating back to the safety
of the cliff was to fill her eyes with Taunier. He balanced
on a thick root just ahead, his hands waving as he fought
the Outer Darkness with small, bright bursts of fire. The
flames shed light on the kneeling children as they pieced
together Arnun's roots.

On the cliff behind them, Thriss breathed a slender
blue jet as she circled Arnun's trunk. The Fire Herd and
the little pip were their only source of light and warmth in

the frigid gloom. Hanna drew another fragment from her pocket and watched Tymm's soiled fingers with wonder as he pressed the piece snugly into place. Broken things were just a puzzle to him—things he could rejoin with grace and ease and glue, only here no glue was needed, for Arnun melded the pieces and filled them with vibrant life, once they were properly joined.

The root bridge lengthened, and still the void extended on and on. *You have far and far to go to find the light beyond the dark.* Had Evver known they would walk out over the abyss on nothing but roots? Had he seen ahead and glimpsed her doing this, the way she'd glimpsed the Wind-taken building Arnun?

A song began as they built the root bridge, and the one leading the song was Arnun, her voice deep as the night:

> *"Show me your heart, Kwen,*
> *Show your heart to me.*
> *Show me your heart, Kwen,*
> *Life in the great World Tree.*
> *Long have I journeyed to find you,*
> *Long have I waited to see,*

All that I love remembered,
Held in the great World Tree."

It was a love song, but the love was more than that of a husband and wife. It was the love between those who'd been torn apart, those who longed beyond all things to see each other again. Ahead of the group, Taunier herded his blazing light. If the roots should fail to reach the World Tree in Noor, could she let him disappear without ever reaching out to him? Would the last thing she saw be simply his back?

Hanna stood and walked carefully along a thick root. Fall to the left or right and she would plummet to her death, but she had to walk this far. The song had circled round again, the words repeating the refrain:

"Long have I journeyed to find you,
Long have I waited to see,
All that I love remembered . . ."

It was a thousand miles and a hand's reach to touch him on the shoulder. Taunier turned slowly and looked down at her.

"Hanna?"

"If this is hello, then hello. If this is good-bye . . ."

She framed his face with her hands, brought it closer to hers, kissed him on the mouth. He did not draw back as she had feared but leaned into her, his lips barely parting.

"Show me your heart, Kwen,
Show your heart to me."

Light danced about their heads. Taunier put his hand behind the back of her neck and drew her closer to him. His lips tasted of salt and fresh rain on green leaves. His skin was cool as wind, but his mouth was warm. And there was fire there.

They were still lost in the kiss when a towering white tree loomed ahead. And as Arnun's tendrils touched Kwen's roots, a spear of brilliant light pierced the dark below. In Taunier's embrace, Hanna watched the breaking dawn spreading golden light east to west. It seemed as if a great black cloth were being drawn back as mile on mile of luminescent colors washed over Oth. Mountains, meadows, and valleys appeared below. Hanna glanced to the left. Beyond the base of Mount Esseley, the Yannara

Sea shone copper bright and turquoise, the colors of dragon scales.

One by one the children wiped off their hands and stood, eyes wide. Hanna waited breathless as the rent between the worlds healed and the Outer Darkness died away to the birthing of the light. Across the lands below, the folk of Oth who had slept in darkness until the waking of the world would rise now from dreamless sleep to a new day.

Arnun's long black roots entwined the great white tree. Taunier and Hanna's fingers interlaced, and they were the first to step from Oth to Noor.

"Show me your heart, Kwen-Arnun." The song went on, though some dragons stopped their singing to thump their tails and cheer as the Kanameer and the Fire Herd crossed back into Noor in the place where the two worlds joined.

In Noor the ground trembled as the World Tree grew dizzily upward, breaking through earth and intertwining in the sunlit sky.

Black tree. White tree. Root to root. Stem to branch to trunk embracing. Oth and Noor together, fitting as two hands fit, as lovers fit. And all was yes and yes.

THIRTY-NINE

SALT WATER

Those tears were hard-won treasure saved up over a lifetime.

—GREAT-UNCLE ENOCH

Hanna sang with the dragons encircling Kwen-Arnun, where the great World Tree branched high into the sky. Five or six hundred feet tall, the black-and-white-entwined trunk reached higher than any cathedral, growing beyond measure of any living thing she'd ever seen in either world. The mighty branches forked out to millions of smaller ones leafed in green and gold.

Beneath the World Tree, the ground swelled with life. Flowering grasses spread green over the parched desert land. There was beauty all around, but Hanna couldn't take it in while Miles was still missing. In the hours since their return, they'd not let silence fall. Miles's life was held within the songs, and so they sang. Guided by Meer Eason's ervay, children's and dragons' voices harmonized.

Hanna paused to sip from Taunier's water pouch and let the healing coolness spill down her throat before passing it to Tymm. She looked at the children in their tattered clothes. Their hair was tangled, their faces smeared with dirt; still, their mouths were open wide as they sang. Without them, the worlds would not have been joined. She felt a sudden pang of gratitude. *I'll bring each and every one of them home,* she thought. *We owe them that.*

Meer Eason leaned against a terrow. Even with all the help he was getting, it was clear the Music Meer couldn't go on much longer.

Hanna left the circle to walk around the World Tree's trunk, its girth like a castle; it would take time to pace all the way around. She'd gone only a little way when Thriss landed on her shoulder, and Taunier and Breal joined her.

"Miles," she said as she walked beneath the boughs. "You awakened Kwen. The Wind-taken rebuilt Arnun, and we've rejoined the worlds. Why won't you come out?"

She was talking as if her brother could hear her words right through the wood. If Miles could still hear Eason's ervay, the children's wavering choir, and the dragons' rich, wild voices, then why would he not hear her?

Tears darkened her dusty leather boots as she rounded the tree. "Come back, Miles. Come back because I say so and because I can't do without you."

She ran her hand along the patterned bark. "Remember the way Enoch was caught inside the oak for fifty years? You don't want to be imprisoned like that, do you?"

How long before Eason's strength gave out? How long before they must all let go of the song, knowing at last that Miles could not return?

Hand in her pocket, she wrapped her fingers around the cool surface and drew out the small brown bottle of tears. *The Kanameer will know what to do with them* . . .

The Kanameer will know. "Enoch gave me this bottle," she said hoarsely. She pulled out the cork stopper. "He sent this for you all the way from across the sea. All the way from home."

Hanna let two droplets fall on Kwen-Arnun's roots.

"These are Enoch's tears."

She kept walking as she tipped the bottle, sprinkling

a drop here and there along the base of the tree. "He gathered them the day you and Gurty and I freed him from the oak."

She was partway around the trunk now, still sprinkling drops in twos and threes. "Some would say they're only salt water and worth nothing at all. But they were hard-won tears. You were with me when Enoch came out. We saw him laugh and cry and dance all at the same time. He was like a wild man. Do you remember?"

White roots and black drank in every drop, songs for the listening, tears for the drinking. "Enoch told me to tell you these tears are sorrow and joy, all in a little brown bottle."

The bottle was nearly empty. She poured the last few drops on her hand and tossed them into the branches. Sunlight caught the droplets clinging to the twigs. Golden leaves rustled.

Empty. She knelt down with Taunier and Breal, placed the small brown bottle snugly between Kwen-Arnun's roots, and added her tears to Enoch's.

Taunier put his hand on her shoulder. She thought of Granda and the Falconer who died last year, of the dragons who were shot down, of Kanoae, who'd never return to the meer's school on Othlore. *But not Miles,* she thought. *Please not my brother.*

Meer Eason leaned against a terrow's side. The ervay's song was fading. Hanna stilled her body. There was a growing silence beyond the tune, a hushed breeze in the leaves, a wave breaking a long way from shore, the far-off steps of a loved one walking mile upon mile to the place where the other waits. The silence was in the wind, the waves, the steps not heard by the ear, but felt in the heart and breath. Hanna held her breath, listening.

The silence was broken by a little thud. A small, round fruit fell from the World Tree and rolled up to Hanna's boot. It was silver, about the size of a juicy plum.

"Catch!"

Hanna leaped up with Taunier just in time to see another small globe hurtling down. She caught it, laughing, and gave it to Taunier. Both drew farther back, shielding their eyes against the sunlight. High up in Kwen-Arnun's branches, half obscured by leaves, Miles sat swinging his legs.

"Try the fruit, Taunier! It's delicious!"

Taunier took a huge bite and chewed appreciatively. He rolled his eyes and smacked his lips.

"Come down here before you fall," Hanna shouted cheerfully. She spun around and around just to fling the joy outward. It was too much to keep hold of otherwise.

"Just a minute." Miles climbed even higher. "There's more fruit up here."

"Toss me one," shouted Tymm.

"And me." Cilla waved her arms. More children crowded under the branches, jumping up and down.

"I want some."

"Me, too."

"Give me some."

Miles laughed. "All right. There's plenty for everyone. Heads up."

FORTY

DRAGONS' BRIDGE

Kwen-Arnun, the great World Tree,
Reached green arms east,
Reached green arms west,
And dragons all flew free.

—DRAGONS' SONG

Breal's Moon rose above Yaniff, full and round and silver as Arnun's fruit. Beneath Kwen-Arnun's branches, Miles joined the gathering for the dragons' crossing.

Taberrells and terrows smacked their tails against the ground. He felt the pounding in his feet, the drumming deep as the earth's heartbeat. Thriss crouched on Hanna's shoulder, flicked her tail against Hanna's back in rhythm with the others. And on Miles's right, Meer Eason stood tall with Taunier, resting his hand on Tymm's shoulder.

Miles fingered the pearly Arnun seeds in his pocket. Sweet, luscious, life-giving, the silver fruit had restored

Meer Eason's strength. "They taste like peaches," he'd said.

"Not at all," Zabith argued. "They're more like papayas." Whether they were more like one or the other didn't matter in the end, for everyone agreed they were the finest fruit in all of Noor and likely Oth as well. As the sun rode across the sky, they'd gorged themselves on the fruit, washed their sticky hands in the river, and saved thousands of pearly Arnun seeds for future planting.

Now, in the bright moonlight, Miles could see more fruit twinkling high in Kwen-Arnun's branches. His mouth watered. He couldn't get enough of it. Before the towering tree, he felt the spreading branches like a splitting in his chest. He lifted his hands and spread his arms wide. Hanna, Zabith, Taunier, and Eason followed the gesture. Meers greet touching their foreheads, but this was the way to honor the great tree.

They had little to wear to mark the occasion, so Hanna loaned Taunier her terrow-scale cloak. The cloak flailed in the breeze as, one by one, he lit the children's torches. Hanna's slender crown caught the torchlight, and her face shone in the flitting gold. *She is changed*, Miles thought. He couldn't name the change, but he could see it in the confident way she held her head, the way she returned his glance, gazing straight into his eyes with ease. He read love and sorrow there. The dragons were leaving.

"We will begin," said the Damusaun.

In her claw, the Dragon Queen held the wing bone of a long dead warrior, retrieved from the cave of bones. He knew the bone had belonged to her brother, Therros, the Wanderer. She'd sung at the entrance of the cave and again when she took it from the rocky shelf. *I will take you to rest in Shangor Mountain, where the foothills meet the sea. Where the waves speak.*

Miles fingered the ervay at his side, remembering the queen's haunting song. He would learn to play it if he could. It was a private song from sister to brother, but he would find the notes. The Damusaun had kept the promise she'd made her brother when he'd died in the dragon wars. She would bring the inner branch of his wing bone to rest in Oth.

After he'd left the cave with the Damusaun, he'd seen more elder dragons entering to gather wing bones. All the warriors, the living and the dead, would enter Oth tonight.

Tails drummed the earth louder as two terrows

marched down the long line. They gave a last look at Noor, the world they'd known all their lives, and turned to Kwen-Arnun. The taberrells and terrows behind them breathed bright blue flames as the Damusaun chanted, *"Eldessur kimbardaa.* You are called. Come home to yourself."

The terrows addressed Kwen-Arnun. "Dragon Bridge, *Vessa kemun dey.* Open the way for us."

The World Tree sighed, and its branches lowered, touching the earth at the terrows' feet. They climbed onto the boughs one after the other, their golden scales shining amid the leaves in starlight, torch, and dragon fire.

The younglings stepped up next, accompanied by Kaleet. Their parting took longer, for the smallest of them was afraid of the great tree. Still, they spoke to Kwen-Arnun, asking for passage, and they went. More stepped up, all turning before they parted, but none choosing to stay behind.

The Damusaun was last to approach the World Tree. No dragons were left to drum their tails for her or send their warm blue fire, but the moon and stars glowed over Yaniff, and the children who had bound Arnun with their hands held their torches high to light her way.

The queen turned to look back at Noor as the rest

had done. Miles's eyes burned. He wanted to say, *Don't go,* but he couldn't ask her to stay.

"I see you share your terrow cloak with the Fire Herd, Kanameer," she said bemusedly. "It's only right. You both did all that was asked of you and more."

"Will you ever come back to Noor?" Miles hadn't meant to ask her that, but he couldn't bear the thought that he might never see her again.

The Damusaun tipped her head, the gesture neither a *yes* nor a *no,* but a *we shall see.*

She lowered her long neck. "Thriss," she said gently. "Come now."

Thriss flicked out her tongue, hesitating.

Hanna's voice was hoarse. "She's right, Thriss. It's time for you to go."

The queen added, "You will have lots of pips to play with in your new home, little one."

Miles thought of the egg the Dragon Queen carried. Soon Thriss would have an infant queen to frolic with.

"Go on, now." Hanna gave her pip a push, though her eyes were brimming. The pip licked her cheek, wrapped her tail around a lock of hair, and swung herself over to the Damusaun.

"Ouch!" Hanna winced, then gave a quick, startled laugh. Thriss folded her wings and sat atop the Dragon Queen's neck. Now that the Damusaun had the last pip, Miles thought she would call the bough down for entry, but she faced him, saying, "And now your gift for me."

Miles hesitated, feeling her heated breath. Hanna had a terrow to send to Oth, but he had nothing in his hands or his pockets except for a handful of seeds and Enoch's empty brown bottle: not a proper gift for the Damusaun.

"I have none." Miles waited out the silence that followed, hoping it would pass quickly. It didn't.

"You do not tell the truth," said the Damusaun.

Was she calling him a liar? A jolt of anger shook his spine. He gulped a breath of crisp night air to quell the burning.

The she-dragon recognized his fire. It was a thing they shared. Learning to control his inner fire was the gift he'd taken from his dragon shifts. The queen watched him without blinking and waited for him to settle.

"You have many gifts to offer, Miles," she said. "And you gave the one that matters most inside the heart of the World Tree."

Miles couldn't hide his surprise from her. He'd told
no one about his transformation in the heart of the tree.
It was too personal somehow and would be hard to
speak of. But the Damusaun had known about his long
struggle with anger. She seemed to know this, too, and it
was much more secret. He'd let go of everything to find
Kwen's heart, let go even of himself. And somehow, by
doing that, he'd come into his own.

He was just now beginning to understand how the
Damusaun had led him away from the fear of his own
power to bring him here.

"Do you remember the one I spoke of the day you
were blue-palmed?" she asked.

Miles gazed up at the constellations, where Mishtar's
Ship sailed east of Breal's Moon.

The Dragon Queen brought her face down close
enough for Miles to see himself doubly reflected in her
eyes. "I see you know the one I mean," said the Damusaun.
"*Essha*, shape-shifter," she whispered. "You were hiding
your powers when we first met on the ship. And it took
you time to come into yourself."

Miles blinked. He was all the stronger for her con-
stant challenges, her harsh discipline, her restraint. Only

now did he see that she was his teacher, that she had been his teacher all along. Now she was leaving him.

The Damusaun raised her voice so all could hear. "Long ago, the dragon's friend, the Mishtar, took up arms to fight alongside the dragons, but when the war was over, he put away his sword and turned his hand to music.

"Here is the new Mishtar. He joined the Kanameer, the Fire Herd, and the Wind-taken to bridge the worlds for us. But in the days to come, the new Mishtar must bridge the way between men and dragons. He must learn our history and play dragon songs wherever he goes." She looked down at Miles. "Do you accept this?"

Her question sent a tremor across his skin. He shook, and it was as if the world was shaking. For once he did not try and control it.

The bright moonlight, and the starlight falling from Mishtar's Ship, fell on the Damusaun's proud face. It crossed the ground between them, the very edge of it touching the backs of his hands.

"I accept it."

There was no cloak or crown for the new Mishtar to wear, only this moonlight and the cold and glittering stars above. That was enough.

"Now, Mishtar," she said. "Your gift."

Miles took out his ervay and polished the silver flute on his sleeve.

Taunier clicked his fingers. The soft glow above his hand illuminated the broad trunk as the Damusaun asked entry from the World Tree.

"Old Friends Parting" was a simple tune, but the song floated easily from the ervay as the Damusaun climbed the bough. She left too quickly and too soon. As the twin pipes played, they all watched her disappear beyond the shimmering leaves.

They sailed homeward the next day with crates full of Arnun fruit, and folk celebrated in every land when the Wind-taken children arrived home. There was such food and feasting as they had never had before, and the Arnun fruit was by far the sweetest delicacy at every table.

Back on Enness Isle, after Mother had hugged all three of her children for the tenth time and wiped away her happy tears, she got out her mixing bowls, made her special crumb cake, and served it on the green platter Tymm had mended the day Hanna first saw the dragon.

Hanna cut her younger brother a thick slice of cake

and smiled as he stuffed a huge hunk of it in his mouth. Tymm gobbled it up and asked, "May I have another?" His mouth was still so full he sprayed crumbs across the table at Da.

Da swept the crumbs up with the side of his hand and gave a hearty laugh. "Do you hear that, Mother? What do you say to the boy?"

Mother clucked her tongue but took the knife from Hanna and sliced her youngest boy a second piece. And before she knew it, she was handing out seconds to Hanna, Miles, and Taunier, which was not like her at all, but then it was a celebration.

Many shining seeds were gathered as the Arnun fruit was devoured at table after table throughout Noor. The children who'd been called by the Old Magic knew what to do with them. In every land, the Wind-taken returned to the fallen forests, where they planted the Arnun seeds. Under their tender care, new Waytrees sprang up in Othlore Wood, in the forests of Emberlee and Reon, and every land where the children lived.

On Enness Isle, Hanna hiked up Mount Shalem with Taunier and her brothers. She knelt by a fallen Waytree, the shiny white seeds in her palm glistening like pearls. A green-scented wind blew her hair as she planted them and scooped brown earth on top.

Less than an arm's length away, wood beetles were chewing patterns in the pine log. The decaying ancients here in Shalem Wood would enrich the soil and nourish Arnun's seeds. In time, the trees of Enness Isle would grow tall again.

She joined the others on the ridge overlooking the bay. "Da wants us to bide with him through lambing season."

"It's only right we do before we go to Othlore," said Taunier.

Miles placed his hand on Breal's furry head. "I can stay on until then."

Hanna was glad they'd both stay on. She wanted to see the lambing season out before sailing to the meer school with them.

The sun came out from behind the clouds. "Look." Tymm pointed at the morning moon.

Hanna looked out over the water where the moon shown pale white as an Arnun seed. Taunier took her hand. His palms were damp with soil. So were hers, but they linked fingers all the same.

† † †

New trees with patterned black and white bark sprang up all over Noor. The trees' roots were deeper than most Noor folk guessed, deep enough to find the ancient world songs and help Kwen-Arnun bind Noor and Oth together. The saplings were called Kwen-Arnun trees, but as they grew in height and girth, towering in forests across the land, many Noor folk simply called them honey trees, for their fruit was the sweetest in the world.

In the beginning when eOwey sang everything into being, Kwen-Arnun, the World Tree, held the world of NoorOth together. Kwen, white-barked and strong, embraced his tree-wife, Arnun, her branches black and shining. Male and female under the NoorOth sun, trunks and branches intertwining, together they were one.

Kwen-Arnun's roots grew deep as the earth, binding all to all. Then eOwey created dragons with hearts of fire to guard the sacred World Tree. Green taberrell dragons and golden terrows wheeled above Kwen-Arnun night and day and tended the rich soil beneath the giant boughs.

In the second age a great quake shook the world of NoorOth, breaking Kwen-Arnun in two. As the World

Tree fell, NoorOth split into two worlds. As NoorOth loosened into the seen and unseen worlds of Noor and Oth, the rift tore a black hole in the heart of the Old Magic, and a Wild Wind awakened with the breaking of the worlds.

Storms blew over Oth, where Kwen's tree-wife, Arnun, was shattered on the ground. Her shining black trunk lay in pieces. Tempests swept through Noor, where Kwen fell, his branches twisted, his broken heart turning slowly to stone.

Yet the worlds of Noor and Oth did not completely split apart. For trees of every kind rose up, all descended from Kwen-Arnun. eOwey called them Waytrees and sent more dragons to protect them. As the years passed, the Waytrees grew taller, and their roots were deep enough to bind the broken worlds.

—*The Way Between Worlds*

GLOSSARY

Abathan—Peace.

Abb nayn kwii onan. Zuss—We gift you with our warmth. Awaken (DragonTongue).

Anteebwey—Devil.

Attenlore—Enness Isle as it appears in Oth.

Azure trees—The most ancient Waytrees of Noor.

Breal—Legendary hero who killed Wratheren, the serpent who swallowed the moon.

Breal's Moon—The first full moon after an eclipse. In the legend, the darkened moon represents the moon swallowed by Wratheren. The way between worlds is more passable on Breal's Moon, a traditional time to cross from Noor to Oth and back.

Brodureth—The Oak King of Oth who has turned to stone. Brodureth once served as the ancient western dragons' bridge between Oth and Noor.

Damusaun—DragonTongue for Queen. The Damusaun is the revered Dragon Queen.

Deya—Tree spirit.

Dreamwalker—A sleepwalker with powerful dreams that can foretell the future.

Eldessur kimbardaa—You are called. Come home to yourself.

eOwey—One who sang the universe into being, also called the Maker.

Ervay—A Y-shaped flute with two pipes made of sylth silver.

Eryl—Human male. Term deyas attach to a male's name. Example: *Mileseryl.*

Esh ell ne da. Ne da rumm pe—Listen to my heart. My heart beats for you.

Esper—A wind spirit or wind woman of the west, also called Wild Esper.

Essha—Listen with understanding.

Grandtree—Ancient Waytree that houses a deya.

Isparel—Wind spirit of the east.

Kanameer—Servant of magic (DragonTongue).

Kaynumba, eOwey, kaynumba—"The ending comes, O Maker, the ending comes." A death knell sung to honor the dead.

Keth-kara—The sacred sound eOwey voices to each individual while they are in the womb. Literally, sound that helps to form the person. A keth-kara can be sung when one is in need of healing, but only when in great need.

Kith—Friend or spirit friend.

Kwen-Arnun—The World Tree that was split in two at the breaking of the worlds. Kwen, the male half of the tree, fell in Noor. Arnun, the female half, fell in Oth.

Lyn—Human female. Term deyas attach to a female's name. Example: *Hannaeryl*.

Masayan trees—Trees that grow in the dragonlands of Oth.

Meer—Literally "one who wields magic." A title given to one who has studied magic and is blue-palmed.

Mishtar—Hero who fought alongside dragons and eventually helped to negotiate an end to the dragon wars. Also the first High Meer of Othlore.

Noor—Name of the world.

Noorfest—Holiday celebrated at winter solstice.

NoorOth—Name when the two worlds were one.

Noorushh—Wind spirit who rides the sea winds.

Oth—Name of the magical Otherworld.

Otherworld—Another name for Oth.

Othic—Ancient language formed when Noor and Oth were one world.

Othlore—Island in Noor where meers and apprentices study magic.

Quava-arii—Combines two Othic words for loss and renewal into a term translated as "ever changing." The symbol rune for the word is a spiral shape with a crescent in the middle. The crescent stands for loss, the spiral for renewal.

Shriker—Name of cursed dog, a shape-shifter who was out for revenge.

Sprite—Tiny winged fairies of Oth.

Sqyth-born—One whose eyes are different colors, as in one blue eye and one green. Also called *sqyth-eyed*. The word *sqyth* was formed from *sqy* (sky) and *-th* (from *ear-th* or *O-th*).

Sylth—Winged fairies of Oth that are human size.

Taberrell—The largest of the dragons, with blue-green scales and golden chests. Females have a ring of purple scales around their necks. Males have a red ring.

Terrow—Smaller dragons with golden scales and same neck rings for male and female.

Tesha yoven—Bind the broken (DragonTongue).

Therros—Name of the Dragon Queen's brother. The word in DragonTongue means "wanderer."

Thool—Dark brown drink served hot and sweetened like cocoa.

Thriss—Othic word meaning "courage."

Twarn-Majas—The dragonlands in Oth.

Vessa kemun dey—Open the way for us (DragonTongue).

Waytree—Ancient, deep-rooted trees large enough to house a deya spirit.

Wratheren—Legendary serpent who swallowed the moon, from Breal's heroic tales.

A			N	
B			O	
C			P	
D			Q	
E			R	
F			S	
G			T	
H			U	
I			V	
J			W	
K			X	
L			Y	
M			Z	

ACKNOWLEDGMENTS

Dear reader,

This book would not be in your hands were it not for the gifted mentors, colleagues, and friends listed below. I owe my warmest thanks to Regina Griffin and Ruth Katcher for extraordinary story insights, sharp eyes, and pruning shears. Thanks to Nico Medina and all the people of Egmont USA who continue to do six impossible things before breakfast every day; to Paul Young for the gorgeous cover illustration; to Susan Burke for early consults; and to my agent, Irene Kraas, who is my lioness.

I'm ever grateful to Justina Chen, who graciously opened her mountain cabin in summer and winter for writing retreats (so many authors' books bloomed there); to

Indu Sundaresan, who read the part of the Dragon Queen aloud and gave her a fierce and noble voice. My thanks to the Diviners: Peggy King Anderson, Judy Bodmer, Katherine Grace Bond, Justina Chen, Holly Cupala, Dawn Knight, and Molly Blaisdell, writers whose divining rods find water in the driest of places; to Jaime Temairik, for her artful rendition of the Othic Alphabet and Web site art; and to photographer Heidi Pettit, for the festive launch party photos (www.litartphotography.net). Praise and gratitude to the intrepid independent booksellers and librarians who keep books alive in the modern-day world—heroes all.

Finally, the Dragons of Noor slap their tails applauding The Nature Conservancy for their Plant a Billion Trees campaign. Readers interested in helping The Nature Conservancy Plant a Billion Trees in the Atlantic Forest of Brazil are invited to visit them at www.plantabillion.org or stop by my "giving back" pages at www.janetleecarey.com.